Hit & Run

Second Edition

Hit & Run

Second Edition

Mike Faricy

Library of Congress Control Number: 2023918908
paperback ISBN: 978-1-962080-53-8
e-Book ISBN: 978-1-962080-54-5

MJF Publishing books may be purchased for education, Business, or promotional use. For information on bulk purchases, please contact the author directly at mikefaricyauthor@gmail.com

Published by

MJF Publishing
https://www.mikefaricybooks.com

Acknowledgments

I would like to thank the following people for their help and support:

Special thanks to my editors, Kitty, Donna and Rhonda for their hard work, cheerful patience and positive feedback.

I would like to thank Ann and Julie for their creative talent and not slitting their wrists or jumping off the high bridge when dealing with my Neanderthal computer capabilities.

Special thanks to Ann for her patience.

Last, I would like to thank family and friends for their encouragement and unqualified support. Special thanks to Maggie, Jed, Schatz, Pat, Av, Emily and Pat for not rolling their eyes, at least when I was there, and most of all, to my wife Teresa whose belief, support and inspiration has from day one, never waned.

Prologue

I was running late and pulled into a parking place in front of the Yarmo Liquor store. A young guy was playing his violin attached to an amplifier at the entrance to the parking lot. He smiled and nodded as I drove past. The amplifier was on a two-wheeled dolly. He looked about eighteen or twenty, and I thought his music sounded awfully nice. His hand-written cardboard sign said he was raising money to help his mother. I watched as a car stopped and handed him a dollar, or maybe it was a five-dollar bill. The driver made a comment and pulled onto the street. I listened for another half-minute and hurried into the liquor store.

"Hey, Lorenzo, how's it going?" I said to the guy behind the counter as I rushed down the far aisle. I grabbed two bottles of Sean Minor Sauvignon Blanc and got in line behind a fat guy buying a case of beer.

"Better give me a half-pint of bourbon, too. What kind you got?" he said.

Lorenzo turned toward the rack of half-pints behind him and read off the brand names. "We got Jim Beam, Dickel, Kentucky Gentleman, Evan Williams, Heaven

Hill, Virgin, Ancient Age, JD Black, and Kentucky Tavern."

"What's the price?"

Come on, man. I got a date tonight, I thought. Lorenzo shot me a look and recited the prices to the guy.

"Mmm-mmm, that expensive? I guess I'll just stick to the beer tonight," he said and handed a twenty to Lorenzo.

Probably not his first night shacking up with a case of beer. I watched him as he waddled out the door. With a massive belly hanging over his belt, I guessed the guy hadn't been able to see his feet in ten years.

"Just these two bottles, anything else, Dev? Maybe a half-pint of bourbon?"

"No, thanks, but I'm good," I laughed. "I'm running late for my date."

"Well then, I better ring you up." He scanned the barcode on the bottles, and I inserted my credit card into the terminal. I input my code and waited for a moment. Suddenly there was a loud buzz, and the terminal screen read 'Card Denied' in red letters.

"That can't be right."

"Pull the card out and insert it again," Lorenzo said.

'Card Denied,' the screen read again. Nothing changed except the buzz sounded even louder.

"Oh, Christ," the guy in line behind me groaned just under his breath.

"Sorry, go ahead and ring this guy up while I dig out another card," I said.

Lorenzo nodded, shoved my wine bottles off to the side, and rang up the next guy. Once his card was approved, he said thanks to Lorenzo, gave me a look and headed out the door. I handed two twenties to Lorenzo.

"Sorry about that, Dev. You might want to give them a call and see what the problem is. That's thirty-five-fifty. You want a bag?"

"Is there a charge?"

"No, Dev, the paper bag is free."

"Yeah, then, I'll take it."

He handed me the change and placed the wine bottles in a paper bag. "Enjoy your evening."

"Thanks. I intend to." I hurried out to my car and placed the bag on the passenger seat. I glanced over at the violinist. He wasn't playing at the moment. Instead, he was talking to two guys who looked like they might be giving him a hard time. One was wearing a black leather vest. The other was wearing a gray hoodie sweatshirt with the sleeves cut off.

The guy in the leather vest suddenly pushed the violin player. He stumbled back but didn't fall. *This is just the way my day is going.* I climbed out of the car and headed in their direction. I wasn't running, but I wasn't wasting time either. The violinist saw me coming. His look caused the other two to glance over at me.

"This ain't got nothing to do with your dumb ass," the punk in the leather vest said. "I'm warning you, dude, 'less you want some of this," he said and slammed his fist into his left hand.

"You been warned, bro," the hoodie sweatshirt said.

I held my hands out to the side and said, "Hey, look, it might be a good idea if you two just left this guy alone. I like his music. Come on. He's here trying to make some cash to help his mother. Probably worked harder today than either one of you has all year. Go on, take a hike, please. No need to cause trouble."

"Little late for that, now, ain't it? Teach him, Bumpy," Leather Vest said to his pal.

Bumpy, the idiot in the hoodie, nodded and spun halfway around, swinging at me. I ducked, grabbed him from behind by the hood, and at the same time kicked his legs out from under him. He seemed to levitate and then dropped to the ground, bouncing his thick skull off the asphalt.

Leather Vest did a little dance and took a swing. I blocked it and punched him in the throat. When he reflexively grabbed his throat with both hands, I kicked him square between the legs, hard. He doubled up, slowly sank to the ground, and curled into a fetal position.

The hoodie slowly rose on all fours. I planted my foot on his shoulder and pushed him down. "It would be best if you two pieces of shit stay right where you are until we leave. I don't want to see you here again. You hear me? I said, did you hear me, dumb ass?"

Hoodie nodded and said, "Yeah, yeah, I got it."

"What about you? You hear what I said? I don't want to see you here, ever again."

Leather Vest groaned and nodded.

I pulled the four one-dollar bills out of my pocket and handed them to the violin player. "You need a ride?"

He shook his head. "Thank you, sir. My car is just over there."

"Thanks for playing. That was really nice. I enjoyed it."

He smiled, nodded, and unplugged his violin. He placed it in a case, put the case on top of the amplifier, and pushed the two-wheel dolly over to an old blue Toyota. I walked back to my car and watched until the Toyota was out of sight. Bumpy and his idiot pal were on their feet. Neither one looked very happy as they limped down the street.

I pulled onto the street and hurried over to Sandie's house. She was cooking dinner, and I figured two bottles of wine would be just the thing to get her in the mood, not that she needed any help.

She lived just up Davern hill from the Sibley Plaza shopping center where Yarmo's was located. Six minutes later, I pulled in front of her brick house, a two-bedroom rambler. I took a couple of deep breaths to get rid of the denied credit card and the wanna-be gangster stress and headed up the sidewalk. With any luck, we'd just skip dinner and head right into her bedroom. I rang the doorbell, wondering if she'd be wearing anything when she answered the door.

One

Sandie was wearing blue jeans and a short-sleeve white blouse with an embroidered pair of lips above her left breast. "Oh, thank God, you're here, Dev. I was beginning to worry,"

"Crazy afternoon. Brought your favorite Sauvignon Blanc. Maybe we just start with that and see where we end up? We could have dinner at midnight," I said, handing her the paper bag.

She lowered her voice and said, "Sounds great. I only wish. My folks are here. They're in town for a memorial service, and they're going to be in the spare bedroom for a couple of nights."

"They're staying with you? Here? Tonight?"

"Oh, calm down. You'll love them."

"Can't wait to meet them," I lied.

She gave me a warning look and said, "Come on, they're in the kitchen." I followed her through the living room and into the kitchen. "Mom, Dad, this is Dev Haskell. He's the private investigator I was telling you about."

Sandie's mom turned on her kitchen stool. She was a nice-looking woman. I guessed late fifties or possibly sixty, orange hair, brown eyes. "Oh, well, we've heard so much about you. Nice to finally meet you. I'm Eleanor, but everyone calls me Elle."

The man with the crewcut next to Elle slid off his stool and held his hand out. "Bert Thomson, Sandie's overly protective father. Nice to meet you, Dev." His introduction sounded more like a warning.

"Nice to meet you, sir," I said as we shook hands.

"Grab a seat, Dev. I'll put this wine in the refrigerator. You want a glass?"

"I'll have whatever you guys are drinking."

"So, Sandie told us you're a private investigator," Bert said.

"Yeah, I've been doing that for a number of years."

"Were you a cop before that?" Bert asked.

"No, I know a lot of folks on the police force, but I was never on it."

"Chase a lot of bad guys?"

"Just the opposite, actually. I double-check work histories on employment applications. Occasionally investigate someone for an insurance company. You know, false medical expenses, that sort of thing."

"Sounds like he should check out your brother," Bert said.

"That's enough, Bert. Don't pay any attention to him, Dev," Elle said.

We chatted about everything and nothing. Bert ran a small concrete company up in northern Minnesota. Elle was a third-grade teacher, looking forward to retiring in twenty-two months. Sandie took dinner out of the oven, lasagna and garlic bread. We ate in the dining room after Bert led us in prayer. It was a pleasant enough dinner. After I helped clear the table, we had chocolate brownies for dessert. We chatted in the living room for another half hour, and after saying how nice it was to meet Sandie's folks, I said goodnight.

Sandie walked me out to the car.

"Thanks for coming, Dev. Sorry my folks were here. I mean, I love seeing them. I just wish they would have called first. I was looking forward to a night with just the two of us."

"Hey, relax. It was nice to meet them. They seem really nice."

"Hope you didn't feel interrogated."

"No, I get it. If you were my daughter, I'd want to know who you were going out with too. You know parents, they still think we're fourteen, and they need to know what we're up to."

"Or worse, they do know and don't like it. Well, thanks for being so understanding." She stepped forward, gave me a big kiss, and said. "I'll make it up to you."

"Counting on it," I gave her a hug and headed home.

Morton, my golden retriever, met me at the front door. I followed him into the kitchen, grabbed his leash, and we took a long walk through the neighborhood. Once home, we settled down in front of the TV. After watching a movie I'd seen before, we went up to bed and slept through the night. I was up before my alarm went off.

I was washing the breakfast dishes when Morton wandered downstairs an hour later. He stretched as he entered the kitchen and then stood next to me for his morning head scratch. I let him out into the backyard, filled his food and water dishes, and he was back inside ten minutes later.

We were in the office well before my officemate, Louie Laufen, turned up. When I saw him park across the street behind my car, I filled his mug with fresh coffee and set it on the picnic table he used as a desk. Our office is on the second floor, and you have to climb a rickety set of stairs to get up to that level. I could hear the stairs creak as Louie slowly made his way up to our office.

He opened the door and stood in the doorway, catching his breath. He was red-faced from the stair climb. Not surprisingly, since he could stand to lose maybe a hundred and fifty pounds. He gave me his standard wave and settled into his desk chair. He never says anything for the first five minutes after his arrival. He catches his breath, sips some coffee, and, I think, debates internally whether he really wants to work.

"So, it appears you survived your hot date with Cindy last night."

"Actually, it was Sandie, and yes, I survived since it was anything but a hot date."

"Oh, God, was this one of those 'we need to talk' nights?"

"No, fortunately, nothing like that. Her folks showed up unexpectedly, and they're spending a couple of nights at her place. Apparently, they're down here for a memorial service. Needless to say, other than the lasagna she made, there was nothing hot happening."

"Oh, sorry to hear that. I know you were looking forward to the night."

"Hopefully, I won some points by being a nice guy. Her folks seemed nice enough. What did you do?"

"Just the usual, left The Spot right around 9:00. Grabbed some fries and a couple of quarter pounders on the way home and settled in to watch the news."

"Sounds about like my night, well, except for the quarter pounders," I said and glanced out the window behind my desk. A guy was climbing out of a dark blue Ford Mustang. He'd parked in front of my car, wrote down my license plate number, and came across the street to our building. A moment later, I heard the stairs creak at a much faster pace than Louie made.

The door opened a moment later. "Hi, I'm looking for Dev Haskell."

"You serving a court order?" I asked and focused on the envelope in his hand.

He smiled and said, "You're Mr. Haskell?"

"Yeah, give it to me."

"Not a court order, sir."

"Then what is it, a restraining order? Can't be an eviction notice. I own my place."

"I believe it's an invitation, sir, but the envelope was sealed, and I can't be sure. It's from Mr. Grumley."

"Grumley? I don't know anyone named Grum— wait a minute. You don't mean a guy named Arthur Grumley, do you? I went to high school with a guy named that. More or less the class prick."

He nodded. "Yeah, that sounds like Mr. Grumley."

"Tall guy, glasses, brownish hair?"

"Sounds like him. Grumley stands about six-two. He does wear glasses. His hair is brown with blonde highlights. I think it's probably dyed. End of my knowledge."

"You work for him?"

He shook his head. "No, sir. Just delivering this for him and charging his firm, by the way."

"His firm? He's a lawyer?"

"No, some kind of tech guy."

I glanced over at Louie, who was nodding and typing away on his computer. I took the envelope from the guy. "Okay, thanks, I guess."

"Thank you, sir," he said and headed out the door.

"You don't know who Arthur Grumley is?" Louie said.

"Actually, I do know. Unless he's changed, he was a spoiled little rich kid who thought very highly of himself and was a real pain in the ass in high school. We called him Arty-Farty. Haven't seen him since gradua-tion, and based on what that guy said, it sounds like he hasn't changed."

"I'd say that's fairly accurate. Along the way, he parlayed his family's inheritance or trust fund into an online marketing company, Grumley Creativity. They got some pretty big-name clients, sports teams, pro golf-ers, and a couple of NASCAR Racers. Take a peek," Louie said and turned his desktop screen toward me.

I stepped over to read what he'd found. He was right. A number of big names were listed as clients with photos and then testimonials from them. I shook my head.

"Amazing, the guy I knew in high school was a real self-absorbed jerk."

"Well, I'm guessing so are these people he's listed as clients. It's probably a perfect match. What's in the envelope?"

"Oh, yeah, I guess that would help." I slipped a pen knife into the envelope, a number ten business envelope with the name Grumley Creativity and a PO box address in the left-hand corner. I opened it and pulled out a sheet of paper. An address in block letters with a phone num-ber was centered and, below that, a handwritten note.

I read the two-sentence note to Louie, "Haskell, hoping you can join me tomorrow for a 1:00 p.m. busi-ness lunch at my place. Call if you can't make it." The address was on Quinlan Avenue North in Stillwater, a town twenty minutes east of the city on the St. Croix River.

I turned the sheet of paper over, thinking there might be something on the back, like a map or an indication of what the business meeting was about. There was nothing.

"So, are you going?"

"Why in the world would this guy want a business meeting with me? I don't know or need anything techy."

"Dev, maybe he's got someone hacking into his system or breaking into his house. Maybe it's some kind of investigation that he'd like to keep quiet, and he thinks you're the best guy for it. God, meet the guy and have a free lunch. If nothing else, you can always say no. On the other hand, since he's a millionaire, what if it was some kind of deal that led to all sorts of opportunities?"

TWO

I left the office at 12:15 the following day, allowing plenty of time to get to Stillwater and Arthur Grumley's place. Good thing, five minutes from my office, I hit a highway construction zone. It took ten minutes to get through a two-mile stretch. I eventually made it to Stillwater only to learn, by following my GPS instructions, that Quinlan Avenue North was, at no surprise, on the north end of town, actually still within the town's limits but not in any sort of heavily developed area.

A 'private' sign directed me to the paved trail that led to Grumley's house. I made my way through a forest of birch trees for four or five minutes and suddenly pulled into a large open area overlooking the St. Croix River fifty feet below. The house looked to be a hundred years old, a massive two-story brick structure with a slate roof, copper gutters, four large chimneys, and an attached four-stall garage. A parking area with angled white lines was in front of the mansion, just off the circular drive that led to three outbuildings. Four cars were already parked there. I pulled into an open space between two of the cars.

I climbed out of my car, looked around, and walked over to the granite steps leading up to the front door. Or was it the back door? I climbed the steps, and when I rang the doorbell, I could hear it chiming inside.

A moment later, a man opened the door. He looked to be about forty and was dressed casually in slacks and a nice shirt. "You wouldn't happen to be Devlin Haskell, would you?" he said.

"Yes, I am. Believe me. No one else would want to be me."

He laughed at that and said, "Mr. Grumley is expecting you. He's in his office. If you'll follow me, please," he stepped to the side so I could enter. Once he closed the door behind me, he nodded and said, "This way, please."

The place reminded me of Tubby Gustafson's house. Only it was easily twice the size. At least there weren't a bunch of armed guards out in front of the place, and I hadn't been patted down before I entered. Still, there was an elegant entryway with white marble tiles on the floor. Walnut paneled hallways led off the entry in three different directions, and a massive, elaborate staircase rose up to the second floor.

We walked halfway down one of the halls, and he stopped, knocked on the door, and opened it. "Sir, Mr. Haskell is here for your luncheon appointment."

"Oh, wonderful, right on time. Thank you, Tony. Dev Haskell, it's been a long time, my friend, a very long time," Grumley said, stepping around from a large, carved antique desk. He wore a gray three-piece suit with a red tie. He looked essentially the same, a few pounds heavier than when we were seventeen but certainly not fat. His brown hair had blonde highlights like the man said yesterday. He stepped toward me with his hand outstretched. "Thank you for coming. I really appreciate it."

"Happy to oblige, Arthur. I have to tell you, your note really surprised me. We haven't seen one another since high school, and even then, we didn't talk very much."

"Well, we ran in different groups. Come on, sit down and let's catch up over lunch." He indicated a polished wooden table with a wave of his hand. We walked over, and I pulled out a side chair. Grumley settled into the gold embossed chair at the end of the table that looked more like a throne than a dining chair. "So tell me, Haskell, what have you been up to?" As he spoke, a dachshund appeared out of nowhere. Grumley picked it up and placed it on his lap.

"Oh, I did a semester of college, but wasn't really wild about that. Spent some time in the service. Started my own investigative firm and have been working at that ever since."

"Yes, which is one of the reasons I contacted you. I'd like you to take a look at something for me, but we can get to that later," he said as a door on the back wall opened and a dark-haired woman walked into the room carrying a silver tray with food.

"Oh, perfect timing, Carmen. Thank you."

She smiled, nodded, and set the tray next to Grumley. Two plates loaded with what looked like roast chicken breast, vegetables, and mushrooms were on the tray.

Grumley took one of the plates, passed it to me, and said, "Help yourself."

I grabbed the plate as Grumley reached for the bottle of white wine on the table. The label on the wine bottle was in French. He filled his glass and then filled mine, although not quite as full as his. He raised his glass in a toast. "To old times," he said.

"Yes," I agreed. I raised my glass toward him and took a sip. It was actually pretty good. I took a bite of the chicken breast. It was delicious. "Mmm, this is very good."

"Oh yes, we import it from France, Bresse poulette," Grumley said using a heavy French accent. "I own a farm over there just outside of Bourg-en-Bresse. We raise chickens, the world's best, literally. Once I had this dish, I knew I just had to play a part."

"Of course. Why not? Are you over there often?"

He smiled, shoved another forkful of chicken into his mouth, and said, "Mmm, not as often as I'd like. One of the problems with running an award-winning business. You always have to stay ahead of your competition." Grumley fed the dog from his plate. For the rest of the meal, he'd eat two forkfuls and then pick up a small piece of chicken between his thumb and forefinger and feed the dog.

The lunch was excellent, the wine was perfect, and the dessert, creme brulee, was the best. I listened to Grumley for the better part of forty-five minutes and three glasses of wine, telling me how wonderful he was and how everything he did was incredibly fantastic. Once Carmen cleared away our dishes and set another bottle of wine on the table, he finally got down to business.

"Well, I suppose you're wondering exactly why I contacted you, Haskell."

"I thought it was to introduce me to this wonderful chicken dish. By the way, I'd love to get the recipe."

He gave me a look and shook his head. "Actually, no, Haskell, that was just one of the many benefits of dealing with me. The reason I wanted to meet with you is to discuss the possibility of you performing an investigation on my behalf."

"Are you having an employee problem, or is someone attempting to hack your system?"

"I think those are two areas a bit out of your range. No, actually, this is more of a personal matter. You see, a number of years ago, a woman forced herself on me and became pregnant."

"What? I mean, I'm sorry. That's just such a surprise." *Because you're such a self-impressed jerk, what woman would have the hots for you?*

"I know what you mean. One of life's surprises, in fact, maybe the only time I ever really made a mistake. But be that as it may." He reached into the inside pocket of his suit coat and pulled out a folded sheet of paper. "I'm keeping the original, of course. But you may keep this copy should you decide to take on the case," he said, unfolding the piece of paper and placing it in front of me.

I glanced at the wrinkled, yellowed paper. It was a copy of a birth record as opposed to a birth certificate dated December 6, 2003. The record was from Seton House, a home for unwed mothers that had been operating for at least a hundred and fifty years. The line for the father's name had the word 'None' typed in. The mother's name was blacked out. The line for the child's name had two words 'No Name' typed on the line. The baby was listed as male, with a weight of seven pounds and six ounces. There was a case number along the top of the certificate.

"Did you black out the mother's name?"

"It's really not that important. What I want is the name of the child. As you can see from the certificate, he was born the year we graduated from high school. I happen to know he was adopted from the hospital when he was two or three days old. Given that the birthdate is on the certificate, it would seem to be a logical path to discover who adopted him and what his name is. He would be nineteen now, so no longer a child. I'm sure I could find this out myself, but, obviously, I'd prefer to keep my involvement private."

"How long have you had this thing?"

"Yeah, I know. It's a Xerox copy. The mother gave it to me a month or two after the birth. She wanted me to see that I wasn't mentioned. Only saw her one time after that."

"Have you tried to contact the biological mother?"

"No point in trying. She passed away some years ago. All I have is this copy of the birth record. That's why I immediately thought of you. I'm not interested in the mother. As I said, she passed away. I would like to see if the boy is okay. If he needs financial help or something, maybe I could play a small part. Of course, I'd like any knowledge of my involvement to remain private. To that end, I've had a contract drawn up," he said and reached into the inner pocket on the left side of his coat. He pulled out an envelope and handed it to me.

Just like his lunch invitation, Grumley's address was in the upper left-hand corner of the envelope. It was also in the middle of the envelope along with a postage stamp. I opened the envelope and pulled out a five-page contract. I quickly went through all five pages. The fifth page had two signature blocks. Grumley had already signed and dated his name.

"Would you like a pen, Haskell?"

"Thanks, but I always have my attorney double-check things before I sign. I don't see a problem, but I want to play it safe."

"Very well, don't let me keep you from your law-yer," Grumley said, pushing his chair back. He set the dachshund on the carpet and stood. "I figured that might be the case. Just mail it back to me once you've signed it."

I slipped the contract back into the envelope and stood. We shook hands for a half-second. Grumley pulled his cellphone out and pushed two numbers. A minute later, the same guy who had answered the front door stepped into the room. "Sir?"

"We've concluded our meeting, Tony. If you would be so kind as to show Mr. Haskell to the door. Wonderful to meet you and catch up after all this time, Haskell. That unsigned contract will be valid for forty-eight hours. I look forward to hearing from you."

"I'll get back to you. Thank you for lunch. Very delicious."

"Of course, it's French," Grumley said and then added a phrase in French that was lost on me. He could have been telling me to get screwed, and I wouldn't have known.

I followed Tony out of the room. He led me back to the entryway and held the door for me. "Thanks, Tony. Nice to meet you."

"Enjoy the day, sir," he said, then closed and locked the door as soon as I stepped out.

Three

I asked Louie, "So, what do you think?" I asked. He shook his head and flipped the pages back on Grumley's contract. "It seems reasonable enough, except for the part where he gets the title to your house and one of your fingers if you don't find this kid by the end of the week."

"What, he has that in the damn contract?"

"Just joking, Dev. Calm down. The thing seems reasonable enough, maybe a little bit of overkill as far as keeping quiet about him. That said, it's not uncommon in this kind of circumstance that a biological parent doesn't want their name mentioned. There could be a variety of reasons. Maybe the kid or the family that adopted him has serious problems. He could have a wife who would be upset to find out he'd fathered a child. It could be any one of a number of things. You said he's wealthy?"

"Appears to be very wealthy. Some tech thing, Grumley Creativity is the company."

Louie nodded and said, "Oh yeah, we looked it up online. Not that it means anything. Anyway, I don't see a problem with signing this thing. Did you discuss fees?"

I shook my head. "No, never came up, not even in general terms. He liked to tell me how successful he was, and I was happy to listen and make some mental notes."

"What'd you learn?"

"If what he said is true, and I've no reason to doubt him, he's worth millions. He's also the same person he was back in high school. Very impressed with himself and not really interested in anyone else."

"Well, good luck. Maybe increase your fee and see if he blinks. Nothing like a good-paying client to make the world seem sunny and bright."

"So you don't have any problem with me signing this thing?"

"No, the main thing is you have to keep your investigation private. You can't mention his name. If you do find the kid, about all you can do is turn the information over to Grumley. I know he told you the mother is dead, but if you find out her name, you might want to verify that. Just make sure you don't mention Grumley's name if you learn who she is and she's still breathing. Once you sign that contract, make a couple of copies before you send it back to him."

"Of course," I said, turning to the back page, signing and dating the contract. I brought my fee schedule up on my laptop, raised everything by thirty percent, and printed off three copies. I raised the lid on my printer and made two copies of the contract with both signatures as well as the birth record. I placed the contract back in the envelope, added the sheet with my fees, and sealed the envelope.

"You going to be here for a bit, Louie?"

"Yeah, I'm here until I head over to The Spot for a beverage. You want me to keep an eye on Morton?"

At the moment, my Golden Retriever, Morton, was stretched out on his pillow. He was sound asleep in his mid-afternoon nap. "He'll be out for another hour or so. Hopefully, I'll be back by then. I want to go over to Seton House and see what I can find out about this birth."

"Seton House, time to update, Dev. They closed their door back in 2016."

"What? They're a home for unwed mothers. What do you mean they closed their door?"

"Just that. The news report said they were merging with some other organization later that year. Apparently, being an unwed mother isn't as difficult or as embarrassing in today's world as it was twenty years ago."

"Merging? That can't be right. Let me check it out." I Googled Seton House. Yeah, unfortunately, once again, Louie was correct. They closed their doors in 2016. Seton Services were now a part of Catholic Charities, and they were located over on University Avenue. I could only hope they might be able to give me a name on the birth record.

Louie smiled and said, "I'll watch Morton while you see if you can get some answers."

"I think I already know what the answer is going to be, but I'll check it out just in case."

The Catholic Charities Seton building on University Avenue is a three-story concrete structure. The entrance is actually in the back under a blue awning, so I pulled in next to the building and parked. The door buzzed open a moment after I pressed the bell. I walked in and headed for the reception counter.

"Good morning. If you'd sign in, please," the woman behind the counter said. The three-ring binder used to sign in asked for my name, car make, color, and license. Once I filled in the information, she handed me a visitor's badge and said, "How may I help you?"

"I have a birth record from Seton House, dated 2003," I said, handing a copy of the birth record to her. "There's no name for the father, and the mother's name has been blacked out. I'm trying to find the child, now an adult, if he's alive."

"I'm afraid we can't help you. The mother apparently did not want her name to be known, which is why it's been blacked out."

"If that's the case, why wouldn't it just say none, like where the father's name should be."

"Most likely because she didn't provide the father's name. She may not have known his name, or he asked that his name not be given. That's not at all uncommon."

"Is there someone I could talk to regarding this?"

"I can see if someone is available. If no one is available, you'll have to make an appointment."

"Okay, hopefully, someone can see me."

She input a three-digit number on the phone and a moment later said, "Hi, Gary. I have a gentleman out here with questions on a birth record dated December 6, 2003. Would you be able to meet with him? Yes, he did. All right, thank you," she said and hung up.

"He's just finishing up. If you'd like to take a seat, he should be out in five or ten minutes."

"Yeah, okay. That's great. Thank you," I said and sat down.

Gary Carlsrud introduced himself five minutes later. "Come on back to my office, and let's go over this," he said.

I followed him back to a room furnished with a desk, a credenza, and two file cabinets. A pair of black plastic chairs were placed in front of his desk. I took a seat as he settled behind his desk and said, "I understand you're adopted and want to find information on your biological parents."

"Not exactly," I said as I handed him the birth record. "My name is Dev Haskell. I'm a private investigator. I've been hired by the biological father, who wishes to find his son. Based on the birth record from Seton House, the child would now be an adult, age nineteen."

He pursed his lips and said, "Unfortunately, the father's name isn't listed here. Who crossed out the mother's name?"

"I thought that was done by Seton House."

He shook his head, "If we did it, the same format as the father's would have been followed. The word 'None' typed in."

"Then I'm not sure. It may have been the father who blacked it out, but I honestly don't know that."

"Here's the problem," he said, handing back the birth record to me. "As it stands, we've no way of substantiating if indeed your client is the father. If you knew who the mother was and she requested the information, we might be able to obtain it. I'm afraid you're dealing with state laws here that are very specific."

"So you can't provide me with the information?"

"I'm afraid not. At least not without the documented father and/or mother requesting it. If his name isn't listed on the birth record, we can't supply the information. If you could get the mother to—"

"Unfortunately, she passed away some years back."

"Oh, dear. I'm sorry, but there's really nothing we can do."

I thought about that for a moment and couldn't come up with anything. "All right, Gary. I appreciate your time."

"Wish I could tell you more, but that's it. The laws are very black and white and with good reason in these instances."

"I get it. Okay, thank you. I'll see myself out."

He smiled and said, "Don't take it the wrong way, but I have to escort you." He walked me to the door beneath the blue awning, we shook hands once again, and I stepped out into the sunshine.

Four

I climbed back into my car in the parking lot. I wasn't that far from the police station, so I pulled out my cell phone and called my pal Aaron LaZelle, my lieutenant pal in the police department. I called his private number.

"Hi. This is Aaron. I'm unable to take your call at the moment. Please leave your number, and I'll get back to you as soon as possible."

"Hi, Aaron. This is Dev. Amazingly, I don't have a problem. Give me a call when you're able. I think it's my turn to buy dinner. Which McDonald's do you want to meet at? Thanks," I said and headed back to my office.

Morton was still asleep when I returned.

"That was fast. I'm guessing you didn't get any information," Louie said.

"You guessed right. Since the father isn't listed on the birth record and the mother's name has been blacked out, there's nothing they can do. I left a message for Aaron LaZelle to see if he would have any ideas."

"What about the county or the state?"

"Even if they could help, the best they could do would be to give me a list of boys born on that date. I looked it up. There's seventy thousand babies born every year in the state. Cut it in half, so thirty-five thousand boys. A birth certificate, if you can get it, costs twenty-six bucks. I don't have the information or the biological connection to obtain a birth certificate, so that's out. Unfortunately, I don't even have the information to physically obtain a birth record. But I checked online, and birth records are only available up to 1934, so that's not an issue. I'm starting to think I may be screwed on this," I said.

"And the baby was born at Seton House in 2003?" Louie said.

I thought about that for a moment. "That's the premise I was working under, and for a number of years, they would deliver the babies, but at some point, they moved the delivery to St. Joseph's hospital just because they were in a better position to deal with any potential problems that might develop during delivery. You know, the hospital would probably have records, maybe. Why didn't I think of this before? You know anyone over there at St. Joseph's?"

Louie shook his head. "No, I don't. Although, if you could find someone there, possibly they could help. I don't know. It sounds like a pretty slim chance."

"It sounds better than the one I didn't have a few minutes ago." I thought for a while, drumming my fingers on the desk before I came up with a name, Maureen

Connolly. We'd dated a few years back for three or four months before she'd dumped me. She was a nurse at Regions Hospital, not at St. Joseph's, but maybe she knew someone there. I called her number.

"You have reached Maureen Connolly. I'm unable to take your call right now, but if you'd like to leave a message, this is a secure line. I'll get back to you just as soon as I can. Thank you and have a nice day."

"Hi, Maureen, a voice from the past, Dev Haskell. I'm just calling to see if you might be able to connect me with anyone working at St. Joseph's hospital. I believe you're still at Regions but hoping you might know someone. Hope all is well with you. Thank you."

I called Grumley next. Just like every other call I'd made, I got dumped into voicemail. "Arthur Grumley," the recording said, and then I heard the beep to leave a message.

"Hello, Arthur. This is Dev Haskell. I signed the contract and mailed it back to you along with my fee list. Any questions, please feel free to call me. I'm working the case now, attempting to obtain the county or state birth record. Feel free to call with any questions."

As I disconnected, Morton stood, stretched, then gave me a look and walked to the door. "Duty calls," I said to Louie and grabbed Morton's leash. We took our usual route, three blocks around the neighborhood. Morton sniffed every other fence gate and left a personal message on the three fire hydrants along the way. I kept trying to come up with some way to obtain the birth record for Arthur Grumley's biological son, but nothing seemed to make sense. Once back in the office, I unhooked the leash from Morton's collar and tossed him a biscuit. He hurried over to his pillow in the corner so he wouldn't have to share just as my cell phone rang.

'Maureen Connolly' came up on my cellphone screen.

"Hi Maureen, thanks for returning my call. Gee, it's been years since we talked."

"Hi Dev, let me just state I've been happily married for four years. We have a darling daughter almost two, and I'm pregnant with our son, who is due in three months."

"Oh, that's wonderful news. I'm very happy for you. Who did you marry?"

"A perfect gentleman from Wisconsin, William Nelson. He's a prosecutor with the city attorney," she said, sounding as if she was giving me a warning rather than just providing information.

"Great, good for you, Maureen. You deserve someone nice."

"Yes, I certainly put in my time on the other side of that equation."

I decided not to pursue that last statement. "Umm, the reason I called is I'm working on a case for someone. A biological father, who is attempting to get the birth records of a child, a newborn boy who was adopted a day or two after his birth almost twenty years ago. The problem is, the father isn't mentioned on the birth record, and the copy I have has the mother's name crossed out."

"Does he know who she is?"

"I believe so, but she apparently passed away some years ago. The child was born in 2003. He would be 19 years old now. My client is a wealthy individual, and he wants to see if there's anything he can do to help the child. The mother was receiving care from Seton House when she was pregnant, and I believe they had moved the delivery services to St. Joseph's hospital prior to the boy's birth, so I'm thinking they might have the birth record. But with the father not mentioned on the birth record and no name for the deceased mother, it's been impossible to obtain any record."

"So, how do you expect to find anything at St. Joseph's?"

"It's a long shot, but the date of birth was December 6, 2003. Even if there are no names on the birth record, I'm thinking the adoptive parents might be listed. I was hoping you might know someone there that I could talk to and explain the situation." There was a long pause.

"Hello? Maureen?"

"Yeah, give me a minute, I'm thinking. Well, I kind of know someone there in accounting, but I don't think she would be much help."

"Would it be all right if I called her? Maybe she would know someone I could talk to."

Another long pause. "Well, I suppose you could try to call her. I better not give you her private number. Her name is Monica Bennett. But like I said, she's in accounting, so she wouldn't be in the records department."

"I'd like to try her. It's better than nothing, and I've really run out of options. If she can't help, I'll just have to contact my client and tell him we've hit a wall."

"And this is so the biological father can help the adopted boy?"

"Yes, it is."

I heard her take a deep breath, and then she gave me the number. I wrote it down, repeated it to her, and said, "Thanks, Maureen. I really appreciate your help. Wishing you all the best on your delivery. Healthy mom, healthy baby."

"Thank you, Dev. If you talk to Monica, please don't mention my name. I don't want her to think I'm passing her name out to everyone. And I hope you won't take this the wrong way, but things are really going well for Bill and me. I think it would be best if I didn't hear from you again, ever."

"That's not a problem. I won't…" but she'd already hung up.

Louie glanced over and said, "Did you get a contact?"

"Yeah, at least I think so. I'll find out in just a moment." I dialed the number and listened to three rings.

"St. Joseph's Hospital. How may I help you," a woman said.

"Hi, I'd like to speak to Monica Bennett. I believe she's in accounting."

"One moment, please, and I'll connect you." Apparently, Maureen had given me the general number. Still, I had a name, so that was better than when I'd started. The phone rang four times, and I was ready to leave yet another message when suddenly a woman answered, "Accounting."

"Hi, I'm calling for Monica Bennett."

"Speaking."

"Hi Monica, my name is Dev Haskell. I'm hoping you can help me. I'm trying to get the birth record for a man born at St. Joseph's and adopted two or three days after his birth."

There was a long pause before she said, "I don't think I'd be able to help you. I'm in accounting. What did you say your name was?"

"My name is Dev Haskell, and I—"

"Dev Haskell? Did you date Maureen Connolly for a while?"

"Yeah, off and on. But that was some time ago, and she—"

"I'm sure you don't remember, but we met at a party. A wedding shower actually for me and my ex."

"Do you live in a condo overlooking the river?"

"Well, we did. It belongs to my ex. Thankfully I don't live there anymore. Everyone in the place was older than my parents, way older. It's nice to hear from you. Still, I don't know how I could help you. As I said, I'm in accounting. How'd you get my name anyhow?"

"Oh, I remembered meeting you at the wedding shower," I lied. "I didn't realize you were in accounting."

"I try to keep it quiet," she said and laughed. "We should get together sometime. It'd be fun to catch up."

"You busy tonight? I'd love to buy you a glass of wine."

"Tonight, yeah, I can do that. You know where the A-Side Public House is?"

"I do. In fact, my office isn't too far from there."

"See you there at 7:00?"

"I'll be there. They get busy at night, so I'll call in a reservation for 7:00. Oh, this will be great, Monica. I look forward to seeing you again and catching up."

"Thanks for the call, Dev. See you tonight," she said and disconnected.

Louie looked over and raised his hands, suggesting, *So, what happened?*

"She's going to meet me for a glass of wine tonight."

"Yeah, I got that part, but can she check the birth records?"

"It doesn't sound like it, but maybe she can line me up with someone who can."

Louie shook his head and said, "It sounds like you're grasping at straws."

"That's exactly what I'm doing."

Five

The A-Side Public House is a converted fire station about three blocks from my office and The Spot bar. I brought Morton home and took him on another walk. I tossed him a biscuit once we got back to the house, and I headed down to the A-Side. For the life of me, I couldn't recall what Monica Bennett looked like. In fact, meeting her in her condo overlooking the Mississippi River was, at best, a hazy memory. Not because I had too much to drink, but it was just one of those events you don't recall after a few years.

I got to the A-Side fifteen minutes early and settled in at a table. I was hoping I'd be able to recognize her from a distance. It worked. A half-hour later, I spotted her as she walked into the place. She was wearing tight, ripped, cut-off shorts and a white top with straps. Her hair was longer, a light blonde, and pulled back in a ponytail. She stepped out to my table on the sidewalk a minute or two later. She was even more attractive closeup. I stood as she approached and held out my hand.

She gave me a peck on the cheek and said, "Well, Dev Haskell, it's been a while. Oh, sorry I'm late. I had to finish up a report at work and was waiting for one of our idiots to get me their numbers before I could total everything up. How have you been?"

"Nice to see you again, Monica. Thanks for coming. I hope I didn't ruin your evening by asking you to help me out."

"What? Oh, no, happy to help if I can. Plus, I hear things about you every so often, and I've always been curious."

"Let me tell you," I said as we both sat down, "I'm the most boring guy in town."

"Mmm-mmm, that's not what I hear. Far from it, in fact."

"Yeah, well, don't believe everything you hear. I just crossed my fingers and hoped you were still at St Joseph's," I lied.

"Oh, yeah. I'll probably be there forever. Most days, I like it, and on the days I don't, I usually get to leave at 5:00, so I can't really complain."

"That's a good way to look at it," I said just as our server arrived.

"Would you like something from the bar?"

Monica looked at me.

"Go ahead," I said. "Whatever you'd like. I'm buying."

"Oh, okay. I'll have a classic mojito, might as well make it a double."

"And sir?'

"I'll just have a Summit IPA."

"Will you be ordering dinner?"

"Are you hungry, Monica?"

"Sure, I could do dinner."

The server placed two menu's on the table and left.

"Now, you don't have to buy me dinner," Monica said.

"I know I don't, but I'm going to. Take a look at the menu, and we can order when she comes back with our drinks."

"I already know what I'm getting. They have wonderful cheeseburgers."

"Sounds perfect," I said and set the menu off to the side. "So, you think you might be able to help me out getting this birth record?"

She nodded. "Yeah, I think so, although I won't actually be doing it. One of the guys in records has been there forever. He always brings me a little treat at the end of the month when we're closing accounts. Cookies, caramels. One time, he came back from a trip to Germany and brought me a box of marzipan. Do you know what that is?"

"I do, and I love the stuff. There's a bakery in town that has a marzipan torte. I think they call it the Princess Torte."

"Better not tell me where they're located. I'll be there tomorrow getting one for breakfast," she said and laughed. "Anyway, he's really nice, and I'd be happy to ask him if he could get the birth record. I know they get requests, well not every day, but I'd guess maybe three or four a month."

"This deal is a little different from the usual requests they probably get. In this situation, my client is the biological father. I have the birth record here." I pulled out a copy from my back pocket, unfolded it, and handed it to her. "It's a little more complicated than usual. As you can see, the father is listed as 'None,' and the mother's name is blacked out. What I've run into is that since the father's name isn't on the record, he can't get a copy. Even if the mother's name was on there, my client told me she passed away a number of years ago. Which means she's not available to request a copy of the birth record."

"So, what do you do?"

"Well, what I'm hoping is if I could get a record from the files, maybe her name is on there. That said, the baby was apparently adopted two or three days after being born. Maybe there would be a record of the adoptive parents or even the name of the baby on the record. I just won't know until I see it."

"Mmm-mmm, you were right. It's complicated," she said and smiled. "But that doesn't mean it can't be done." She studied the copy for a moment. "Oh, and there's a file number on this, so you'd think it would be easy to get. God, I might even have access. I can check in the morning."

"Your mojito," the server said, placing a tall, chilled glass in front of Monica. A slice of lime and a sprig of mint adorned the top. "And your IPA, sir. Have you had a chance to look at the menu?"

"Monica?"

"I'll have the double cheeseburger with fries and coleslaw."

"I'll have the same," I said and handed over the menus.

Once the server left, I said, "So you think this guy you know might be able to help if you don't find it?"

"If I can't access the records, I'll pay him a visit, smile, and ask him nicely."

"Oh, that would be so great. Honest to God, Monica. Hang onto that copy of the record and show it to him. If this works, I would be forever in your debt."

"Oh, interesting," she said, raised her eyebrows, and took a sip of her drink.

We chatted over dinner. I had another beer. Monica had two more mojitos. I wondered if I should let her drive, but after the third time she told me she didn't need a ride, I let it go. I walked her to her car, got a hot kiss, and watched her leave. It was a little after 10:00, and I debated heading up the street to The Spot, then decided the wiser decision would be to just go home.

I had just let Morton back in the kitchen and was putting my breakfast dishes in the dishwasher when my cellphone rang. I pulled it from my pocket, the name Billy Flores was on the screen. He's a pal who owns a restaurant called Ranchero Flores.

"Hey, Billy. How's it going, man?"

"If things were going well, I wouldn't be calling you, Dev."

"What's the problem?"

"I got a couple of young wanna-be gangsters coming around looking for protection money."

"Protection money?"

"Yeah, you know the drill, suggesting it would be a shame if graffiti was spray-painted on the building or cars in the parking lot, hassling my wait staff and customers when they leave, that kind of shit."

"You call the cops?"

"Yeah, they've come by a couple of times. At least, I think it's them. I told the idiots not to hang around out front, but they're back the same night, two or three of them standing out front trying to look tough. I want to go out there and shoot one of them, send a message back to whoever is doing this shit."

"Don't shoot one of them, Billy. You'll go to jail, and they'll cause an even bigger problem."

"That's why I'm calling you, Dev."

"You going to be at the restaurant today?"

"I'm here now, and I'll be here until 11:00 tonight when I lock up."

"I'll stop by. Any time better or worse for you?"

"Maybe swing over sometime between 2:00 and 5:00. We'll have time to chat. I can give you a late lunch or an early dinner. Whatever works once you're here."

"I'll call ahead if something comes up. Otherwise, I'll stop by this afternoon."

"Thanks, Dev. See you later."

I put Morton in the car, and we drove down to the office. Louie wasn't in yet, and the coffee pot had been on all night. There was barely enough to cover the bottom of the pot, and the office smelled like burnt coffee. I turned off the burner and dumped the remnants down the sink. We probably hadn't cleaned the glass pot in five or six months, so I grabbed a sponge, and scrubbed away, then turned it upside down to dry.

I was seated at my desk watching through the binoculars as a woman got dressed and put on her makeup in the apartment across the street. Louie pulled up outside just after 9:00. I watched him out the window as he climbed out of his car. I put the binoculars back in the desk drawer and made ten cups of coffee. I turned on the pot just as red-faced Louie opened the office door. He gave me a little wave and headed for his desk chair.

"Just got the coffee going. I'll pour you a mug when it's ready," I said.

Louie pushed his mug across the picnic table and nodded.

His mug was half-full of yesterday's coffee. I dumped it down the sink, rinsed the mug, and then wiped the inside with a paper towel. The paper towel ended up black, so I gave it a second rinse, then cleaned my mug while the coffee percolated.

"Any luck with your dinner last night?" Louie asked as I filled his mug.

"Maybe. I'd forgotten how attractive this Monica was. She's a hot number, and God bless her, but she's going to try to get a copy of the birth record. If she can't, she knows someone in their records department who might be able to help. Turned out to be a nice night just talking and having dinner."

"Sounds like it went a lot better than you expected," Louie said and took a sip of his coffee. "Mmm, thanks, needed this."

"Late night at The Spot?"

"Late night, but not at The Spot. Stopped in for one just to fortify myself. Then headed off to poker night with some law school pals."

"How'd you do?"

"Better than usual. I only lost twenty bucks. I think of that as a successful evening."

"That's why I don't play cards," I said. "I'll wait on the table, serve pizza and mix drinks. But if I pick up the cards, I'm always the guy everyone wins money from."

"That's why you should join us. Everyone would love to win money from you."

I spent the next few hours running into a number of dead ends trying to access the birth record on my computer. Just before the noon hour, my cellphone rang, Monica Bennett.

"Hi, Monica. How's your day going?" I said, not wanting to sound anxious.

"Hi, Dev. Guess what I've got?"

"Hopefully, not a headache from the three mojitos last night."

"Not funny, dopey. No, I've got that birth record you've been trying to get."

"What? You got it. How in the world did you do that?"

"Well, I went online and tried a couple of things, none of which worked. So, after the better part of an hour, I just did what I should have done to begin with. I picked up the phone and called Stanley."

"Stanley? Is he the guy in the records department that's your big fan?"

"Yes, he is, and now I'm going to owe him, big time. He put me on hold for a couple of minutes and then told me to come down to his office. I went down there, and he had a printed copy waiting for me."

"Is the woman's name on there?"

"Yes, it is, along with her date of birth. I can see why she was at Seton House. She was just barely eighteen."

"What's her name?"

"Oh no you don't, Dev. You owe me, and I need to be paid."

"Paid?"

"Yes. I'm going to cook dinner tonight, and you're going to bring some wine and dessert. Well, unless you already have something planned, in which case we can meet up some other night."

"No, I'll be there, and listen, why don't I bring dinner? I can pick something up. I'll still bring the wine, oh and a dessert, too. You won't have to do anything. I can—"

"Stop. I'm cooking dinner. You bring the wine, a white because we'll be having chicken, and bring a dessert."

"Yeah, okay, I will. What about Stanley? Do you want to ask him? I could—"

"Hey, are you picking up on what I'm putting down? I'm arranging a private evening for the two of us. No, Stanley will not be there. If you want, you can bring a bottle of wine for him that I'll give him tomorrow, and I'll tell him that it's from me. Be prepared to stay late."

"Okay, yeah, believe me, I'm prepared. I mean, I will be. Oh, thanks, Monica. This is fantastic. Thank you so much."

"It's going to be my pleasure. I'll see you tonight, promptly at 7:00. Let me give you my address."

I wrote down her address and read it back to her just to be sure I had it correct. "See you tonight, Monica, and thank you."

"As I said, it's going to be my pleasure." With that, she disconnected.

Louie was leaning back in his desk chair, grinning. "So?"

"God bless her. That guy she knows in records department gave her a copy of the birth record. It's got the mother's name on it."

"What about the baby's name?"

"She didn't say. She's cooking dinner for me tonight and told me to be prepared to stay late."

"What?"

"Yeah. That's what she just said. I'm quoting her. Oh, this is going to be great. I've got to bring wine and a dessert. Probably should bring a dessert we can eat in bed."

"Yeah, good idea. Something fancy like Hostess Cup Cakes or may a Tootsie Roll Pop. Do you know what flavor she likes?"

"Very funny, not. No, I know exactly what I'm going to get. I'll run up to Wuollet Bakery and get two slices of their marzipan torte. She was all excited about it last night when I described it to her. She'll love it. Oh, and I'm supposed to bring the wine, too. I better get that as well. You going to be here for a little while?"

"Go on and get that stuff. I'll watch Morton. If you get tied up, we'll be over at The Spot no later than 5:00."

"I'll be back within the hour."

"Take your time. I'm here all afternoon."

"You know, if it's okay, what I might do is run over to Ranchero Flores. It's a restaurant down on West Seventh. I have to meet with Billy Flores, the owner. It shouldn't be more than a thirty-minute meeting. Let's say the whole thing might take an hour, ninety minutes tops."

"Yeah, good, go. Maybe toss a biscuit to your buddy Morton before you take off."

"Thanks, Louie. Let me just call Billy and make sure he's going to be there." I brought Billy's cellphone number up on my screen and pushed the button. He answered on the second ring.

"Dev?"

"Hi, Billy. I wanted to check in before I come over. Is now a good time?"

"No, were you listening? I said anytime after 2:00. I'm still dealing with the lunch crowd. Give me another hour, okay? Can you do that?"

"Yeah, not a problem. I'll see you then," I said and disconnected.

I phoned Arthur Grumley, thinking I'd bring him up to date on our good luck. I hung up before I was dumped into his voicemail, thinking it might be wise to hold off until I actually saw the birth record. For the next thirty minutes, I picked Louie's brain for possible ways to track connections to the deceased mother. Louie finally said he had to get back to work. I tossed Morton a biscuit and headed to the bakery for the marzipan torte.

Seven

I decided to get three pieces of the torte, two for this evening and the third for whenever Monica wanted to eat it. The girl at the counter placed the three pieces in a white bakery box and wrapped a red plastic ribbon around it. I carried the box out to my car and placed it on the floor of the passenger seat.

From the bakery, I drove to Solo Vino, my favorite wine store and just a block from my house. I got four bottles of Sean Minor Sauvignon Blanc, chatted with Chuck, the owner, for a couple of minutes, and then pulled into my driveway. I placed the wine in the refrigerator so it would be nicely chilled for this evening.

It was getting close to 2:00 when I drove down to West Seventh Street. Ranchero Flores wasn't too far from Sibley plaza. As I drove past, I gave a quick look for the violin player but didn't see him. I pulled in front of Ranchero Flores. If I could get a parking place in front of the restaurant that suggested to me that the noontime crowd was thinning out and Billy would be able to sit down and explain his situation. I caught his eye just as soon as I stepped in the front door. He gave me a nod and continued talking to the woman facing him.

"Do you have a reservation, sir?" a young guy asked. He stood an inch or two taller than me, looked an awful lot like Billy, and was holding a half-dozen menus in his hands.

"No, I don't have a reservation. Say, you wouldn't happen to be Billy's son, Miguel, would you?"

He grinned and said, "Guilty as charged. You know my dad?"

"Yeah, Dev Haskell. I'm a pal of your dads. We've known one another for a hundred years."

"Oh yeah, sorry I didn't recognize you. I was out kind of late last night, and my dad got me up at 6:00 to cover for someone this morning," he said and held out his hand.

We shook hands, and he led me to a booth looking out on the street. It was in an isolated corner of the restaurant, and no other customers were seated around it. "My dad told me you were coming in. Can I get you something from the bar?"

"Thanks, but I think just some coffee when you have a chance. No rush."

Billy was still talking to the woman when Miguel returned with my coffee. "You interested in something for lunch? We've got a special this week on chicken fajitas."

"Oh, thanks, Miguel. I'd love it, but I've got a big dinner tonight, so I'd better hold off. You still going to college? Where is it, Iowa State?"

"Yes, sir, down in Ames. I'm just home for the summer."

"How's that going?"

He smiled and glanced over to make sure his father wasn't behind him. "Let's just say I'm counting the days until I can go back."

"Believe me. I get it. Good for you. Keep those grades up."

"You sound like my dad, except he's not that nice. He tells me if school doesn't work out, I can always come back home and work for him."

"He knows what he's doing."

"Yeah, I get it. That's a real incentive to keep the grades up."

"Miguel, get those two tables cleared and set them for tonight," Billy said from behind. "How are you, Dev? Did you order something? We've got a special on fajitas."

"Thanks, Billy. Miguel tried to talk me into them, but I've got dinner plans for this evening, so I better take a pass. The coffee will do me just fine."

"Thanks for coming," Billy said as he slid into the booth across from me.

"So, tell me what you're dealing with," I said.

"A bunch of numbskulls who think they're tough guys. They told me they'd make sure there weren't any problems. Said they heard guys were looking to rifle through cars in our parking lot, steal purses from women, or maybe spray paint something on the building."

"Can you identify them?"

"No, they called me on the phone. Called my cell-phone, as a matter of fact, so someone who knows me had to give them that number."

"You talk to the police?"

"Yeah, they stopped by, and I told them about it. Gave them the phone number that called me. They called back a day later and said it was one of those burner phones, and it couldn't be traced. Probably already thrown away."

"You have any problems here?"

"Like I told you on the phone, not yet. There were two or three guys hanging around out front for a couple of nights. I chased them off, told them I'd called the cops, and they left. Haven't seen them since, but just one or two incidents in the parking lot or out front, and it could cut my business in half."

"Yeah, I don't doubt it. Have you seen them at all during the day?"

He shook his head. "No, just the two nights they were out there. Both nights, it was dark, you know, maybe nine, nine-thirty. The dinner crowd is winding down by then, but I've still got a lot of folks at the bar. Maybe it's just a couple of dumb shits watching too many movies, but like I said, one or two incidents and suddenly the word is out on the street, and no one wants to come here."

"Yeah, I get it. The guys that were out front, what did they look like?"

"Well, there were three of them one night, two the next. The first night there was a big guy, dark curly hair cut short on the sides. He was wearing a t-shirt, some piece of shit band I never heard of. I had the impression the other two were taking orders from the big guy. They looked like a couple of putzes. One was wearing a black leather vest, no shirt. The other was wearing a gray hoodie sweatshirt with the sleeves cut off."

"Oh, God. I got into it the other day with those two over at Sibley Plaza. They were hassling some kid playing a violin and asking for donations to help his mother. He wasn't bothering anyone, playing nice music, and those two jerks started pushing him around, so I went over and asked them to stop."

"What'd they say?"

"Oh, they started giving me a hard time. They both ended up on the ground. That might be why you haven't seen them lately. That said, they had no problem coming after me, so it would be best to be careful."

"Idiots," Billy said and shook his head.

"Hey, on a happier note. The last time I saw Miguel, he was about two feet shorter. He looks great."

Billy smiled. "Yeah, he's doing very well. Of course, he's got this lovely girlfriend. You just hope the two of them behave."

"Oh, yeah, behave just like we did at that age."

"And you're still doing today," Billy said.

"Which reminds me, I had better head out. If it's okay, I'll swing by a few evenings, might mention it to some cop pals. Hopefully, nothing will come of it."

"Anything you can do will be much appreciated." We shook hands, I gave a wave to Miguel and headed out the door. I walked around the building to the parking lot. There were just a few cars, and everything seemed fine. Of course, it was still a sunny afternoon, although it was just as bright when I left the Yarmo liquor store the other day, and those two idiots were hassling the violin player.

I decided to do a quick drive through the Sibley Plaza parking lot, just in case they were hanging around there, but I didn't see them or the violin player for that matter, and I drove back to the office.

Both Morton and Louie were apparently in the middle of their afternoon naps. I got on my computer and sent an email to Arthur Grumley, telling him I may have found a break in the birth records search and would know more tomorrow. Morton woke ten minutes later, promptly got off his pillow, and stood by the door. He looked over his shoulder at me as if to say, 'What's taking you so long?'

I grabbed his leash, and we went out for a walk, quietly closing the door behind us. When we came back, Louie was wide awake, working on his computer.

"Oh, I must have dozed off for a moment. Didn't hear you two leave."

"Yeah, we tiptoed out. If you fell asleep, you must have needed it."

"Either that or the brief I'm working on is so boring it put me to sleep."

I placed a call to Billy Flores toward the end of the afternoon. Everything was fine on his end. I headed home and took Morton on a long walk. I grabbed a shower, shaved, pulled on my best pair of jeans, and found a clean shirt in the back of my closet. I tossed Morton a biscuit, told him to "Wish me luck," then drove over to Monica's.

Eight

I pulled in front of Monica's house at exactly 7:00. Her house is in an area of town known as Tangle Town due to the winding and curved streets in a twenty-block area. The larger area is referred to by locals as Mac-Groveland. Mac, coming from Macalester College, located just two blocks from Monica's house on Princeton Avenue. Her home was a two-story stucco bungalow with a front porch and a neatly trimmed front yard.

She was seated on the screened-in front porch and waved at me as I climbed out of the driver's seat. I walked around to the passenger side and pulled out the four bottles of chilled wine in the insulated carrier case and the white bakery box with the marzipan torte. She was on her feet and opened the porch door for me as I approached the front steps.

"Oh, right on time, very impressive, Dev."

"I do my best. Here's our dessert, the marzipan torte. A dessert piece for each of us tonight and then an extra one for the lady of the house whenever you like."

"Mmm-mmm, thank you," she said and kissed me on the lips as she took the bakery box from me. She took a step back, and it looked like she was wearing the same pair of tight, ripped, cut-off shorts and tonight, a white tank top with crisscross straps.

"I like your outfit, really nice."

"Thank you, hoped you would," she said.

"Now, I've got the wine here. This case is insulated, so you don't have to put the bottles in the refrigerator if you don't have room."

She looked in the case. "Four bottles?"

"I thought it would help to put us in the mood. Actually, one of the bottles is for your work friend, Stanley. Thanking him for the birth record."

"I've got it right over there on the couch." She nodded toward a manila folder on the wicker couch she'd been sitting on. "Why don't you fill the wine glasses, and I'll take this out to the kitchen," she said, indicating the bakery box. "I'll be back in a minute."

I pulled out one of the wine bottles and filled both wine glasses. God bless twist-off caps. I placed the bottle back in the insulated case and set it on the porch floor. I was tempted to open the manila folder, but I heard her coming back from the kitchen, so instead, I settled into a wicker chair.

"Oh, Dev, that torte looks beautiful, and those are big pieces."

"Wait until you try it. If you like marzipan, you'll love it."

"Mmm-mm," she said, raising her wine glass. "Here's to you and a lovely evening."

We clinked glasses and sipped the wine. She took a cracker from the crystal tray, added a spreadable cheese, and handed it to me. "Hope you like Brie."

"I do, thank you."

We ate cheese and crackers and emptied one of the bottles of wine over the course of the next forty-five minutes. "Are you okay with eating dinner out here?" she asked. "It's such a lovely evening. I made a really simple meal, just chili and garlic bread. I would love to eat out here," she said.

"Hi Monica," a younger couple called as they walked past, pushing a stroller.

She waved and called, "Have a nice night. Hope he sleeps through."

"Yeah, eating out here would be perfect," I said.

We were on the second bottle of wine. Or, more accurately, Monica was. I had been slowly sipping my second glass, which was still more than halfway full. The empty chili bowls and a crust from Monica's piece of garlic bread was all that remained of dinner. Just now, Monica was in the process of inhaling her piece of the torte. Much as I liked it, I was just nibbling at my piece and waiting for her to show me the birth record.

She finished her slice, drained her wine glass, and then licked her fork in a sexy way. "Don't you like your torte?" she said, eyeing my plate.

"Oh, I do, but I was enjoying watching you devour that piece. Would you like the rest of mine?"

"Oh, I really shouldn't," she said as she snatched the dessert plate from my hands. I refilled her wine glass, emptying the second bottle.

"Mmm-mmm, it's so good. I can't thank you enough, Dev. I just love this."

"You know, I should probably take a look at that—" My cellphone suddenly started ringing.

I was going to ignore it, but Monica said, "Go ahead and take the call, baby. I'm running to the bathroom." She grabbed her wine glass and headed into the house.

I pulled my phone out, Billy Flores. "Yeah, Billy, what's up?"

"They're back, Dev. Three of them. Right out in front of the place. I've already seen a couple pull up, take a look, shake their heads, and drive off. Can you come over? If I go out there, I'll end up getting arrested for assault."

"Maybe they'll leave in a little—"

"Dev, they've been out there for at least an hour. They're saying shit to customers when they leave the restaurant. This isn't good."

"Okay, I'm on my way. Be there in ten minutes," I said and disconnected just as Monica stepped back out to the porch. It wasn't lost on me that the button at the top of her sexy cut-off shorts was still undone. I wondered if that was intentional or just a wine-induced mistake.

She leaned over and gave me a lingering kiss on the lips, then settled onto the wicker couch and set her empty wine glass on the table. I opened the third bottle of wine and filled her glass almost to the top.

"Hey, Monica. I'm really sorry, but I just got a call from a client. I have to run down to his place and deal with a problem. I'll be back before you can finish that wine."

"You have to go?"

"Just for a couple of minutes. I promise I'll be right back."

"You better hurry back, baby, or I'm going to start without you," she said, raising her eyebrows. She reached for the wine glass and took a healthy sip. "Don't keep me waiting."

"Oh, believe me, I won't. I promise," I said and literally ran to my car.

Nine

It was just after 9:00 when I got to Ranchero Flores. I saw the three guys on the front sidewalk as I drove past. The same two idiots that had hassled the violin kid were out there with a larger, heavier set guy who looked in pretty good shape. There wasn't a parking place in front, which was actually good. I pulled into the parking lot in back and entered the restaurant through the rear entrance.

The place was reasonably full, but at this hour, it was mostly people drinking rather than eating dinner. I spotted Billy standing behind the cash register near the front door. He saw me as I headed toward him.

"You see those bastards out there?"

"Yeah, two of them, the leather vest and the dumb shit in the hoodie, are the same guys I mentioned who were hassling the kid playing the violin. Did you talk to them tonight?"

"Not really. I stepped outside for all of ten seconds and told them to get the hell out of here, said I'd called the cops."

"And did you call them?"

"Yeah, that was forty-five minutes ago. Haven't seen 'em yet."

"Well, we're over a hundred cops short on the force, and they're probably answering higher priority stuff. No one's fault. It's just the way things are now. I'll go out there and talk to them. Hopefully, convince them to leave."

"Do you have a gun?"

"No, and don't even think of going out there with one. It will just lead to more trouble."

"Okay, I get it. You be careful," Billy said.

I nodded and headed out the front door. The three guys were facing the restaurant. They were leaning against a shiny, dark-green car. I think it was a BMW, and I was pretty sure it wasn't theirs. As I stepped outside, the guy in the leather vest glanced over at me and said, "Goro, look, that's him. The guy that jumped us in the plaza parking lot."

"Hey, guys, I'm hoping we don't have any trouble tonight. Look, you're making life tough for my pal here. You're hurting his business, and he works very hard. Tell you what, maybe head down the street to one of those wild and crazy joints. Find some girls, and you'll have a lot more fun than standing out here, trying to scare folks off."

"You think you're some tough dude, you and your pals jumping my friends the other day," Goro said.

"Me and my pals? I didn't have anyone with me. They were shoving some kid around who was playing the violin. He had a sign that said he was raising money to help his mom, and he was playing nice music. I just asked your pals to leave him alone."

"That ain't what I heard," he said and rolled his shoulders, making me focus on his muscular chest and very large biceps. Not that I hadn't noticed them before. "They told me they were just walking past. Heading for the bar and you and your pals started giving them a hard time. Well, you ain't got any pals with you tonight, now do ya?"

"No, I don't, and I didn't the other day. I just told you what happened."

"Yeah, and I'm thinking you better get your dumb ass out of here while you can still walk."

"Not gonna happen. I'm asking really nice. I don't want any trouble, honest."

"You just got more trouble than you're gonna be able to handle," he said and took a step toward me.

I wasn't sure what I was going to do. Fear can be a big motivator. Just now, I was wishing I had a gun. I waited for him to come closer, but he didn't move. The other two idiots backed up a step or two.

Suddenly, a voice behind me called, "Is there a problem here, gentlemen?"

I turned and looked at the two officers standing in front of the squad car.

"Good evening, officers. I was just suggesting to these gentlemen that they're making the patrons of this establishment uncomfortable."

"This here is a public sidewalk. You don't own it, and besides, officer, he threatened to shoot us."

"That would be pretty hard to do since I don't have a gun. They've been hassling the customers coming in and out of here for the past hour. They told the owner they wanted protection money to make sure no one damaged any cars in the parking lot or spray painted the building."

"We never said any of that shit."

"Might be a good idea if you three found somewhere else to spend the evening. Let's just break it up. You three head down the street, and you, sir, should probably head back inside. No need for any trouble tonight, guys."

"This ass wipe is the only one causing trouble," the guy in the vest said.

"Well, you're making it sound like the only way we're going to solve this is to bring everyone down to the station, and we can sort things out there. You sure you want to do that?"

"Just take this prick—"

"Last time, I'm going to ask nicely, sir. Next step is to pull the cuffs out, and we all go down to the station."

"But we ain't—"

The cop pulled out his handcuffs and dangled them.

The muscular guy raised his hands and said, "I've got other things to do tonight." He glanced at me and said, "I'll see you around." He turned and headed down the street.

"Hey, Goro? Goro?" Leather Vest called.

"We need to go," the guy in the hoodie urged. He grabbed Leather Vest by the arm and pulled him away. They picked up speed and caught up with Goro halfway down the block.

I turned to the cops. "Thanks, guys, sorry for the hassle. I'm sure you have other things to deal with."

"You're Haskell? A pal of Lieutenant LaZelle's?" one of the cops asked.

"Yeah. Have we met before?"

He shook his head. "No, someone mentioned you and LaZelle. What's the deal with those three?"

"They've been hassling the owner, wanting protection money. Standing out here chasing away people coming in. They told the owner there was the possibility of graffiti ending up on the building or on customers' cars. They told him they could make sure it didn't happen."

Both cops shook their heads. "Small-time punks," one of them said.

"Well, thank you for showing up. I was afraid I was going to have to deal with that big muscle-bound guy."

"You think you could take him?"

"Oh, yeah, I'd just let him beat me until he got tired, and then I'd get him."

They chuckled at that. "Probably a good thing we arrived when we did."

"It's always a good thing."

We chatted for a couple of minutes and shook hands. I got their names, thanked them again, and went back inside the restaurant.

"Perfect timing on the cop's part," Billy said as soon as I stepped inside.

"Yeah, you got that right. I think those guys are gone, at least for tonight. Any problems, give me a call, Billy."

"Hope I didn't ruin your evening."

"Relax, this was more important. The cops will make a note of those three and spread the word on their so-called protection scam. I'll touch base with you tomorrow."

"Thanks again, Dev. Next time bring a girlfriend over, drinks and dinner on the house."

"Thanks, Billy. I just may take you up on that. Which reminds me, I better head out." I went out the rear door, climbed in my car, and left. I drove down the street for a mile or two, looking for the three guys, but didn't see them anywhere. I drove up to Snelling Avenue and hurried back to Monica's.

As it turned out, I didn't need to hurry. Three empty wine bottles, the empty chili bowls, dessert plates, a half-dozen crackers, some Brie cheese, and my wine glass were still on the coffee table out on the porch. Monica's wine glass and the fourth bottle of wine were missing. I did notice that the manila folder was still on the wicker couch.

The door on the porch that led into the living room was open, and the lights were still on. I picked up the dishes, bowls, crackers, and cheese and headed into the kitchen, expecting to find Monica. She was missing in action. I checked the refrigerator for the fourth bottle of wine. It wasn't there.

I figured she had probably taken it up to bed. I debated going upstairs and decided that probably wasn't the best idea. If she hadn't passed out yet, she was about to. Instead, I rinsed off the dishes, placed them in the dishwasher, washed my wine glass, and set it in the sink rack to dry. I placed the bakery box with the third piece of torte in the refrigerator and found a notepad to write a note.

It was almost 10:30, but I put 9:35 as the time on the note and wrote;

'Hi, Monica. Just back. Sorry I had to run off. Police came, and everything worked out. Thank you for a wonderful evening, a delicious meal, and your most enjoyable, beautiful self. I've turned off the lights and locked the door. Call me tomorrow so we can set a day and time that I can make it up to you.

Sweet Dreams,

Dev'

I set the note in front of the coffee pot on the kitchen counter. I turned off the kitchen and living room lights, closed the door onto the porch, and made sure it was locked. I turned off both porch lamps, grabbed the manila folder, and headed home.

Morton met me at the front door. I let him outside one last time, and once he was back in the house, we headed up to bed. I thought about Monica for two or three minutes before I fell asleep.

Ten

I was up early the next morning, showered, shaved, and stepped into a clean pair of jeans and a hardly wrinkled shirt. Once downstairs, I poured myself a coffee, settled in at the kitchen counter, and pulled the manila folder from Monica in front of me. God bless her. With any luck, I'd be able to move forward on this project, find Arthur Grumley's biological son, and bill him thirty percent more than anyone else.

I opened the file. There was the line for the father with the word 'None' typed in where Grumley's name should have been. The line for the baby's name was the same, 'None.' The mother's name was typed in, and I read it a half-dozen times, then double-checked the babies birthdate, December 6, 2003. I read the birth mother's name again, Diane Donnelly. That couldn't be right. I counted back from December. She would have been three months pregnant in June.

Diane Donnelly was the name of my girlfriend for the last half of my senior year in high school. But we never had sex. Well, I mean, we parked in the car after dances and parties, but that was just an hour or two of mostly kissing. We both remained dressed and never did anything that would have led to pregnancy.

I looked at the mother's date of birth, November 4, 1986. I wasn't sure of the year, but the fourth of November had been Diane's birthday. I counted back seventeen years from 2003 twice. The second time I used my fingers just to be sure, and it still came out as 1986.

We were the hot high school couple. Diane had red hair and sparkling blue eyes, and she was beautiful. I remember being in the car when she dumped me the night of our graduation. Instead of passionate kissing, she said, "I want to go home, Dev. This just isn't working out." After ten minutes of pleading, I drove her home. I still remember that I asked if we could talk, and she just shook her head and ran into the house. Two days later, when I knocked on the door, I was told she was gone for the summer and not to stop by. I never saw her again. I dropped out of the U the following December and joined the army. Smart, gorgeous Diane was killed in an auto accident while I was in Iraq. I visited her grave once when I was home on leave just before my second tour.

Arthur Grumley was the father? That just couldn't be right. I double-checked the dates twice more, but nothing changed. Morton suddenly barked. He'd been standing next to my kitchen stool for God knows how long, and I was completely oblivious. I gave him a quick scratch behind the ear and let him outside.

I turned on my laptop and Googled Diane. The only thing that came up was her obituary. Her graduation photo was the picture in the paper. 1986 to 2006. Even though the image was grainy and black and white, her hair looked red, and her blue eyes seemed to sparkle. We were going to travel the world. Diane wanted to be a movie star, and I thought it would be cool to be a singer in a rock and roll band. Strange how things work out or, in Diane's case, don't.

Morton scratched at the back door, and I let him in. Rather than head for his food dish, he wagged his tail and bumped his nose against my thigh. I bent down to give him a head scratch. He raised his head, I guess making sure I was okay. Then he licked the tears from my cheeks.

Eleven

We made it down to the office well before Louie. I got the coffee going and then was on my laptop searching for anything on Diane. Other than her obituary, I was coming up empty-handed. Morton wandered over two different times to check on me. I gave him a couple of very good head scratches and a hug which seemed to put him at ease. He was up close and personal with his rawhide bone when Louie made it up the stairs. I'd already filled Louie's coffee mug and set it on his picnic table desk.

"So, how was dinner with your lady friend?" he said once he'd caught his breath.

I shook my head and said, "Things were going great until I got a call from Billy Flores. I had to run down to his place and get some idiots to move on. By the time I got back to Monica's, she had gone to bed. I left her a note, locked the place up, and went home."

"So much for making plans," Louie said. "What was the problem with Billy Flores?"

I gave Louie a more in-depth version, adding the police showing up and the muscular guy telling me he'd see me around.

Louie shook his head. "Unfortunately, it sounds like they're not finished. Life being what it is nowadays, they'll probably be back at a later hour, either slitting tires or spray painting graffiti in the middle of the night."

"Yeah, I'd say you're probably right. In fact, I should head over there this morning and touch base with Billy."

"You haven't heard anything from your wine lover this morning?"

"Monica? No, nothing. I'm sure she's at work nursing a hangover. The last thing she needs is a call from me this morning. If I don't get in touch, it'll just make me look like a nice guy."

"Yeah, and we know that's a tall order."

"You going to be around for a bit?" I asked.

"I've got to leave at 11:00 for a court appearance. Go ahead and take off."

"Thanks. I'll head over to Ranchero Flores and see if we can't come up with a plan." As soon as I got out of my chair, Morton looked up and hurried over to me.

"What's with him this morning? It's like he's checking on you."

"He's got my back, is all. Don't you, Morton?" I said and gave him a head scratch. "I'll take him with me. That way, you won't have to do anything if I don't make it back in time."

"It's not a problem, Dev, honest."

"Thanks, but he can sack out in the car. Good luck in court this morning."

"Thanks. With any luck, I can talk my client into accepting whatever the sentence will be and not call the judge names as he's being escorted out of the courtroom."

I took Morton on a quick walk and then put him in the back seat. When I climbed in behind the wheel, he leaned forward and licked the back of my head. "Oh, thanks, Morton. Don't worry. I'm okay. I just all of a sudden have a number of things to check out."

There was still a breakfast crowd at Ranchero Flores. No parking places on the street and, thankfully, no guys hanging around the front of the building. I pulled into the parking lot and took one of the two remaining spaces. I took a biscuit out of the glove compartment and handed it to Morton.

He snatched it from my hand and settled into the corner of the back seat, chomping the biscuit in three quick bites. Apparently, sharing and caring only went so far and didn't apply to dog biscuits.

I wandered in through the back entrance and headed toward the front of the place. Billy was standing behind the cash register. "Oh, look who's back. Come on. You get a breakfast, all you can eat. No charge. Thanks again for your help last night."

"They didn't come back?"

He shook his head. "No, I saw the police drive by twice, so no trouble."

"Good, but I'm afraid they may not be finished. Let me grab a booth, and when you have time, let's see if we can't come up with a plan."

"We'll be emptying out in the next half hour. People will be heading to work or whatever they do for the rest of the day. Come on, let me get you seated, and you can enjoy your breakfast, then we'll talk."

He led me to the same booth as the other day, the one in the isolated corner of the restaurant that looked out onto the street. The booth was set for two with silverware rolled in a cloth napkin, glasses of ice water, and two coffee mugs. Billy placed a menu on the table and said, "I'll send a server over in just a moment."

I was still reading the menu when the server said, "Hi, Dev." I looked up to see Miguel.

"Hey, working the early shift too, I see."

He glanced over his shoulder to make sure his father wasn't nearby. "Yeah, I'm here twenty-four-seven. Like I told you, counting the days until school starts."

"Keep those grades up, and it's a path to do whatever you want. Believe me, I know what happens when you don't do that."

"You know what you're going to have?"

"Yeah, I think I better try the Huevos Rancheros."

"Good choice. Coffee?"

"Yeah, black, please."

"Back with your coffee in just a minute." It was more like thirty seconds when Miguel was back and filled my coffee mug.

I sipped coffee and watched the customers. Billy was right. The place was gradually clearing out. From time to time, I glanced out the window. I didn't see anyone resembling the punks from last night. I did see a police car drive past. It was impossible to know whether or not that was due to last night's situation, but either way, it was nice to see them.

A young blonde girl approached with a plate. "Compliments of Billy," she said and set the plate with a caramel roll down in front of me. I glanced across the room, and Billy gave me a thumbs-up.

"Oh, perfect. I need sweetening," I said.

She flashed a quick smile, suggesting she'd heard that line before, and said, "Your breakfast will be out in just a minute."

The caramel roll was covered in warm sticky caramel. It was delicious, and I devoured it in about two minutes which was a good thing because, just as I finished, the girl was back with my breakfast order. She topped off my coffee and said, "Is there anything else I can get you? Hot sauce, maybe?"

"No hot sauce. This will be perfect." I started in on the two eggs over easy, black beans layered with corn tortillas and hash-browns smothered in salsa verde. Everything was topped with a large dollop of sour cream.

Ten minutes later, Billy slid in across from me just as I pushed my cleaned plate off to the side.

"You like it?"

"It was very good, Billy. God, if I ate breakfast like this every day, I wouldn't be able to fit in this booth."

"Hey, I want to thank you again for coming down here on such short notice last night. I don't know. Maybe I overreacted. But they were right outside, and when I saw the car pull up and that couple took one look at those jackasses, shook their heads, and drove away, I knew I had to do something."

"You've got cameras covering your parking lot and the front of the building, so that's going to serve as a deterrent to anyone with any brains."

"Yeah, but the way you put it doesn't seem to apply to these idiots. I don't know, I'm thinking of maybe hiring a security service, but that adds another aspect to the deal. I don't need people coming in here and wondering why I have a bouncer."

I nodded. "I think that makes sense. You know what might work? What if you had someone in here acting as a customer? Eating dinner, maybe having a dessert. Say they came in here around 8:00 and hung around until close."

"But the problem is these jerks are outside."

"So, if they're out there, you could give him the nod, and he'd step out, and they'd leave."

"One person? Dealing with those three? And, who knows how many others they have and what they might do? Besides, who is going to sit here every night? That would cost me an arm and a leg."

"Yeah, there would be a cost, but I think that would be temporary, and then maybe the guy just makes an occasional appearance. You know, he'd be here just enough so that if they're watching, it would make sense for them to go cause trouble somewhere else."

"That sounds good. You know anyone who would fit the bill?"

"It just so happens that I do. I haven't talked to him yet, but if he's up for it, I could probably have him here tonight."

"Well, if you think it'll work, I'm willing to give it a try. Who is this guy, anyway?"

"He's Luscious," I said and smiled.

Billy gave me a look. "You're not going to the other side on me, are you, Dev?"

"What? No, Billy, the guy's name is Luscious, Luscious Dixon. He played for the NFL a few years back. He's big. One look, and you wouldn't want to be on his wrong side. Now, he loves his food. So, I'm thinking, if you give him a meal or two every evening, maybe put him in one of these booths that look out onto the street and pay him a modest wage, he'd be up for it."

Billy seemed to consider that and then said, "So part of his payment would be a meal?"

I nodded. "Yeah, but it might be two meals or even three. You could work on giving him some healthy items, green beans, salads, and maybe a soup. As far as

I know, he's never met a food he didn't like. Last time I checked, he was making a daily appearance at McDonald's."

"And if there was a problem, I mean if these guys got rough, he'd be able to deal with it?"

"Let me put it this way, Luscious was a defensive end on three different NFL teams, all during the same preseason. He never played as much as a minute in any game, which seems in itself to be an NFL record of sorts. He has a number of issues; apparently, one of them being anger management, which helps to explain the felony convictions and his habit of quickly becoming a marketing liability to whatever team he signed with. If I remember correctly, I think his record was seventy-two hours with the San Francisco 49ers. Ultimately, it was decided Luscious drew the sort of attention the entire league was better off without. The anger issues, felony convictions, and the bad-boy profile made obtaining regular work for Luscious somewhat difficult in the NFL."

"Anger issues?"

"Only when he's hassled. Say, for example, by the three guys last night."

"And you'll vouch for him?"

"Oh yeah. Now, I still have to check and see if he would be interested. But I think he probably would be."

Billy nodded and said, "Okay, let's give it a try. How about we make a week-long contract. If that works out, we can extend it, and if it doesn't, well, at the end of the week, he's finished."

"That sounds good. I'll give him a call, and hopefully, he's available."

"Much appreciated, Dev," Billy said and extended his hand. "Hey, breakfast is on us, and I'm still waiting for you to bring your latest heartthrob in some night. All expenses paid."

Twelve

Morton was asleep in the back seat when I went out to my car. I glanced around. There were three security cameras covering the parking lot. I climbed in the car and buckled up just as my cell-phone signaled a text message coming in. I pulled my phone out and checked the message. Monica. I clicked on the message.

'Oh, Dev. I am so, so sorry. I can't believe I was that stupid last night. Too much wine. Too eager to get to know you 'better'. I'm hoping you grabbed the folder with the birth record because I couldn't find it this morning. I'll call you after work. Busy day and I've got a headache. Monica'

I sent her a short text. *'Hang in there, and I enjoyed being with you last night.'*

I glanced at the time on my cell. It wasn't quite 10:00. Maybe too early to phone Luscious. I pulled onto Highway 5, headed across the Mississippi River, then took the exit for Highway 62 and the Mendota Bridge. Resurrection Cemetery was on Lexington Avenue, just off of 62. It had been sixteen years since I'd been at Diane's gravesite, and a lot of people had taken up residence around her grave in that time. I had to stop in the office and get directions, but that only took a couple of minutes. In short order, I remembered my way, drove up a slight rise, and pulled alongside the family gravesite.

Morton paced back and forth across the backseat. I clicked his leash onto his collar and let him out. The family gravestone was made of shiny black granite with the name Donnelly in gold letters. Diane's parents' names were listed along with their birth dates but no date of death, which suggested they were still alive. Diane's gray granite grave stone was in front of the family stone. It was a simple rectangular granite stone set in the ground. Diane's name, along with her birthdate, November 4, 1986, and the date of her death, May 26, 2006, was in white engraved letters. In the upper right corner was the image of a dove in flight.

I got a lump in my throat and shook my head. Morton somehow picked up on it, gave a little whine, then rubbed his head against my knee. I bent down and gave him a good hug. "She would have liked you, Morton." We lingered for another couple of minutes and then went back to the office.

Louie was gone, and Morton settled onto his pillow and focused on his rawhide bone. I was on my computer clicking on the images of houses on Pinehurst Avenue in the Highland Park section of town. I thought Diane Donnelly had lived in the second house from the corner, but on clicking the images on Google Maps, it turned out to be the third house. I tossed a biscuit to Morton and closed the door behind me.

The Donnelly family had lived in a three-story brick home on Pinehurst Avenue. The first floor had been all hardwood floors covered with rugs as opposed to carpet. I pulled in front of the house and stared for a minute or two. The house looked the same as I remembered, except that the pine tree in the front yard was about twice the size. I finally took a deep breath, got out of the car, walked up to the front door, and rang the doorbell. A moment later, I heard a door open inside, and then the front door opened.

"Yes?" a gray-haired woman said. She had the same sparkling blue eyes as Diane. I hadn't seen her in twenty years, but she looked the same except for the gray hair. She was maybe a little shorter, or had I just grown that much?

"Mrs. Donnelly?"

"Yes."

"I'm sure you don't remember me. My name is Dev Haskell, and I was in high school with your—"

She got a funny look on her face. "Yes, you were in school with Diane. I remember. Oh my God. I'm sorry, we had heard you were dead. That you were killed in Iraq."

"No, ma'am. I was over there when Diane died, but…"

"Oh, well, here, excuse me. Where are my manners? Come in, come in, please," she said and unhooked the screen door. I stepped inside, and she said, "Oh, this is so nice to see you. Here, come into the kitchen. Can I get you some coffee?" she asked as I followed her into the kitchen.

"Yes, a coffee would be very nice. Thank you."

We cut through the dining room and then through a swinging door into the kitchen. The room looked the same as I remembered, with cherry wood kitchen cabinets. The countertops were still white, but now they looked like they were quartz instead of the Formica from when I was last here.

"Let me just call Bill. He'll want to see you. He's out working on his roses. Just a minute."

"Oh, don't bother him if he's—"

"Oh, he'd never forgive me."

She hurried out the other door to the kitchen. I remembered the back room as a den paneled in knotty pine with comfortable chairs, a TV, and an upright piano.

"Bill, oh, Bill. We have a guest in the kitchen," I heard her call.

I could hear their voices a moment later but couldn't make out what they were saying. They both stepped into the kitchen. "Well, Dev Haskell. This is a surprise. We thought you weren't with us anymore," Mr. Donnelly said and came around the kitchen counter and gave me a hug.

He was thinner than I remembered, with salt and pepper hair, but his voice sounded exactly the same. I remembered him saying more than once, "Now, not too late, tonight."

"How very nice of you to stop by, Dev. Really, this is a surprise. A wonderful surprise."

"Thank you. It's nice to see the two of you. You both look wonderful."

"We're here to tell the story," he said.

"Sit down, Bill. I'll get the coffee," his wife said as she set three mugs on the counter and took the coffee pot off the burner.

Thirteen

Mrs. Donnelly smiled. "Well, Dev, you look none the worse for wear. So what are you doing now?"

"Thank you." I nodded as Mrs. Donnelly pushed a mug of coffee across the counter to me. "What am I doing? Well, after high school, I enrolled at the University of Minnesota. I lasted a semester and decided it wasn't for me. I enlisted in the army, did a couple of tours overseas, and then got out."

"We had heard you were killed in Iraq."

"Yeah, a real screw-up. Actually, what happened was my folks had an officer knock on their door and tell them I had been killed. Fortunately for me, it was a guy with a similar name, Devon Haskens, from down in Lubbock, Texas. I never knew him. I learned later he was in the Army's Transportation Corps, killed by a roadside bomb just two weeks after he was in country. I found out about it when I called my folks a couple of days after the officer had knocked on their door. One of the crazier phone conversations I've ever had. I, umm, didn't know about Diane's passing until I was home after my first tour. I'm really sorry."

Mrs. Donnelly nodded. "Thank you. We still have the card you sent from overseas, along with all the others from people. Such a shame. She had really found herself and was going back to school, night classes in finance, when she was killed."

Mr. Donnelly looked at her and was about to say something when she reached over and placed her hand on top of his. She shook her head slightly. "So, you made it back in one piece, thank goodness. Did you go back to school on the GI Bill?"

"No, I was interested in police work. But the more I looked at it, the more it reminded me of being in the army, and at the time, that wasn't what I wanted. I ended up getting licensed as a private investigator, and I've been working for myself at Haskell Investigations ever since."

"So you're a private eye?" Mr. Donnelly said.

"Yeah, but I'd be the first to tell you it's nothing like you see on TV or in the movies. A good part of my work is checking out people's job applications. You know, did they actually work at a place for five years, were they really the employee of the month, that sort of thing."

"Interesting. Who would have thought?" Mrs. Donnelly mused.

"Yeah, I know what you mean, but I enjoy the work. I work hard at it, and thus far, it pays the bills."

"Good, for you. It's important that you like what you do. Long term, that's healthier for you than making a lot of money, and at the end of the day, you hate what you're doing, and you're unhappy."

"Yeah, well, actually, the reason I stopped by is I came across something, and I wanted to ask you about it. If you don't want me to go any further, I'll stop. I mean no disrespect."

Mrs. Donnelly suddenly placed her hand on her husband's again, only this time she didn't let go.

"Go on," Mr. Donnelly said.

"Okay. I was contacted about a week ago by a wealthy guy who was in the same high school class as Diane and me. Although, I never really knew him. He apparently fathered a child back in 2003. The child was adopted two or three days after being born. The birth was through Seton House, but it took place at St. Joseph's hospital."

The Donnellys both appeared to be pressing their lips together. Mrs. Donnelly's eyes began watering.

"If you want me to stop, I will. I just—"

Mr. Donnelly shook his head. "No, no, Dev, we knew this was bound to happen sooner or later. Go on," he said and wrapped his arm around his wife.

"So this guy gave me a copy of the birth record, and where his name should be, the record just says none. It said the same thing for the child's name, and the mother's name was blacked out, so all I really had was the birthdate. I went through a couple of people, and I was finally able to get a copy of the original record with the mother's birth name."

A tear ran down Mrs. Donnelly's cheek. "It listed Diane, didn't it?"

I pulled the folded copy from Monica out of my pocket and handed it to Mr. Donnelly. He didn't open it. He took a deep breath, exhaled, and said, "We'd thought for a long time that you had gotten her pregnant, but she kept insisting it wasn't you. We never found out who it was and, well, then she was killed in the hit and run and—"

"Wait. A hit and run? The information I had said she was killed in a car accident."

Donnelly shook his head. "She was killed in a hit and run, just outside of St. Catherine's College, on Randolph. She was taking night classes and was crossing the street to her car when some son of a bitch—"

"Bill, please," Mrs. Donnelly said.

"—ran over her and just kept on going."

"Were there any witnesses, evidence, something, anything?"

"There was a woman who said she saw the incident out her apartment window. One of those apartment buildings across the street from the college, but that was as far as it went. Nothing ever came of it. They said she died instantly. All sorts of traumatic injuries. Another driver stopped, but he didn't have anything to add. Cops spoke to both people, but as I said, nothing ever came of it."

"Oh, I'm so sorry."

"When she had the baby, we, well, let me back up," Mrs. Donnelly said. "When we learned of her pregnancy, we sent her to spend the summer with my sister and her husband in Afton. Right from the start, it was understood by all of us that the baby was going to be adopted. Through Seton House, a lovely couple met with Diane and the two of us, and the adoption was arranged months before the baby was born."

"It was hard on all of us," Mr. Donnelly said, "and it took Diane a good year at least to pull out of a postpartum depression, but she did it."

"Yes, and began working for an accounting firm, an entry-level position, but part of her salary included an option for night classes. She was almost finished with her second year when she was killed."

"It wasn't even dark out. Some son of a bitch drinking, talking on his damn phone, or looking the other way. Once he ran her over, he sped up and disappeared around the corner."

I shook my head and made a mental note to check the case files. "So, it sounds like the family that adopted the baby interacted with Diane and you."

They both nodded. "They were very kind," Mrs. Donnelly said.

"They made a very difficult situation bearable," Mr. Donnelly added. "They offered to pay for her medical costs. Insisted she make regular visits to the obstetrician. Visited Diane weekly and always brought her fresh fruit.

They had a garden, well, a farm actually, but they had a large garden and made sure she had fresh greens and eggs. It was really amazing. They were wonderful people. If the baby was going to be adopted, and long term that was the best option for Diane as well as the baby, they were the perfect couple."

"I'll be right back," Mrs. Donnelly said and hurried from the room.

"I'm sorry to bring this up. I know it has to be hard," I said.

Mr. Donnelly shook his head. "No, Dev, in a way, it's cathartic for both of us. We've been quiet about it for too long. Clearly, Diane's death was a hit and run. Was it intentional, someone she knew? We've no idea, and I've kept that thought locked up inside since the day it happened. Marilyn can't bear to hear me mention it, and I guess I'm at the point where our hearts have been broken enough by this. No good can come from me bringing that aspect up, so it's best to move on.

"Look what I found," Mrs. Donnelly said, coming back into the kitchen with two envelopes. She handed both envelopes to me. "Go ahead and open them up."

The envelopes were from 2003 and 2004. Each envelope had a Christmas stamp in the upper-righthand corner for thirty-seven cents. The words 'Seasons Greetings' were centered at the bottom of the envelope. They were addressed to Diane at this address on Pinehurst Avenue, with no return address.

I opened the first envelope. There was a Christmas card and inside the card was a color photo of a tiny baby wrapped in what looked like a Christmas blanket. The baby was held by a blonde woman with a dark-haired man sitting next to her. Both adults were all smiles.

"That's the Whites, Patrick's adoptive parents," Mrs. Donnelly said, and just like that, I had the child's name. She said a couple more things, but I was too focused on the name and the fact that he couldn't have been more than two and a half weeks old in the photo.

I turned to the second card, and once again, there was a Christmas stamp in the upper righthand corner of the envelope. This time the photo was of a little boy standing in front of a wingback chair. He was wearing blue sleepers. The one-piece kind with a zipper down the front and white plastic soles on the feet. His hair was reddish and still thin, but he was definitely from Diane's gene pool. I couldn't tell what color his eyes were.

"Are you still in touch with these people? What are their names?" I asked even though I'd read them on the Christmas cards.

"Kevin and Colleen White, and the baby is named Patrick," Mr. Donnelly said. "They lived out in the Prior Lake area. He was a farmer. I think she taught school."

Mrs. Donnelly nodded. "Yes, she taught second grade. Diane got to help choose the baby's name. We lost touch with them after her death. It was just too much, and as long as we knew the baby was in good hands, we thought that was enough. Now, well, I'm afraid we'd be inserting ourselves, and I'm sure they've done a wonderful job. He must be ready to graduate high school pretty soon."

"Actually, he'd be nineteen. I like that he has that hair. It's probably just like his mother's, beautiful," I said.

They both nodded but didn't say anything.

"Well, look, I should get out of your hair. Thank you for your time. It's been wonderful to see you," I said, picking up the birth record, folding it, and returning it to my pocket.

"You said you've met the father, the man who impregnated our daughter?" Mr. Donnelly said.

"Yes, I have."

"Well, thank you for not mentioning his name. No telling what we might want to do to him. He left Diane in an awful predicament. As far as connecting him with the child, I'd be careful. I can't see anything positive he'd have to offer, and the lad, Patrick, would be better off not accepting anything. You're an adult. It's your decision. Just so you know where we stand."

"I appreciate that and thank you again. It was wonderful to see you both."

Mrs. Donnelly smiled and said, "Wonderful to see you, Dev. You're always welcome here."

"Thank you," I said.

They walked me to the door. We said another round of thank yous, and I headed to my car. As I drove off, they were still at the front door, Mr. Donnelly's arm around his wife and her head rested on his shoulder.

I thought it was funny that they never mentioned Grumley by name, but then apparently, Diane never told them his name. Did it make any difference? No, not really, except that right now, I was wondering exactly how much I was going to tell Arthur Grumley.

Fourteen

Louie was still out of the office. Morton was asleep on his pillow. As I entered the office, he opened one eye, saw it was me, and went back to sleep. I settled in at my desk and paged through my Rolodex, until I landed on the card for Luscious Dixon. There were three different addresses on the card. The first two were crossed out. I called him on my cell phone and was in the process of leaving a message when he called back.

"Hello, Luscious, long time no see," was how I answered his call.

"Same from this end, Dev. How you been?"

"Couldn't be better. How are you?"

"Good, real good. Got me a job."

"A job? What are you doing?"

"I do a training and weightlifting class for a gym every day. I'm in the best shape I've probably ever been in. Feeling good. I even got a little money in the bank."

"Oh, that's great news, Luscious. I'm happy to hear that. Congratulations. Well deserved."

"Thank you, Dev. Now to what do I owe the pleasure of your phone call?"

"Well, I had a short little gig I was hoping you'd be interested in. But it's really great news you've got that weightlifting job."

"Well, hold on, now, Dev. That just keeps me busy in the morning. What is it you were thinking of?"

Perfect. "Here's the deal, Luscious," I said and went on to fill him in on the Billy Flores situation.

"I can do that, Dev. I'm not busy in the evenings. Oh, and get this. Guess what I got?"

"Hopefully not Covid," I said.

"No, Dev. But I'm independent now. I got me a driver's license, and I got my own car."

"You're driving yourself?" I asked, thinking I wasn't sure that was such a good idea, at least from the 'safety of the city' point of view. "Oh, that's, umm, really great news, Luscious."

"Yes. It is. So how about this, you said around 8:00, why don't we meet down at that restaurant a little before 8:00 tonight? You can introduce me to your man Billy. We'll go over what he wants, and if it sounds okay, I'll be happy to help out."

"Luscious, that's great. Thank you. I'll call Billy, tell him we'll be there tonight. You sure you want to drive?"

"Yeah, honest, Dev. I like getting myself to places. Now I don't have to depend on others. I can come and go as I like, and I've never even had an accident."

"Sounds great. Here, let me give you Billy's address. There's a parking lot in the back where you can park and a rear entrance to the restaurant. I'll see you there tonight at 8:00, Luscious."

"See you there, Dev. Looking forward to it, and thanks for thinking of me."

I got to Billy's well before Luscious. I was waiting in what, apparently, had become my usual booth. Miguel was my server, and at the moment, I was sipping a beer. Luscious stepped in the rear entrance at maybe 8:20. I gave him a wave, and he headed in my direction.

I have to say that more than one head turned as he came through the dining room. He was dressed in jeans and a short-sleeve shirt. If I had to guess, I would have said he'd lost close to a hundred pounds. He was big, muscular, and smiling as he headed toward me.

I stepped out of the booth as he approached and held out my hand. Luscious slapped my hand away, gave me a bear hug, and lifted me off the floor. Just about the time I was going to cry 'uncle,' he released his grip and smiled.

"Dev, you still look the same, dude. Great to see you again."

"Wonderful to see you, Luscious. Come on, sit down. You look like you've dropped a ton of weight, and obviously, you've been working out."

He flashed a grin. "That's the beauty of my job. They're actually paying me to work out. I'm there seven days a week. I haven't felt this good in years. Even got me a girlfriend," he said.

"A girlfriend? That's exciting news. What's her name?"

"Oh, I'm not telling the likes of you. I know how you be. Next thing I know, you'll be calling her up, wanting to take her out."

"No, I wouldn't do that to you, Lucious. Honest, I wouldn't."

"Yeah, I know. I was just playing with ya."

Billy suddenly appeared and said, "Good evening, Dev." He shook my hand and turned to face Lucious. Billy was an inch taller than me, and Lucious was a good two inches taller than Billy. Suddenly, my average height was the shortest in the group.

"Hi, Billy. This is the gentleman I was telling you about, Mr. Luscious Dixon. Luscious, this is Billy Flores, the owner of the restaurant."

They shook hands, and Billy grinned, taking in Luscious's size and physique. "Please, let's sit down, and we can talk," Billy said and then waved a hand, indicating I should move over so he could slide in next to me. "Have you ordered yet?" Billy said and raised a hand to Miguel.

Miguel was over with two menus a moment later. I ordered another beer, and Luscious ordered orange juice.

"You got a special tonight, Billy?" I asked as I scanned the menu.

Billy shook his head. "Everything's a special for you guys, on the house, order whatever you like. Dev told me you were with the NFL," Billy turned to Luscious.

Luscious smiled and nodded. "Yeah, three different teams and never played for a single second. That's okay. They gave me a nice package to go away, and I was happy to take it. I don't want the problems all those concussions lead to in later years or have to get my knees replaced. I think I came out better than a lot of guys."

And so it went. Luscious seemed to be a changed individual. Pleasant, funny, a hundred pounds lighter, in shape, and armed with a driver's license. I took a pass on staying for dinner. Luscious ordered a dinner salad. I left when the salad arrived to give the two of them a chance to discuss things without my interference.

When I got home, I called Aaron LaZelle. Amazingly, he answered. "Hi Dev, let me stop you before you tell me what's wrong. This is my first night off in six days. If this is your one phone call, you're going to have to spend the night in a cell, and I'll see you sometime tomorrow."

"So not funny, Aaron. Have you really been working the last six nights?"

"Well, maybe not. What's up with you?"

"I wanted to look up a case from about twenty years ago. Apparently a hit and run. Who should I talk to?"

"Is it officially listed as a hit and run?"

"That's my understanding. I got this information from the parents, so it's possible this is their version, but that said, the little they told me sure sounded like a hit and run.”

“Well, I can have that file pulled for you. What’s the victim’s name?”

“Diane Donnelly.”

“Diane Don—is this the girl you dated senior year?”

“Yeah, last half of senior year. We clicked at a practice for the senior class play. She was in the play. I was a stagehand.”

“She was a redhead, wasn’t she?”

“Yeah, dumped me on graduation night.”

“If I remember, you weren’t too happy about that.”

“I’d say that’s correct, maybe even a bit of an understatement. I recently learned a couple of things about her. If you could have that file pulled, I’d like to look at it.”

“Hmmm, interesting. Tell you what, come on down around 11:00. You can go through the file, and we can grab lunch afterward. You’ll be paying, by the way. Of course, this is subject to neither one of our days going haywire, which usually happens by about 9:00.”

“Thanks, Aaron, much appreciated. I’ll see you tomorrow. Lunch wherever you want to go. You know there’s a McDonald’s about a half-mile from your office.”

“See you tomorrow, Dev,” Aaron said and hung up.

I was tempted to call Monica but decided against it. Maybe give her some time without me pressuring her.

Besides, I couldn't seem to get my mind off of Diane and what her parents had told me about the hit and run.

I took Morton for a walk, and we watched a movie I didn't realize I'd seen before until about ten minutes from the ending when everything suddenly came back to me. Three minutes of the evening news was all I could take, and we headed up to bed.

Fifteen

Things seemed to be pretty much back to normal for both Morton and me. I gave him a good head scratch when he made his morning appearance. Once he was back in the house, he was more focused on his breakfast than checking me out.

Surprisingly, Louie was already in the office and had the coffee made when we arrived. He was in the process of placing a file in his briefcase and heading out the door before we'd even settled in.

"Gotta run. I've got a 10:00 appointment to interview my client, nursing a hangover in the drunk tank. We're appearing before a judge at 11:00."

"A repeat offender?"

"Afraid so, and she's going to be doing some time on this one. Probably lose her license."

"Good luck," I said.

"Multiple past experiences tell me exactly how this is going to go down. Not well for her."

"Hang in there," I said as Louie hurried out of the office. I watched out the window as he waddled across the street, and I thought of all the weight Luscious Dixon had lost and the great shape he was in now.

I debated calling Arthur Grumley and decided against it. I Googled the names Kevin and Coleen White and eventually came up with a number of images. Pictures of what looked like extended family get-togethers, a couple of high school graduations for blonde daughters, and then there was the picture of them with their red-haired son, Patrick. He was wearing a high school graduation robe and had a big smile on his face. If Diane had been gorgeous, this kid was handsome and very good-looking, and I could see a strong resemblance to Diane. Oh, and in the picture, his blue eyes seemed to sparkle. The line below the photo read, "Rusty's graduation."

I couldn't find an address, but there were three pictures of a two-story house with a front porch. Given the area, the house was probably a hundred years old and was painted yellow with white trim. A large red barn was behind the house. I'd been out to the Prior Lake area a couple of times over the years. It used to be all farm country, but I knew that had changed in the last two decades. Now new homes were being built, not starter homes, but million-dollar places on three to five acres with swimming pools and three-car garages. That said, the graduation picture of Rusty was two years old, and he was definitely at a farmhouse with a red barn in the background.

I glanced at the clock on my computer. I was due in Aaron's LaZelle's office in ten minutes. I tossed Morton a biscuit, locked the door behind me, and hurried to my car.

The visitor's parking lot across the street from the police department is a gravel affair pockmarked with potholes. I was able to avoid three of the larger ones and parked in the back of the lot away from the other cars. I hurried across the street, entered the building, and headed for the front desk.

One of the officers looked up as I approached. He had dark hair, gray around the temples, and a salt and pepper mustache. He wore a set of wireless headphones and had a slim microphone running along his left cheek. He watched as I approached and then said, "Dev Haskell? When did we let you out?"

"Hey, Dennis, how are you doing?"

"Still here to tell the story. You here to see LaZelle?"

"Yeah, if he's available. We set up a tentative 11:00 meeting."

"Let me see if he's come to his senses and is busy," he said and punched in a couple of numbers. "Yes, sir, I have a Devlin Haskell to see you. Says he has an appoint-ment. Yes, sir. Thank you," he said and disconnected. "He'll send someone down to escort you. Just grab a seat, Dev. Should only be a couple of minutes."

"Thanks, Dennis," I said and wandered over to the waiting area filled with five rows of black plastic chairs and an assortment of characters. Of course, when you considered the location, waiting in the police department, odds are whatever the situation, it probably wasn't positive.

"Dev Haskell," a guy in plain clothes called a few minutes later. I hurried over to the metal door he held open. A badge and pistol were attached to his belt. As I passed the front desk, I said, "Thanks, Dennis. Good to see you."

"Always nice to see you, Dev," he said.

It was just enough to let the guy holding the door open know that I was okay. "Thanks for coming down to get me." I stepped through and he closed the door behind us.

"Not a problem. You've been here before?"

"Yeah, many times. I've known LaZelle since we were kids."

He pressed the up button on the elevator and nodded. "You're a PI, aren't you?"

"Yes, I am."

"Yeah, I've seen you here before. Tommy Jacabowski," he held his hand out. We stepped into the elevator, shook hands, and he pushed the button for the third floor. The doors opened a half-minute later, and we walked down the hall to Homicide. "I'm just going to let you in and then run, I need to leave. You know where the LT's office is?"

"I do unless it's been moved in the past couple of weeks."

He smiled at that and input a code on the keypad next to the door marked Homicide. Once the door buzzed, he pulled it open and said, "You're good to go."

I stepped into the Homicide office. There were all sorts of desks, maybe a quarter of them occupied. Most of the people at the desks were on the phone. Everyone at a desk had at least one file open in front of them and a stack of files waiting for attention.

I nodded at a couple of guys I recognized and got a few nods back as I headed toward Aaron's office. I kept an eye peeled for Detective Norris Manning. We'd had what could be described as an adversarial relationship for a number of years, but hopefully, that had improved since I was able to help with a problem his son had.

Aaron's office was in a corner at the far end of the room. The two walls protruding from the exterior walls had windows from halfway up the wall to the ceiling. Venetian blinds hung from the windows, and at the moment, they were pulled open. I could see Aaron LaZelle at his desk. A sergeant and Detective Norris Manning were seated in front of the desk. A number of files were scattered in front of them.

I stopped and debated knocking on the door. "You waiting for the LT?" a detective seated at his desk asked.

"Yeah, you got any idea how long they're going to be?"

He shook his head and said, "You're the PI, right?" I nodded. "Yeah, he mentioned you were coming in to look at a file. Go ahead and knock on the door. They're finishing up."

"You sure?"

"Yeah, he's expecting it."

"Thanks," I said and stepped over to the door and knocked.

I waited a moment, and suddenly the door opened. "Hi, Dev. Here you go. Grab a seat out there and take a look. We'll be finished up here in a bit," Aaron said and handed me a thin file.

"Take a seat at Owens' desk," the detective said and nodded toward the empty desk next to him. "He's out for a couple of days."

"Thanks, I shouldn't be too long."

"Depends on what you find. Good luck," he said.

I sat down at the desk. It was cleared off except for the desktop computer, a phone, and a framed photo of a woman and three young kids. I opened the file, and there was a copy of Diane's graduation picture. There were six black and white 8x10 photos of the accident scene taken from a couple of different angles. Two of the photos showed Diane's body covered by a white sheet and two patrol officers with their backs to the camera looking east toward Fairview Avenue. Another two photos were taken approximately from where the body was looking west down a hill toward Cleveland Avenue. I stared long and hard at the body covered by the sheet, then began to read the report.

The case was officially a hit and run. The time of the accident was listed as sometime between 20:10 and 20:25, 8:10 and 8:25 PM. That would have probably been just after an hour-long class that had started at 7:00. I went back to the photographs. Diane was hit as she left the campus. Based on where the covered body was, she was probably thrown fifteen or twenty feet. There was a thick hedge approximately four feet high running along the campus grounds on Randolph Avenue. She would not have been able to cut through the hedge and gain access to the street. In the photos looking west, there was a sidewalk leading through the hedge and then a cross-walk painted on the street. She had probably parked across the street from the campus and would have been headed back to her car. It would have still been light out at that hour in late May. With the campus on one side of the two-lane street, houses, and a couple of seventy-year-old apartment buildings on the opposite side of the street, it wasn't the typical area you'd expect to see a speeding car, not that it didn't happen.

The report had very little information other than the two interviews, along with the names, addresses, and phone numbers of both eyewitnesses. One was the driver of a car, a man named Walter Sheridan, and the other was a woman named Eleanor Monroe. She lived in an apartment directly across the street from the campus. I copied down their names, phone numbers, and addresses.

The detective in charge of the investigation was Roger O'Leary. I'd met him once or twice a few years ago and was pretty sure he had retired. The witness statements were brief. Eleanor Monroe had glanced out her window on the first floor just as Diane was struck by a red car. Walter Sheridan stated that he was driving up the hill on Randolph Avenue when a red vehicle with a spoiler pulled away from the curb and sped toward Diane, who had just stepped into the street. She turned around in an attempt to get back to the sidewalk. The car seemed to swerve and intentionally hit her. Once she was struck, the car sped down the street, ran a red light, and made a right-hand turn at the next corner. Neither witness could identify the driver or had a license number.

Aaron's office door opened. Manning and the Sergeant stepped out. Manning gave me a polite nod. "What do you say to some lunch?" Aaron said as he followed them out and closed the door behind him.

Sixteen

We were finishing up our Coney dogs and Cokes at the Gopher Bar, one of the city's more notable dive bars. The owner and crabby cook is named George. He rarely has anything nice to say to anyone, which is part of his charm. He's always been nice to Aaron and me.

"From the eyewitness account I read in the file, it sounds like the car sped up, aimed for her, and intentionally hit her," I said. "Based on the two photographs of her body and the location, I'm guessing she was knocked fifteen to twenty feet."

"I went through the file but just glanced. Was there an autopsy report?" Aaron asked.

"No, there wasn't," I said and wrote 'autopsy' down in my notebook.

"Well, when she was hit, she probably had three impacts. The first would be the car striking her. The second would likely be her flying up, over the hood, and into the windshield, and the third would be falling off the hood and landing on the street. Based on those photos in the file, she may have bounced off the curb and back into the street.”

“The witness in the car behind said the red vehicle was parked at the curb. It suddenly pulled away from the curb, sped up, and hit her. It sure sounded like it was intentional.”

Aaron nodded and said, “Possibly. Don’t get me wrong. I’m not suggesting it wasn’t. But the odds are, if you’re hit by a car going twenty-five to thirty miles per hour, you’re probably going to die. Pulling away from the curb and speeding up, does that mean the driver was trying to get some distance from the witness’s car? Maybe he was only doing twenty, and the witness was doing fifteen. I’m not saying this wasn’t intentional but keep an open mind.”

“Yeah, I get it. But put that aside for a moment. The one fact that’s a given is that after hitting Diane, her body ends up fifteen or twenty feet from the crosswalk. He doesn’t stop. In fact, according to the witness in the car, the guy speeds up, runs a red light, and makes a right-hand turn at the next corner. That suggests to me that he was aware of what had just occurred. And that, in my opinion, increases by a certain percentage the idea that this was intentional.”

“You going to try to find these two people, the witnesses?” Aaron said.

“The witnesses? Yeah, their addresses and phone numbers were in the file. It’s a number of years ago, but you don't forget something like this, as much as you might want to."

"Be interesting to see if you can even find them."

"Yeah, that long ago. In fact, after lunch, I'm going to check out the addresses, knock on the door of the guy's place, and step into that apartment building. Hopefully, they'll have names on the mailboxes in an entry area."

"Let me know if I can be of any help. You ready to head out? I got a 1:00."

"Yeah, let me settle up with George," I said and pushed away from the table.

Our receipt was a handwritten affair labeled 'Guest Check' across the top and then a pale green area where someone, either crabby George or the waitress, scribbled

2 coney 2 cokes $10.<u>50</u>

<u>Thanx</u>

I stepped over to the bar and handed the receipt and a twenty to our waitress. She was in the process of pouring beers for a table of three guys.

"Thanks," she nodded. "You need any change?"

"Give me a couple of bucks."

She finished filling the beer mugs and pulled two one-dollar bills from the cash register. "Here you go," she said and didn't smile. A seven-dollar tip on a ten-dollar lunch made me wonder if I was in the wrong line of work.

I drove back to the station with Aaron. I took another look at the case file on Diane's hit and run. I knew

I was prejudiced, but I was even more convinced her death had been intentional. At Aaron's request, I left the file with the guy at the desk next to me, and he wished me luck on my way out the door.

I drove over to the College of St. Catherine, called St. Catherine University, as of 2009. Not much had changed on Randolph Avenue in the last sixteen years. The apartment building where Eleanor Monroe had witnessed the hit and run was a two-story gray stucco structure built in 1926 and located on the corner. According to Google, the building had five one-bedroom rental units. Looking from the outside, both first-floor units would have had a clear view of Randolph Avenue.

I was able to step into a small entry with five mailboxes built into the wall and a sign with directions on how to contact a specific resident on the wall phone. The door next to the phone was locked. Unfortunately, there were no names on the mailboxes. There was a sign with the landlord's name, Stevenson & Associates, along with a phone number, and I wrote the number down. I went back out to my car and phoned the number for Eleanor Monroe and crossed my fingers, hoping the number, after all these years, was still good. Thank God. I got dropped into her voicemail.

"Hi, you've reached Eleanor. Can't take your call right now. Leave a message, and I'll get back to you."

"Hi, Eleanor, my name is Dev Haskell. I'm a private investigator in St. Paul. I'm looking into a hit-and-run incident that happened back in 2006. You're listed in the police report as an eyewitness, and I would like to talk to you." I left my phone number along with a 'Thank you' and disconnected.

Walter Sheridan's address was just a few blocks away on Stanford Avenue, so I drove over there. His two-story home was a buff-colored stucco structure with brown trim. The lot had a steep hill with six steps leading up to a curving sidewalk. The sidewalk led to three steps and the front door. I was able to park just across the street. I climbed the steps. The place appeared to be well kept, the grass was cut and edged along the sidewalk, and the hedge along the front of the house was neatly trimmed.

I rang the doorbell, and soon after, an older woman, short, with gray hair and red lipstick, answered the door. She was wearing a dress that looked like it had been styled in the 1970s.

"Yes?"

"Hello. My name is Devlin Haskell. I'm looking for Walter Sheridan."

"What is this about?"

"Mr. Sheridan was an eyewitness to a hit and run incident on Randolph Avenue back in 2006. I'm investigating that incident and would like to talk with him."

"That's going to be a long wait, I'm afraid. Walter passed away in 2018 from a heart attack."

"Oh, I'm sorry to have troubled you. My condolences."

"Thank you. He didn't like to talk about it, the accident. He'd been in Viet Nam and had seen enough injured people to last two lifetimes. He was the first person on the scene. I mean, the car that hit the girl had pulled out in front of Walter, sped up almost as if he intended to hit her, and then just disappeared around a corner. Dreadful, absolutely dreadful. Walter rushed out of his car to help the girl and knew immediately it was too late. There was nothing he could do."

"He was your husband?"

She nodded and said, "Yes, we were married fifty years."

"Well, you must have been ten when you were married."

She smiled and said, "Not quite, but thank you. Back to this dreadful accident. Why are you investigating it after all this time? If Walter called once, he must have called a half-dozen times asking if there was any progress. But, unfortunately, there never was."

"Other than your husband's statement and one other witness, there was never any other information. From what I read in the report, there was no way to trace the vehicle, no license number or make. Other than the description of a red vehicle, nothing else."

"He always maintained the car was driven by a young man. It was a red car like you said. I remember that much."

"Did he ever mention anything specific about the car or what the driver looked like?"

She shook her head. "No, and I remember that frustrated Walter. The truth is, he just had a quick glance from behind when the car pulled in front of him. If the girl hadn't been hit, he never would have remembered the car."

"Thank you for your time, Mrs. Sheridan. May I give you my business card? If something should come to mind, you could call me."

"Well, you can give me your card, but I don't think I would have anything to add. But sure," she said as she pushed the screen door open.

After thanking her and handing her my card, it was time to leave. My cellphone rang on the way back to the office. Since I was driving, I didn't answer. Morton met me at the door when I stepped into the office. Apparently, Louie hadn't returned, so I grabbed Morton's leash, and we went for our usual walk. Thinking things over, I decided to wait to talk with Eleanor Monroe before getting in touch with Roger O'Leary, the detective who had been in charge of the investigation.

Thinking of Eleanor reminded me of the phone call I never answered because I was driving. While Morton examined the fire hydrant for the proper target, I pulled out my cellphone, hoping the call had been from Eleanor Monroe. Unfortunately, it wasn't. Arthur Grumley had called.

"Haskell, Arthur Grumley. Wondering what you've come up with. Last I heard, you were about to get the boy's name. Call me."

I wasn't quite ready to call Grumley.

Seventeen

Louie wandered into the office just after 3:00. "How'd it go?" I asked once he'd recovered from climbing the stairs.

"Things were going pretty much the way I hoped until she thought it was a good idea to call the judge a rather caustic name and then demanded that her right to free speech was being violated. She'll have three days in the workhouse to think about it before she begins her six-month sentence. Her driver's license has been revoked, and I suspect she's in line to lose her job as a school bus driver, so all in all, it made for an interesting day."

"Man, and I thought I had problems."

"How's the search for the adopted kid going?"

"Like most cases, moving forward slowly but surely. The direction keeps changing as the process develops."

"Mmm, so in other words, you're not going to tell me."

"Yeah, something like that," I said just as my phone rang. "Oh, gotta take this. Hello, Luscious. I was just about to call you. How did things go last night?"

"Absolutely boring, which was perfect. I had a wonderful salad, and later in the evening, Billy insisted I have a plate of grilled salmon."

"Sounds great. Did you like it?"

"Oh, yeah, very good. I walked around the outside a half-dozen times. I never saw anything out of line. No reports of cars being broken into, slit tires, or anything like that."

"Good, glad to hear it. Just continue to keep an eye out. I don't like these three idiots who were hanging around the other night."

"Don't you worry, I'll keep my eyes peeled. I just wanted to thank you for getting me this job, Dev. It works perfectly with my weightlifting class in the morning. I can go home in the afternoon, nap if I'm tired, and then I get paid for eating a healthy dinner."

"Good, Luscious, glad it's working out. Any trouble, you call me right away, and I'll be there."

"Thank you, Dev. Very much appreciated. Catch you later, dude," he said and hung up. I quickly dialed Monica's number rather than get the third degree from Louie about Grumley. I ended up leaving a quick message and then went onto my laptop.

I googled the name White and the town of Prior Lake. A number of images came up along with some business names, one of which was called White Acres. I clicked on the site, and there it was, a picture of Kevin White in jeans and a short sleeve work shirt. He was leaning against a green four-wheel-drive vehicle, maybe an industrial lawnmower or something like that. It was definitely the same man in the photo of the couple holding the baby that Mrs. Donnelly had shown me. He was older, and his hair was thinner, but there was no mistaking him.

"You going anywhere this afternoon?" I asked Louie.

"I'm here until my workout over at The Spot."

"Your workout?"

"I'm lifting, Dev," Louie said and bent his elbow on his right arm as if he held a glass he was about to drink.

"I might be gone for a couple of hours. I want to check out a guy west of town."

"Not a problem. I'll be here. If we happen to be gone when you get back, you know where we'll be."

"Thanks, see you later," I said and left. The drive out to the Prior Lake area is all freeway now. I hopped on I35 for twenty-five minutes and took the exit marked Prior Lake. My GPS directed me to turn onto Murphy Boulevard, a gravel road, and a mile down the road, the audio informed me, "You have reached your destination."

There it was, a yellow house with white trim and a red barn behind it. I pulled onto a paved drive that led past the house and to the red barn. Once I was past the house, it was obvious the barn had been revamped and looked like a remodeled office structure. There were three cars and two pickup trucks parked next to the double glass doors that formed the entrance. I pulled in between the pickup trucks and headed for the doors.

I stepped into a large room with three paintings of farm fields hanging from the walls. "Hi, can I help you?" a blonde woman wearing blue jeans and a white blouse with the sleeves rolled up asked.

I'd seen her before, as recently as today, on my computer. "You wouldn't happen to be Colleen White, would you?"

"Yes, I am. I'm sorry, have we met?"

I shook my head. "No, my name is Dev Haskell. I'm a private investigator in the twin cities. I got your name and your husband's from Mr. and Mrs. Donnelly. They're the parents of Diane Donnelly. The biological mother of your son."

She got a strange look on her face and said, "Let me call my husband." Before I could answer, she stepped behind the reception counter and picked up the phone. A moment later, she said, "Kevin, would you come out here, please? No, no, please. Yes, thank you."

"I'm sorry. I didn't mean to upset you. I have a client that—"

"What's the problem?" a voice said, and I turned to look at Kevin White. His hair was maybe a little thinner than in the image I saw online, but it was clearly him. He wore jeans and a blue shirt embroidered with 'White Acres' in yellow.

"Hi, Mr. White. My name is Dev Haskell. I'm a private investigator in the twin cities. I was given your name by Mr. and Mrs. Donnelly, the parents of Diane Donnelly, the biological mother of your son, Patrick."

"Yes, I, we know the Donnelly's. We also know that Diane was killed in an automobile accident a number of years ago. So what is this about?"

"Could we maybe sit down, and I can explain what I know thus far?"

"Are we going to need an attorney? Are we being sued?"

"Sued? Oh, no, sir, nothing like that. Actually, I have some questions with regard to an investigation, and before I proceed, I want to make sure you and your wife are aware of what I'm doing and that you're comfortable with it. I knew Diane Donnelly. We went to high school together and—"

"Are you Patrick's biological father? The guy who didn't want his name on the birth certificate?"

"No, sir, I'm not. Can we maybe sit down, and I can try to explain the situation, please?"

His wife nodded. He took a deep breath and said, "Okay, my office is back this way."

Eighteen

We walked past two other offices. White's office was in the back of the building and had a door on the far wall leading outside. We went through his office and stepped out onto a small patio with cushioned chairs and a table with an umbrella. The patio itself was poured concrete stamped to look like stone. The Whites settled onto a couch, and I sat in a chair facing them. They both looked worried.

"Let me start by saying this has nothing to do with any questions regarding your adoption proceeding. That is perfectly legal and aboveboard. This has nothing to do with Mr. and Mrs. Donnelly, other than the fact that they are very happy you two were there to adopt Patrick and, in the process, were very kind to their daughter Diane."

That seemed to relieve some stress.

"I should also mention that I went to high school with Diane. We were in the same class, and we dated during the final semester of our senior year. I'm not the father of Patrick and would be willing to submit to a DNA test if you wish." A little more stress seemed to disappear.

"I was contacted a few days ago by an individual who claims to be Patrick's biological father and wants me to find him. He does not know Patrick's name, and he does not know where, at this stage, Patrick lives. The boy could be in Europe for all he knows. He knows absolutely nothing about you guys."

"So why, after all this time, is he looking for him?" Colleen asked.

"He told me he wanted to make sure everything was okay and that if Patrick needed help in any way, he would try to help. I will add that he was in the same high school class as Diane and me. I've only met him that one time since we graduated. I did not like him in high school, and I don't think I like him now, but that's my opinion. He apparently is a very wealthy individual. He has a successful business doing programing for online games and marketing. I wanted to talk to you, tell you what I know, and then if you decide you would prefer not to have him involved, I'll just go back and tell him I've hit a dead end."

"But if he's as rich as you say, what would stop him from hiring some other investigator who would find Patrick and pass on the information? No offense, but if you got this information, what's to stop anyone else?" Kevin said.

"I know what you mean. I know Mr. and Mrs. Donnelly, and I could tell them not to give that information to anyone. But, that said, they showed me two Christmas cards with photos of Patrick that you sent. One of the photos has the two of you on the couch. Colleen is holding the baby. You've got your arm around her, and Patrick looks maybe two or three weeks old. The other picture has him around a year old in a blue sleeper standing in front of a chair."

"I remember those. Actually, we sent them to Diane," Colleen said.

"Yeah, but she was living with her folks," Kevin said. "I think she was hit by that car maybe a year later. I just remember we only sent two cards, and she had died before he turned three years old. We really liked her and wanted her to be a part of Patrick's life. At least as much as she wanted to be."

"Well, there's another part to this I want to bring up. Mostly just a theory on my part."

"What is it?" Colleen said.

"Diane was killed in a hit and run. No one was ever charged. In fact, I just went through the police case file from back in 2006. They never had a suspect. There were two eyewitnesses, but their information was sketchy at best. All they knew was that she was struck by a red car. One of the witnesses said he thought it was intentional. The way he described it made it sound like she was coming from an evening class at St Catherine's College. As she stepped into the street, a red car pulled away from the curb, sped up, and hit her, probably killing her instantly. The car ran a red light and disappeared around a corner a block away. There was never a license plate number and never a description of the driver, other than it was a male. Nothing. The case hit a wall and remains unsolved to this day."

"It sounds like you have some thoughts," Kevin said.

"General thoughts, nothing specific. But that's where this is now. You two seem to have gone above and beyond in the adoption process, and you've got a lovely son to show for your effort."

They both smiled, and Colleen said, "Thank you."

"We'd love to have you meet Rusty. He's a great kid. He's starting his second year at the U this fall. He's out on a job site right now, but they'll be back in an hour or two. You're welcome to stay. Relax out here if you want," Kevin said.

"One of his hobbies is growing roses," Colleen said.

"Thanks, but I think I should head back to town before rush hour kicks in. Here," I said, pulling a business card from my wallet. "Let me give you this. Think about what I said. Talk it over and call me in the next day or two if you have any concerns. I'm sorry if I've caused you a headache. I just thought it was important to bring you up to date rather than have someone suddenly appear in your lives, well, and in Rusty's life, too."

Kevin took the card, glanced at it, and said, "Thanks Dev. We'll give you a call, and if there is anything we could do to help in the hit-and-run situation, please let us know. Diane was a real sweetheart, and we are blessed to have Rusty as a son."

"Does he know he was adopted?"

They both nodded. "We waited until he was old enough to understand. It's been what, ten years now?" Colleen said.

Kevin nodded. "We told him, out of all the children in the world, we chose him, which I guess is pretty true," he said, and we all laughed.

Kevin held out his hand, and we shook. "Thank you, Dev. We appreciate you making the effort to get in touch with us. You could have just dumped this on all three of us."

"All five," Colleen said. "The girls would go crazy. They've been Patrick's biggest fans since the moment he arrived."

"Thanks. I won't proceed with this until I hear from you. Give me a call when you come to a decision, hopefully in the next day or two," I said.

"We'll discuss it tonight," Kevin said. "Please give our best to the Donnelly's. We'd love to have them meet Rusty at some point."

"I will. Thanks for letting me interrupt your day. Take care,"

Nineteen

I was just pulling in across the street from the office when my phone rang. I pulled it out and said, "Hi, Sandie. How are things?"

"Hi, Dev. How are things? Well, my folks finally headed back up north after lunch today. I'm in the process of rearranging my kitchen and undoing the changes my mother made while I was at work."

"Sounds like fun."

"The 'F' and the 'U' are correct, but fun isn't the word I'm coming up with. Wondering if you'd have time for dinner tonight? I feel like I owe you after you sat through a meal with my folks."

"Relax, Sandie, they were nice."

"Well, thanks for understanding and sitting through the third degree. I felt like I was back in high school, and they were interrogating my homecoming date."

"Hopefully, I passed."

She didn't respond to that last comment. "Can you make it over tonight?"

"Yeah, I'd love to come. What can I bring?"

"Nothing, I've got wine. I'll be baking salmon fillets. Tell you what, how about something for dessert? You choose whatever you want."

"I can do that. Is 6:00 okay?"

"That would be perfect. I look forward to seeing you," she said.

I stepped out of the car and went up to the office. Louie was typing away on his computer. Morton opened one eye as I stepped in, saw it was me, and went back to sleep. I had just settled in at my desk and happened to glance out the window as a shiny black Mercedes that looked like a jeep pulled alongside the curb in front of my car. The driver stepped out of the car. He was dressed in navy-blue slacks and a light-blue, starched shirt, and I recognized him as Tony, Grumley's butler or whatever he did. He opened the rear door of the car, and Arthur Grumley stepped out. He glanced around, frowned, and then walked across the street to our building. Tony climbed back into the driver's seat.

I heard the stairs begin to creak, suggesting it was too late to run down the hall and hide in the men's room. "Louie, I just saw my pain in the ass client cross the street. He's coming up the stairs. You may want to take off."

"On the other hand, I may find it interesting. Besides, a witness is always a good thing to have on your side."

"Suit yourself," I said. I quickly picked up my notes and the copy of the birth record Monica got for me and dumped them in my desk drawer on top of the Glock pistol I kept. Just as I closed the drawer, the door opened, and Grumley stepped in.

"Well, Haskell, glad I found you," he said. He looked over at Louie behind the picnic table, made a face, shook his head, and headed for my desk. Morton was up and looking at Grumley, who was in the process of running a hand across the back of my client chair. Once he'd done that, he checked his hand for dust.

"Nice to see you, Arthur. Please take a seat."

"I think I'll stand if it's all the same. Since you didn't answer my phone call or my text message, I decided I'd come in. Maybe get some answers this way. What have you found out?"

"I found out a couple of things. There is no record link. If you'll recall, you're listed as 'None' on the birth record. I can't get a copy from Seton House, which has since merged with one of the hospitals in town. I'm currently attempting to access county birth records, but again, I'm being stonewalled," I lied. "I apologize for not responding, but I thought we had a chance with Seton House, and that went out the window yesterday afternoon. I'm back to square one."

He shook his head and said, "Your apology lacks all credibility. I really hoped you'd do better than this, Haskell. I should have known. Apparently, nothing has changed since high school."

"Arthur, the powers that be view this as very private information. The child is just eighteen and—"

"He's nineteen, Haskell, and considered an adult."

"That may be, but without a record link, there's no way I can access the records."

"What about her parents?"

"Her parents? I don't know who her parents are because the birth record you provided had her name blacked out. Do you even know the birth mother's name? You were seventeen or eighteen at the time. Was it someone from high school?"

I expected him to fidget, maybe shake his head no. Instead, he smiled and said, "Oh, sorry, thought I told you. It was your friend, Diane Donnelly. But then, you probably already knew that. Big deal, it was a one-nighter, and she drank so much she barely knew her own name. I dealt with that problem a long time ago. Now, I'm paying you to get the information for me. So do it, damn it," he said and stepped away from the chair.

I had all I could do to stay seated as I felt my face flush. For a moment, I was back in high school, and this son of a bitch had just dissed me and my girlfriend, big time.

Louie looked over with a surprised look on his face and moved both hands up and down, suggesting I should stay seated.

"Hey, Arty-Farty, I tell you what. Get someone else to do this. I quit."

"I knew you were a loser, Haskell. Knew way back when we were in high school, and you were the class clown. Looks like nothing's changed. Too bad. This could have led to some long-term business for you, but once again, you've screwed up. So sit here with this guy and his picnic table and this untrained mutt. You didn't quit. I just fired your ass," he said and headed for the door. "Oh, and one more thing, Diane really enjoyed herself. Told me I was way better than you."

I tore out of my chair. Fortunately, Louie was up before me and stepped between us. "As a legal witness, I have to warn you, you're on very thin ice, Mr. Farty. I suggest you leave now."

"Who in the hell—"

Morton was suddenly on his feet and let off two loud barks followed by a vicious growl. Grumley looked over, wide-eyed, and hurried out the door and down the stairs.

"What an absolutely awful prick," Louie said.

I watched out the window as Grumley ran across the street.

Tony hurried out of the driver's seat and opened the rear door just as Grumley made it to the car. I opened my desk drawer and grabbed the binoculars. Grumley looked up to my window, gave me the finger, and climbed into the car.

Tony closed the door, glanced up and shook his head, then climbed behind the wheel, and they drove up the street. I focused the binoculars on the license plate and repeated the number until I'd written it down.

"Sorry, Dev, I didn't—"

"You kidding? Thanks for stepping in. If you hadn't been here, I'd be looking at a murder charge right now.

And Morton, thank you. Good boy. Good boy," I said and tossed him a biscuit.

"That guy is psychopathic, Dev. Smart move getting away from him. No good is going to come from working with him."

I kept thinking of Grumley's statement. *I dealt with that problem a long time ago.* "I'm going to nail his worthless ass if it's the last thing I do."

"I think it might be a good idea to head over to The Spot a little early today. You up for it?" Louie said.

"Thanks, Louie, but I better not. I need to make some phone calls, anyway."

"You sure? I'll buy the first round. Hell, after that guy, I'll buy all the rounds."

"Oh, thanks, but I'd better not."

"You going to be okay here, Dev? You're not going to go after that guy, are you?"

"Not that I wouldn't like to, but no, I'm good. Thanks, you head over. I have to meet someone for dinner, anyway. I'll see you in the morning."

"Okay. You need anything, call me and Dev, legal advice from a friend. Stay away from that bastard."

"Thanks, Louie, I intend to."

I watched Louie cross the street and head into The Spot. Much as I could have used a beer, ten would not have been enough, and one would have been too many. Once he stepped inside, I sat down at my desk and pulled out my phone.

Twenty

I phoned my friend Dennis Glaizer, who works in the state's Motor Vehicle Division. He answered just as I was prepared to leave a message. "Dennis Glazier."

"Hi Denny, Dev Haskell."

"Hi Dev, and no. I'm not going to look up the information on the gorgeous woman you think was waving at you. Let's be honest here. She was giving you the finger and probably calling the police to report you for stalking her."

"Not to worry, I knew she was giving me the finger. Hey, I wondered if you could help me. I've been going through a cold case file from back in 2006. If I give you the name of an individual, can you check and see what kind of car he might have been driving back then?"

"I suppose I can, as long as he was listed as the owner. If it was a company car, obviously, that wouldn't work. You got a name for the guy, and if you have a current address, that would help."

"Yeah, the name is Arthur Grumley," I spelled out the last name. "Current address is in Stillwater, on Quinlan Avenue North," I said and gave him the house number.

"Okay, just bringing him up. Mmm-mmm a number of vehicles, four current to be exact. A 2022 G-Class Mercedes, a 2021 Cadillac Escalade, a Classic 2005 Ford Mustang GT, and a 2020 Lexus ES. Looks like this guy buys a new car every year. Is he a car dealer?"

"No, I think he's just into cars. I'm wondering about a vehicle back in 2006."

"Hang on. Just a moment, let me scroll back. Yeah, here we are. Apparently, he owned just one vehicle at the time. What do you know, a Ford Mustang GT. That was their souped-up version. Do you remember it, Dev? They had a spoiler on the back."

I'm not a car nut, so I didn't remember it. "Can you give me the VIN number and the license?"

"Yeah, sure, you got a clean space on the wall and a color crayon?" Glazier said and chuckled.

"Yeah, I've got an orange crayon, so go ahead."

He laughed again and said, "Okay, here's the VIN number." He read it off and then did the same with the license plate.

"What's the color of that vehicle?"

"Crimson red. If I recall, that was a special color for the fortieth-year celebration of Mustangs."

"That wouldn't happen to be the same Mustang he currently owns, would it?"

"Hang on checking that vehicle now. Oh, wow. Yeah, it is the same vehicle. Amazing, he's had the thing for almost twenty years. He must really like it."

"Okay, thanks, Dennis, very much appreciated."

"Sure thing, Dev. Hope this helps your investigation. Give me a call sometime. I'd like to get together and catch up."

"Let me get this deal behind me, and I'll give you a yell in a week or two. Thanks again for the help," I said and disconnected. So, Grumley was driving a red Mustang in 2006. It had a spoiler on the back. I'm sure he enjoyed racing through the city streets. Grumley's statement, *I dealt with that problem a number of years ago*, took on an added meaning.

After clicking the leash onto Morton's collar, we went out on our three-block walk. I debated heading into The Spot with Morton. Fortunately, I remembered my scheduled dinner at Sandie's and was responsible for bringing dessert. We headed home, and let Morton into the backyard. Heading upstairs, I grabbed a shower, and pulled on some clean jeans and a sports shirt. I let Morton inside, checked the locks, and pulled a Tupperware container from a cabinet. On the way to Sandie's, I stopped at the grocery store and purchased two packages of eight chocolate chip cookies that looked homemade. Once back in the car, I transferred the cookies to the Tupperware container.

I stopped over at the Yarmo liquor store and picked up a chilled bottle of sparkling Portuguese white wine.

When I stepped out of the store, the violin player from a few days back was just setting up on the median at the entrance.

"Hey," I called and hurried toward him.

When he turned and faced me, I saw his black eye.

"Not so fast," a guy shouted as he climbed from a parked car. He had slicked-back black hair, and he was carrying a baseball bat.

My gun was in my car, and a wine bottle didn't seem like the best match to a baseball bat.

"Is okay, he's my brother," the violin player said and waved him off. "He's watching for me."

"You have a problem?" I asked, indicating his black eye.

"Just a little problem. They not back since."

"The same two guys?"

He nodded. "They come back, we have a surprise for them. My brother, he's good with the bat."

I reached into my pocket and gave him all my cash, two bucks. "You still have my card?"

He nodded again.

"Any trouble, you call me. Thank you for being here and playing. It's very nice."

"I play for you now."

"I'll go back to my car and listen. Good luck." I turned around, gave a wave to the baseball bat brother, and walked back to my car as the air was filled with a wonderful violin solo. I waited until he finished, clapped, and gave him a thumbs-up.

Twenty-one

I drove over to Sandie's and pulled in front of her house. As I stepped out of the car, I glanced around just to see if she had another unexpected family guest. The only other cars I saw were in the neighbors' driveways. Tucking the Tupperware under my arm, I grabbed the wine bottle, and headed to the front door.

Sandie opened the door about fifteen seconds later. She was wearing tight white shorts and a light gray halter top that left nothing to the imagination. "Oh, Dev, right on time. Thank you," she said and gave me a kiss that was a little longer than casual. I could taste wine on her lips. She pulled back and said, "Come on into the kitchen, honey."

"Here," I said and handed her the Tupperware container. "I baked these this afternoon."

"You baked cookies?"

"Yeah, I'm trying to do some different things, you know, bake, eat vegetables, exercise, all that kind of stuff."

"Oh. My. God. I don't believe it. Dev, that is so good. Oh, I'm really proud of you. Well, and surprised, but don't take that the wrong way. That's really great. Can I talk you into a glass of wine?"

"Oh, yeah. That sounds perfect. I brought this just in case we run out," I said and handed her the bottle of wine.

The kitchen counter was set for two. A wine bottle was in the ice bucket. There was a wooden salad bowl on the counter. The oven was on, and two salmon fillets were in a baking pan with slices of lemon spread across them.

"Oh, this looks really good, Sandie," I said as she filled my wine glass and topped hers up.

She handed me the glass and raised hers in a toast. "Here's to a memorable evening," she said as we clinked glasses.

We chatted or, to be more accurate, Sandie chatted, and I kept thinking about Arthur Grumley showing up in the office this afternoon and my phone call with Dennis Glazier where I learned that Grumley was driving a red Ford Mustang back in 2006.

"Dev, I said would you like more wine? I feel like I'm drinking alone here. What are you thinking about?"

"What? Oh, sorry, I was just thinking about the salmon. It's been so long since I've had salmon. I can't wait."

"Well, hold on, it'll be ready in ten minutes. I've been doing all the talking. Why don't you tell me about your day?"

"My day, hmm-mm, let's see. I'm working on a case where a child was adopted years ago, just two or three days after he was born, and I met with his parents. They were really nice people, and the boy has two older sisters who really like him. He's in college now, and things are going well for him, so that was very nice."

"Oh, that sounds wonderful. Never enough of that in any workday."

"I couldn't agree more," I said. I brought myself back to the here and now and really tried to pay attention to Sandie as she chatted over dinner. She had a half-dozen stories to tell about her parents' visit. Her mother wondered why she wasn't married yet, and her father warned her about dating the wrong type of guy. I wondered if he did that because he'd met me, but I didn't bring it up.

I helped clear the kitchen counter, and while Sandie loaded the dishwasher, I scrubbed the two pans and washed the wooden salad bowl. She arranged the cookies on a plate and brought them out to the living room. We had another glass of wine while we ate cookies.

"Oh, Dev, these are really good. You have to give me the recipe."

"Well, I can't really remember it off the top of my head other than I put the chocolate chips in at the end and then put the mixing bowl in the refrigerator for an hour before I baked the cookies."

"Well, of course, send me an email with the recipe. These are really good."

"Glad you like them."

We chatted some more, and Sandie asked me to rub her back. She wondered if I was tired. She asked if I had to be anywhere in the morning. All hints that the night could turn into exactly what I'd normally hope for. Only tonight, I couldn't get Arthur Grumley and what he said about Diane out of my mind.

At 9:45, Sandi looked at me, shook her head, and said, "Well, I've got a meeting first thing tomorrow morning, so I'm going to kick you out. Thanks for coming over, Dev. It was great to see you. I hope whatever case you're working on goes well for you. Good night."

I suddenly found myself in my car and driving home.

Twenty-two

Morton and I were down in the office before Louie. I had just placed a call to Aaron LaZelle when Louie stumbled in and settled into his desk chair. Amazingly, I didn't get dumped into Aaron's voicemail. "Lieutenant LaZelle, Homicide."

"Hi Aaron, it's Dev."

"Dev, what are you calling this number for? This is for important people."

"Oh, sorry, must have tapped the wrong number on my screen. As long as I got you, can you tell me again the name of whoever was in charge of the investigation on Diane Donnelly's hit and run back in 2006?"

"Hang on a second. I think that file is still here, somewhere." I waited maybe a minute before he picked up again. "Okay, got it. You set to write this down?"

"Yeah, go ahead."

"Detective Roger O'Leary. He retired back in, I think, 2016. Seems to be enjoying it. I spoke to him last year at the Christmas party. He and the wife moved out to Afton. I think they've got a place right on the St. Croix."

"You got a phone number for him?"

"Yeah, hang on." I waited another minute. It only seemed like five minutes. "Be with you in just a second, fellas. Okay, you still there, Dev?"

"Yeah, give me that number, and I'm out of your hair."

Aaron read the number to me and finished up with, "Gotta run," and hung up.

I dialed O'Leary's number. "Hello," a man answered.

"Hi, I'm calling for Roger O'Leary. My name is Dev Haskell. I'm a private investigator looking into a cold case."

"Dev Haskell. Oh yeah, I remember. We met a couple of times. You're big buddies with LaZelle, aren't you?"

"Yeah, Roger, wow, excellent memory. I can barely remember my own name some days."

"Not much else getting in the way on this end. We've moved into the small town quiet life," he said.

"That sounds pretty good from where I'm sitting," I said just as I watched a kid out the window as he raced across the intersection on his bike, a car had to hit the brakes and screech to a stop.

"You said you're looking into a cold case. Something I was involved in?"

"Yeah, back in 2006. It was a hit and run and—"

"Oh, I remember. Diane Donnelly was the victim. Young woman taking night classes at St Kate's."

"Yeah, St. Catherine's college in those days. I've read the two eyewitness reports and—"

"You're not really going to get much other than there's a strong possibility, at least in my mind, that it was intentional. If I recall, the Donnelly woman was struck by a red car. No license number. We checked with the usual repair shops, but nothing turned up. The driver ran a red light about a half-block away and disappeared at the next corner. Never found a trace. There were some paint chips placed in evidence. I think they were red."

"You got time for a coffee one of these next days?" I suggested.

"I got all the time in the world. You name the time and the place," O'Leary said.

"Tell you what, I'm going to be checking some things out in Stillwater. Would you be free this morning? I'd gladly meet you in Afton."

"That works for me. We've got a nice coffee shop in town right on St. Croix Trail, Velo du Nord. You can't miss it."

"10:30 work for you?" I asked.

"I'll have a table waiting," he said.

I chatted with Louie for a bit and headed out to Afton. It's a small town on the Minnesota side of the St. Croix River. On the way out to Afton, it dawned on me that this was the town where Diane was sent to live with her aunt when she was pregnant. It was a forty-minute drive, and when I pulled into the parking lot, I was twenty minutes early. That didn't matter. Roger O'Leary was already seated at a table, reading the paper. He'd put on a few pounds from what I could remember, but you'd never call him fat. He happened to look up and gave me a wave just as I stepped into the coffee shop.

"Roger, nice to see you again. Thanks for making the time. Let me get a coffee. You need anything?" I said as we shook hands.

He shook his head and said, "No, I'm good."

I stepped up to the counter and ordered a medium-sized coffee, black. I sat down a minute later.

O'Leary folded his newspaper and took off his glasses. "I was checking my notes," he said and pulled a file from a brown leather bag. "I keep a file on all my unsolved cases. You never know when I might get a call like yours."

"You get many calls?"

"You're the third in six years. Doesn't sound like much, but the previous two led, in some small way, to closing the case. That makes me a happy camper."

"Absolutely, I get it. Let me give you some background on my involvement." I went on to tell him about Arthur Grumley contacting me. Showed him the copy of the birth record Grumley gave me with Diane's name blacked out. I told him about learning the birth mother's name, meeting with the Donnelly's, meeting the White's, and last but not least, the fact that, in 2006, Grumley drove a crimson red Ford Mustang.

O'Leary took a couple of notes while I talked and then said, "I think the next thing you should do is confirm the specific color on those paint chips. That's not going to prove anything other than serve as a possible connection to this individual, and I stress possible. But it builds the case," he said and rubbed his hands together. "When is your next meeting with him?"

"There won't be one. Yesterday when he was in my office and told me he'd dealt with the Diane Donnelly problem a long time ago, I told him I quit."

"How'd he take that?"

"I think he was poised to give me a hard time, and I was ready to throw him down the stairs. Fortunately, my office mate, an attorney, stepped between us, and then the other smart individual in the room, my dog, barked and growled. That got Grumley hurrying out of the office."

O'Leary nodded and said, "Just the little you told me about the guy, it strikes me as strange that, after all this time, he suddenly wants to help out the adopted child. Where's he been for the last two decades? My advice would be to warn the family of this latest incident. You said they live in Prior Lake?"

"Yeah, really nice folks. Along with a large farm, they run a landscaping business for cemeteries."

"The way you describe this Grumley person, it sounds like he's out to protect himself. Is he so wealthy that he's worried about someone wanting a piece of his fortune? Does he have children who would lose a certain percentage down the road if he passed away? I mean, there are a ton of reasons he might be concerned. He's always going to come first in whatever he undertakes. Perhaps that was at least part of his thought process if, and I stress 'if,' indeed he was the driver of that car."

"As you can see, I have no way to prove that, but I can feel it in my gut," I said.

"Let me suggest that you do not want to provide him with the name of the child or the adoptive family."

"Yeah, I get that."

"If I can do anything to help you, let me know," O'Leary said.

We chatted for another ten minutes and then went our separate ways. I was thinking I might drive by Grumley's place, but then what? The more I thought about it, the more it seemed to be a waste of time.

Instead, I drove back to town and pulled in front of the Donnelly home. Bill Donnelly was in the front yard cutting the grass. He turned off the lawn mower when I climbed out of the car.

"Hi, Dev, everything okay?"

"Yes, sir. Just wanted to stop by and tell you that I spoke with the adoptive parents yesterday, Kevin and Colleen White. Their son Patrick is doing well and attending the U. If you'd like, I'd be happy to pass on your contact information. By the way, the boy is a redhead, just like Diane, and they call him Rusty."

Donnelly smiled at that, but there was a touch of sadness in his smile. "Yeah, I think it's been too long.

We'd love to see him, meet him actually. Please feel free to pass the information on."

"I'll do that. I expect a phone call from them in the next couple of days. Listen, I won't keep you from the task at hand. You know, I've got a lawn that needs cutting. I'll pay you five bucks to do it."

He smiled at that and said, "Thanks Dev. We were talking last night. It was really nice to see you."

"Yeah, nice to see the two of you, too. Thanks, and please stay in touch," I said and climbed back into my car.

Twenty-three

I drove back to the office. On the way, I stopped at Rooster's BBQ and got two sandwiches. One for me and one for Louie. The moment I stepped into the office, Morton hopped off his pillow and focused on the bag of sandwiches.

By the time I encouraged Morton with a biscuit, Louie had opened his Styrofoam container. He took a big bite of his sandwich and immediately dribbled BBQ sauce down the front of his wrinkled white shirt. He glanced at the stain. It didn't seem to bother him, and he took another bite.

I had just finished my sandwich when my cellphone rang. The screen read Eleanor Monroe. "Haskell Investigations," was how I answered.

"Hello, I'm returning a call from Mr. Haskell."

"That's me. Is this Miss Monroe?"

"Yes, it is, and please, call me Eleanor. Your message said you were calling regarding that dreadful accident back in 2006."

"Yes, I'm a private investigator looking into the accident."

"Well, from the little I know, I don't believe they ever found the person who was driving that car."

"That's correct. You and another individual were the only people who witnessed the accident."

"Yes, in fact, he stopped his car and got out while I called 911 in my apartment."

"Would you mind telling me what you remember from that day?"

"Well, I can tell you that it all happened in a split second. It was a warm day, and I had the front window open. I just happened to glance out and saw the car strike the poor woman in the street. She wasn't even in the middle of the street, just a step or two from the curb. To my way of thinking, he could have easily gone around her. He was definitely speeding. He hit her. She bounced up onto the hood of his car and then fell off and into the street. Now it's just taken me way longer to describe the incident than it took to happen."

"And you called 911."

"Yes, and then I ran outside. The man who had stopped told me she was dead and not to get too close. He actually held me back. He didn't want me to see her body. I remember he had blood on his hand. His right hand, I think. When the police came we told them what we'd seen. They took our names. I think it was the next day when I got a call from a detective. He came over and interviewed me. There were two of them, actually. I told them everything I knew, which wasn't much. It couldn't have taken more than fifteen or twenty minutes, start to finish. I wish I could have told them more, but that was pretty much it."

"I read your interview. You said it was a red car, a man was driving, and the car ran a red light at the intersection and turned at the next corner."

"That would have been the other person's description. I would have been on the phone at that point or maybe running out of my apartment. I do remember it was a red car, and it had one of those fancy things on the back. You know, on top of the trunk. I can't remember what they're called. Some kind of racing car do-dad."

"That's called a spoiler."

"Mmm, yes, I think that's what it was. I have to say, ever since then, I've never liked red cars."

"I'd say that's understandable, Eleanor. Anything else that comes to mind?"

"No, I'm sorry. It's like it just happened all over again. I saw it, but it was only a split second. I couldn't have gotten a license plate number. If the driver was next to me in a restaurant, I wouldn't know it was him. Just boom and the poor woman was dead in the street. It happened that fast."

"Well, thank you for your time. If you should remember something else, even if it seems insignificant, please don't hesitate to call. You never know. It could lead to solving the case."

"Oh, I only wish. I was a senior in college, just finishing up, and after graduation, I couldn't wait to get out of that apartment. I cracked the whip when it came to teaching my own kids to cross the street. The image of that will be with me for the rest of my life."

"Well, thank you. You've been a big help. All the best to you and your family."

"Thank you. Good luck to you in your investigation. I hope you find whoever did this."

"Me too," I said, and we disconnected.

"Something positive?" Louie asked.

"Well, let's just say nothing negative. The remaining witness to Diane Donnelly being struck by that car. She confirmed everything from her initial interview. Unfortunately, there wasn't much to begin with, other than the car was red and had a spoiler on the back."

I called Aaron LaZelle and ended up leaving a message. "Hi Aaron, this is Dev. Hey, I met with Roger O'Leary this morning. He sends his regards, by the way. He suggested I take a look at the evidence file for the hit and run that killed Diane Donnelly. Specifically, some paint chips to see if they match a 2005 Ford Mustang. If you could set me up with a pass to the property room, I'd appreciate it. Let me know, and thanks."

Morton and I joined Louie over at The Spot. Morton did his usual, nearly pulling my arm out of the socket as he headed along the bar, straining at the leash. He hurried around the end of the bar and sat in front of Louie.

"Oh Morton, how good of you to come. How about a reward for yet another day of keeping Dev on the straight and narrow?" Louie said, then filled his hand with pork rinds and leaned down so Morton could inhale them in half a second. Amazingly, not one pork rind ever fell to the floor.

Mike, the bartender, suddenly appeared with an IPA in a frosted glass and a fresh drink for Louie. "Compliments of Louie," Mike said as he pushed the beer across the bar. I raised my glass toward Louie, he nodded, and we both took a drink.

"Any progress on the Donnelly case?" Louie asked.

I shook my head, "No, not really. The two witness statements check out. Unfortunately, we're still at the stage where all that's really been identified is that it was a red car with a spoiler. But obviously no photographs or supporting statements from anyone. I'm still leaning toward Arthur Grumley as the driver, and I'm going to be checking him out starting tomorrow. I just can't believe he all of a sudden wants to find his biological son so he can help out when he hasn't done anything for almost twenty years."

"Yeah, he's a piece of work, all right. Just be careful. The few minutes I saw him, I would say he's entirely capable of doing whatever it takes to get what he wants. That includes physically threatening or attacking you in some way, shape, or form. From the little you've told me, he would have no problem paying someone to accomplish that task. In other words, watch yourself."

"Yeah, I get it. I—"

My phone rang. Monica. "Oh, I gotta take this," I said and stepped out the side door. "Hi, Monica, what's up?"

"Hi, Dev, sorry I didn't get back to you sooner. I know it's last minute, but I wondered if you'd have time to come over for dinner tonight. I mean, if you don't have something scheduled already."

"Tonight, yeah, I could do that. It would take me maybe forty-five minutes before I made it over there, but if you can wait, I'd love to come over."

"Oh, wonderful. Can't wait to see you. I'm doing chicken. It'll take thirty or forty minutes. I won't put it in until you're here with a glass of wine in your hand."

"Okay. I'll get there just as fast as I can." I stepped back into The Spot and said, "Sorry, Louie, duty calls."

"Everything, okay?"

"Yeah, I think so. I want to check to make sure," I lied and gulped down my beer in about thirty seconds. "I'll see you in the morning." I grabbed Morton's leash, and we hurried out the door. Once home, I let Morton into the backyard and jogged upstairs. I pulled on a reasonably clean shirt and a different pair of jeans. I coaxed Morton inside and headed over to Monica's house. She had just opened the door when it dawned on me that I didn't bring anything.

"Well, that was fast. Come in," she said, grabbing my hand and pulling me inside. Once she closed the front door, she gave me a long kiss, then stepped back and smiled.

"Hey, I'm really sorry, but I was in such a hurry to get over here that I forgot to stop and pick up some wine. Can I run out and get some? I can grab a dessert or something while I'm getting the wine. No problem, honest."

"I didn't call you up so you would have to bring something over. Besides, I have everything here, and I'm planning on moderating my wine intake. I don't want a replay of the last time you were here when I staggered up to bed, and you cleaned all the dishes and everything for me. That was so sweet," she said and gave me a quick kiss. "Come on into the kitchen. We can drink our wine on the front porch, and I'll set the timer for the chicken. Is that okay with you?"

"I'm just here to follow your directions."

"Mmm-mmm, I'm going to hold you to that," she said and led me into the kitchen. Two chicken breasts, covered in spices, were in a bright orange baking dish on the kitchen counter. "If you would open the wine, please. It's on the shelf of the refrigerator door. I'll put the chicken in and set the timer while you fill the glasses."

It took her about two seconds to put the chicken in and thankfully, the wine had a twist-off cap. I filled the glasses, and we headed out to her front porch. We chatted while eating cheese and cracker hors d'oeuvres. We had a lovely dinner and an adventuresome evening. I eventually made it home around 2:00. Morton was asleep in my bed, and I was too worn out to move him.

Twenty-four

When we arrived in the office, Louie was typing away on his computer. He was wearing a clean, starched shirt and a freshly pressed gray suit that had to have just come from the dry cleaners. A fresh pot of coffee was on, and there was a paper plate with a chocolate doughnut resting on my desk.

"Oh, man, Louie. Fresh coffee and a doughnut. To what do I owe the pleasure?"

"Oh, I just thought you've been dealing with enough shit this past week, so maybe we would start the day out right. Besides, I'm in court this morning, and I figured if I did something nice, maybe the gods would look down and smile on me."

"Well, let me do my part and thank you sincerely for the doughnut. Can I top up your coffee?"

"Yeah, now that you mention it," he said and slid his mug to the edge of his picnic table desk. I topped up his mug, filled mine, and settled in at my desk. I took a bite of the doughnut. "Mmm-mmm, delicious."

"Good. Everything go okay on whatever problem you were dealing with last night?"

"Problem? Oh, you mean the phone call. No, that wasn't a problem. That was Monica calling to invite me over for dinner," I said and followed up with a yawn.

"Oh, well, I guess I should consider myself lucky you even made it in this morning."

"You're lucky every day that I'm here." My cell-phone suddenly rang. "Haskell Investigations."

"Hello, Dev. It's Kevin White."

"Hi, Kevin. Everything okay?"

"Oh, yeah, just fine. Colleen and I talked over your situation with the biological father, and without meaning to sound negative, we'd prefer if you did not pass on any information to him. Things have been going very well for the last nineteen years without his input, and the fact that he suddenly wants to insert himself into Rusty's life does not sound like the best thing to happen for either Rusty or us. Besides, we don't have any definite proof that he is indeed the father. I'm sorry if this causes any problems for you, but we—"

"Kevin, believe me, it's no problem on this end. In fact, I resigned from the case the other day. I was planning to call you later today if I didn't hear from you. I support your decision one hundred and ten percent. I do have a favor to ask of you."

"Oh?"

"I spoke yesterday to Bill Donnelly, Diane's father. He said they would love to get back in touch with you and Colleen and to meet Rusty."

"Oh, we'd like that too. Frankly, I think it would mean a lot to Rusty."

"Well, I have their information here. It may be the same as what you have. They're still in the same house on Pinehurst Avenue. I've got a cellphone number for you as well."

"Go ahead and give it to me. I'm at my desk and ready to write it down."

I gave Kevin the Donnelly's phone number and address. I also gave him Arthur Grumley's name so they could be on guard just in case he had someone else investigating. We chatted for another minute or two and disconnected.

Louie was packing up his briefcase and about to head out the door.

"Good luck in court today, Louie, and thanks again for the doughnut."

"Keeping my fingers crossed, thanks. Catch you later," he said and headed out the door. He wasn't gone five minutes when I saw a car pull up and park behind mine. A guy with a shaved head stepped out, looked up and down the street, and crossed. I heard the stairs creak a moment later, and the office door suddenly opened.

"You Dev Haskell? The investigator?" the shaved head said and closed the door behind him. He looked at me in a no-nonsense manner, attempting to take charge. He looked familiar, but I couldn't place him.

"Yes, I am. Let me just make a wild guess. You've been hired by a former client of mine. He probably gave you a birth record with the mother's name blocked out, and where his name would supposedly be, the word 'None' is typed in. He'd like you to locate his supposed biological child, but you're finding it difficult, to say the least, because you can't access any records."

The look on his face suddenly softened. "Yeah, you got it. Anything you can do to help me."

"How long have you known Arthur Grumley?"

He glanced at his watch. "Maybe nineteen hours. I had a phone call from him yesterday and just came from his place out in Stillwater."

"Have you checked him out?"

"No, not yet. I will as soon as I'm back to my office."

I debated how much to tell him and quickly decided not much. "I'm sorry I didn't catch your name."

"Don Humphrey, I'm a PI."

"Yeah, and before that, you were a St. Paul cop. Weren't you?"

He got a surprised look on his face and nodded. "Things going the way they are today, I got out as soon as I qualified for a pension. Been a PI for three years now."

"Grab a seat, Don. Happy to answer any questions you may have."

He sat down, looked at my chocolate doughnut with the bite out of it, and said, "Can you help me?"

"The short version is I hit a number of walls attempting to conduct my investigation. I thought I finally had a shot, and that dissolved overnight, essentially right before my eyes. I tried to explain that to Grumley, but he didn't want to hear any of it."

"He told me you were upset because the woman who was the mother, well, based on the age, I guess the girl was your girlfriend."

"Did he give you her name?"

"Yeah, Debra Donnelly."

"Half right, her first name was Diane. The thing is, I couldn't access any records, and then he came here to my office and started raising hell. Life is too short, and I don't need the hassle."

He seemed to think about that. "You couldn't look at records at Seton House?"

"No. He'd actually have better luck on Ancestry.com or someplace like that. No records I saw listed him as the biological father, which I guess was his choice, but that pretty much ends any access to records for something like 90 years."

I was waiting for him to threaten me and knew my Glock was in the top drawer of my desk just beneath my notes on the case.

"If I could make a suggestion," I said. "If you haven't signed a contract, maybe arrange to be paid on time spent, and after two or three days, send him a bill and tell him you've exhausted all options. That's basically what I did, well, except my resignation was due to him raising hell in my office. I never sent him a bill. I just wanted to be done with him and move on."

He nodded but didn't say anything.

"How's the business been going for you, Don?"

"You know, same shit, different day. To be honest, this case is more than a little weird. I don't know. There's something about Grumley. I can't quite put my finger on it, but I've been cautious right from the start."

"I went to high school with the guy. Even back then, there was something about him. I wish I could help you more, but I never got anywhere."

"Well, thanks for the info. I'm going to try a couple of things, but it sounds like I'll be pissing in the wind."

"Good luck, Don. Let me know how it goes. Hey, you got a card? Something comes up, I could give you a call."

"Oh, sorry, fresh out of cards." We shook hands. He gave a final glance at the doughnut and left. I watched out the window as he crossed the street to his car, a white Jeep Liberty. I had my binoculars out and copied down his license plate as he drove off.

Twenty-five

Louie finally made it back to the office from his court appearance toward the end of the afternoon. It would be an understatement to suggest he was elated. He was thrilled with the results. Apparently, the judge ruled in his favor, and Louie's client was released and sent on his way. As he stepped into the office, he yelled, "Woo-hoo-hoo. Drinks are on me, Dev. We won big time."

"Hey, that's great, Louie. Congratulations."

"I'm heading over to The Spot now. Can you join me?"

"Yeah, that sounds perfect. You head over there. I'll lock up and give Morton a quick walk."

Louie hurried over to The Spot. I locked the office door, clipped the leash on Morton, and we took a quick walk. When we stepped into The Spot, Louie was surrounded by a half-dozen smiling people, all holding freshly poured drinks. Morton dragged me along the bar and around the corner. I unclipped his leash, and he made his way through the crowd and assumed the position in front of Louie.

"Well, Morton. Thank you for helping Dev finally find his way over here," Louie said as he poured half a bag of pork rinds into his hand. "Here's a little reward for all your hard work," Louie said and fed him not one but two handfuls of pork rinds.

Mike suddenly appeared with a beer and slid it across the bar to me.

We talked, laughed, told stories, and suddenly it was time to head home while I could still drive. I caught the last few minutes of the evening news and woke up on the couch just after 1:00. I headed up to bed. Morton was already sound asleep on the bed, and I climbed in next to him. My alarm woke me in the morning.

Despite the previous evening's liquid dinner, I felt fine. I tossed my jeans and shirt in the laundry basket and headed into the shower. Morton joined me in the kitchen an hour later. We drove down to the office, and I pulled to the curb behind Louie's Ford Fiesta. I was amazed he was already here, but then maybe there was something related to yesterday's case that had to be filed, and he wanted to get it done first thing. I let Morton out of the car, and we were about to cross the street when a car came around the corner. We stepped back between my car and Louie's and waited for it to drive by. The guy behind the wheel gave us a thank you wave as he passed.

I just happened to glance over at Louie's rear window and saw what looked like his suit coat hanging on the passenger seat. That seemed strange, and I stepped around to the passenger door to make sure it was locked.

That's when I saw Louie snoring in the backseat. He looked like the proverbial ten pounds in a five-pound bag. All scrunched up with his massive stomach hanging over the edge of the backseat.

I knocked on the window and didn't get a reaction. I tried it again, with the same result. Finally, I pounded on the window, and Louie's nose began to twitch. At least he was alive.

"Louie. Hey, Louie, wake up. Louie, rise and shine. Louie." As I shouted, I pounded on the window and the side of the car. A bus drove past with a number of people staring out the window at me, probably wondering exactly what in the hell I was doing.

I pounded again, and this time, Louie's eyes fluttered open. He looked up at me, then seemed to study the interior of the car for a long moment before he slowly sat up and rubbed his eyes. Eventually, he unlocked the door and climbed out. His eyes were bloodshot. He definitely needed a shower and a shave, but he was okay, all things considered.

"You spent the night in your car?"

"Apparently. To be honest, I have no recollection of how I ended the night. Oh God," he said and arched his back as he turned his head from side to side. I heard audible cracks from his spine and shoulders. "I wonder how I got in there."

"Probably a good idea you didn't drive, although you might have been better off sleeping in the office. Tell you what, I'll head up and get the coffee going while you avail yourself of the bathroom. We better get some coffee in you before you get behind the wheel.”

“Yeah, probably a good idea. I’ll see you up there. Oh, maybe leave the aspirin bottle on my desk.”

“Not to worry. Don’t forget your suit coat and make sure you’ve got your car keys.”

He stuck his hands in his trousers, pulled out what looked like a slice of pizza from the left pocket, and then his car keys from the right pocket. “Here, Morton,” he said and handed the slice of pizza to Morton before I could stop him. Morton inhaled the pizza in two quick bites, then licked the sauce off Louie’s hand.

“Get cleaned up, Louie. You’re lucky the cops didn’t find you. They would have arrested you for loitering,” I said as Morton and I hurried across the street. We stepped inside the building, and Morton suddenly began to hesitate. I had to pull on the leash a couple of times to get him to move. “Come on, Morton. Let’s go. Come on. What’s with you? Let’s go,” I said and gave the leash a yank. We headed up the stairs, and halfway up, Morton stopped. I wondered if he was picking up the scent of something from the hairdressers just across the way from our office. Maybe burning hair, or could it have been a reaction to that slice of pizza?

“Come on, Morton. It’s okay. Let’s go. We’re all right.” I gave a couple of tugs on the leash to get him moving again. “Come on, Morton. That’s right. It’s okay. Let’s go. We finally made it to the top of the stairs, and I pulled my key out. Just one problem. I didn’t need

my key. The door was open about six inches. There was
a large boot print on the door, just next to the doorknob,
and two pieces of the broken doorframe trim were on the
floor. Someone had broken into our office.

Twenty-Six

The drawers on the file cabinet were all pulled open. A mound of files had been dumped on top of Morton's pillow. All the drawers on my desk had been pulled out and dumped onto the top of the desk. My computer was still there, as was Louie's. I quickly rustled through the pile of files and various notes on my desk. My Glock was still there along with the half-dozen naked pictures of Linh, a woman I'd dated a couple of years ago, although the pictures were lined up and had clearly been viewed. My pair of binoculars rested on the windowsill, suggesting someone in the apartment across the street had come home late last night and never pulled the shade.

I sifted through the pile and realized the few documents and notes related to Grumley's biological son, Patrick 'Rusty' White, were missing. All my contact information for the White's, the Donnelly's, and Monica was nowhere to be found. I immediately came to the conclusion this had to be the work of Don Humphrey.

Louie walked in a few minutes later. For the first time, I noticed what was probably a pizza stain across the lapel of his gray suit coat and down the front of his shirt. He apparently lost his tie at some point yesterday evening. He sat down at his desk, oblivious to the door having been kicked in, the pile of files on Morton's pillow, and the pile of debris covering my desk.

"Did you find the aspirin yet?"

I walked over to the coffee maker on the top of the file cabinet, grabbed the bottle of aspirin, and set it on the picnic table. I grabbed Louie's coffee mug, dumped the contents down the sink, rinsed it out, filled it with water, and set it next to the aspirin bottle. Then I set about making coffee.

While the coffee brewed, I began to return the files to the cabinet. The office was usually in some state of disaster, but the file cabinet had always been orderly. That came as a blessing as I returned the files to the proper drawers in alphabetical order. Ten minutes later, the coffee was ready, the file cabinet was arranged, and Morton was able to settle onto his pillow with what remained of his rawhide bone. Louie had washed down four aspirin with the mug of water, so now I poured him a mug of fresh coffee. I did the same for myself and began to sort through the mess on the top of my desk.

In sort of a reverse mathematical equation, the pile on my desk was easily a tenth of the size of the file cabinet pile. It took me at least ten times as long to sort through the various items one by one and arrange them in a semblance of order.

I pulled a fresh file from the box, labeled it 'Linh,' and carefully placed the six photos of her in the file for future reference.

"You rearranging things?" Louie asked as he got to his feet and headed toward the coffee pot. He wasn't kidding.

"God, how much did you have to drink last night? Louie, someone kicked in the office door and went through all my files. They stole all my paperwork that had anything to do with Grumley."

"Are you kidding? Really?"

"Did you notice the boot print on the door, where they kicked it in? The pile of junk on my desk? Or all the files dumped on Morton's pillow?"

"I guess I did, at least I think so. Someone broke in here last night?"

"Yeah, check out the doorframe. The board that holds the door in place is still on the floor in pieces."

Louie leaned forward and glanced around his desktop screen. "Holy shit."

"Yeah, you aren't kidding. I'd better make some phone calls and warn people." The first person I called was Aaron LaZelle, and I ended up leaving a message. "Hi Aaron, Dev. Hey, someone kicked in our office door last night and went through all my files. They stole everything I had on the Arthur Grumley case. Please give me a call when you have a moment. Thanks, Dev."

I phoned Kevin White next and gave him the news.

"So they've got our name, address, and phone numbers?"

"Yeah, I'm afraid so. I have an idea who might be responsible but just be extra careful for the time being."

"They do much damage to your office?"

"No, just kicked in the door, knocked some trim off the doorframe."

"Have you fixed it yet?"

"No, I wanted to give you and the Donnelly's a call before I started in on that. Then I want to check out the idiot I think is responsible for this. Fixing the door trim is somewhere further down the list."

"Don't worry about that. I'll send someone over."

"Oh, thanks, but you don't have to do that, Kevin."

"You're right, Dev. I don't have to do that, but I'm going to. Someone will be there this afternoon. I'll have them call before they arrive. They'll put a little more secure system in place."

"You sure? We can just tack the trim back up. Well, as soon as I find my hammer, and—"

"Say no more. You've just convinced me this is necessary. Thanks for the call. Someone will be over there this afternoon." Click

I phoned the Donnelly's next and got a busy signal. I phoned Monica and ended up in her voicemail. "Hi Monica, just wanted to thank you for the other evening. Most enjoyable. When you have a moment, please give me a call. My office was broken into last night, and some files were stolen. Talk to you later. Thanks."

I tried the Donnelly's number again, but it was still busy. "You going to go home and get cleaned up?" I asked Louie.

"What would be the point? I've got a couple of things to do this morning, and then I might head home around lunchtime, maybe talk myself into a nap in bed this afternoon."

"I'm going to run an errand for about an hour, and I'll be back. Someone's coming over this afternoon to repair the door trim. If you head out, don't worry about Morton. I should be back shortly."

I climbed in my car and drove over to the Donnelly house. Thankfully, Don Humphrey's white Jeep Liberty wasn't parked in front of the place. I rang the doorbell. Mr. Donnelly answered.

"Haskell?"

"Hi, Mr. Donnelly, sorry to bother you. My office was burglarized last night, and if you have a moment, I'd like to run a couple of things past you."

"Oh dear, that's not good. Yeah, sure, come on in. Let me just check with my supervisor, Marilyn. Oh, Marilyn," he called and headed toward the kitchen. I followed. His wife was seated at the kitchen counter talking on a phone mounted on the wall. The phone cord was at least ten feet long. I remembered the one in my folks' kitchen. It had been years since I'd seen one in use. As Donnelly entered the kitchen, he signaled his wife to finish her phone call.

"Oh, well, apparently Bill needs some direction, Mary Jane. Let's talk again this afternoon. Yes, I will. You do the same. Bye, bye, bye," she said and hung up the phone. "What is it that's so important it couldn't wait, Bill?"

"You were talking to Mary Jane for over an hour and—"

"Yes, and you watched the baseball game last night for over three hours."

"Dev Haskell is here," he said as I stepped into the kitchen.

"Oh, well, why didn't you say so? How nice to see you again, Dev," she said, then shot her husband a look.

"Nice to see both of you, ma'am. Sorry to interrupt your day. I wanted to let you know that my office was burglarized last night and whoever did it stole all my notes and files on Diane. That would be the birth record along with your phone number and address, as well as my information on the White family."

"Burglarized? Oh dear, but why would they steal that information?"

"I'm not sure unless whoever did it wanted to find out information regarding the adoption of the child."

"Did they take anything else? Money? Other files?"

"There wasn't any money to take, and at this point, I've not been able to identify anything else that's missing."

"And what do the police say?" Mr. Donnelly asked.

"Well, we just spoke on the phone, so not much," I lied since I never reported the break-in. "The door was kicked in. That's being repaired today."

"Did they dust for fingerprints?"

"No sir, they said there was no point and—"

"No point? Do they ever watch anything on TV? They should always dust for fingerprints. It's the first thing they should do."

"Yes, sir. I've got a call into them now to come back. Just waiting for a reply. You know how busy they are."

Donnelly shook his head, "Gad, the world's gone to hell in a hand basket."

"Bill," Mrs. Donnelly said.

"Well, it is."

"Anyway, I just wanted to let you know. Hopefully, nothing will come of this, but maybe be extra cautious and on guard. If someone phones or knocks on the door, let me know, and I'll be over right away."

"Oh dear, and we were so happy to learn about the little boy."

"I hope you're finally able to meet him at some point. From everything I hear, he's a very nice guy, and his parents are wonderful." Mrs. Donnelly's eyes were suddenly moist. "Well, I'll let you get back to your day. Wonderful to see you both. Sorry it's under these circumstances. Any changes, I'll let you know."

Mr. Donnelly walked me to the door. We shook hands, and I left.

Twenty-seven

When I returned to the office, Louie was gone, and Morton was asleep. I phoned Aaron LaZelle again. This time, he answered.

"Yeah, Dev. I just heard your message and was about to return your call. How bad's the damage?"

"Hi, Aaron. Damage isn't that bad. Whoever did it kicked in the door and knocked the trim off on one side of the doorframe. I got someone coming out this afternoon to fix it. What's more important is that my file on the case I was working on was stolen. That appears to be the reason for the break-in."

"This is the one where you were trying to find the kid who was adopted at birth?"

"Yeah, Diane Donnelly's baby. The client was such a jerk I had a real concern about what his intent was. I honestly couldn't see him trying to help the kid. Anyway, it gets more involved from there, but I've got a question for you."

"What's that?"

"I resigned from the adoption case. Told the guy I quit. I didn't send him a bill. Yesterday a guy came in, and he told me he's taking over the case and had some of the same concerns about the client that I did. I didn't give him any information on my sources. In fact, I didn't even tell him what I'd learned. I recognized him as someone who had been on the force. He told me he just wanted to get out, and he retired as soon as he qualified for a pension."

"What was his name?"

"Don Humphrey."

"Humphrey? Large sort of guy?"

"Yeah, not huge, but solid. He's got a shaved head."

"And he told you he had retired?"

"Yeah. Why? Is he still on the force?"

"No, and he hasn't been for three or four years. He was fired, a laundry list of infractions. I gotta tell you, based on his record here, I'm pretty sure he wouldn't be able to get a Private Investigator's license."

"Really? He seemed nice enough, but then when I asked him for a business card, he didn't have one. He didn't know anything about the specifics of the case, but that was before my files went missing. I've warned all but one person I talked to regarding this, and I've got a call in to her."

"And you said all your files were stolen."

"It was actually just one file with the contract and then a bunch of notes. The problem is the names, addresses, and phone numbers of people I've dealt with were in the file, and I'm not convinced my client was interested in helping the kid out."

"What do you think he was going to do?"

"Okay, I have no proof on any of this, but I think he might try to get the kid, now nineteen, to sign some sort of document where he rejects any opportunity for inheritance. If that doesn't work, he might do something worse. I have nothing to base this next speculation on, but I think Arthur Grumley, the apparent biological father, is responsible for Diane's hit and run death back in 2006."

"Is this why you want to review the evidence in that cold file?"

"Yeah. The two witnesses both identified a red car with a spoiler on the back. Grumley owned a 2005 red Ford Mustang that was licensed to him in 2006. I know that's not enough to go on, but if the paint chips matched a Ford Mustang, it brings everything just that much closer."

"Were these thoughts part of the file that was stolen?"

"No, I haven't written any of this down yet, another reason I want to look at that file. Up until recently, I was more worried about Diane's parents and the adoptive family."

"Might be a good idea to alert the witnesses to the hit and run."

"Well, one died three or four years ago, and the other one I've only spoken to on the phone. I'll give her a call as well."

"Yeah, better play it safe, Dev. Come on over this afternoon, and I'll escort you down to the property room."

"Are you going to be around this morning?"

"I am unless something comes up."

"I could be there in fifteen minutes."

"I think that might work. Hopefully, I'll be here."

"Thanks, Aaron," I said and disconnected.

It was closer to a half-hour by the time I pulled into the visitor's parking lot across the street from the station. I dodged the potholes, parked, and hurried across the street and into the station. The desk sergeant phoned Aaron, and for the first time in at least two years, he actually came down from his office and escorted me downstairs to the property room.

"Thanks for doing this, Aaron. I didn't mean to pull you away from whatever you were working on," I said as we rode the elevator down to the lower levels.

"Not a problem, happy to help. I called the property room, so hopefully, they already have that file pulled. I did a quick look at your friend, Don Humphrey. He's not licensed, and there's nothing that suggests he's presented himself as licensed. I'm wondering if your former client, Grumley, contacted him and lined things up."

"Could be. You didn't happen to find an address or a phone number on Humphrey, did you?"

"Well, of course, we have that information, but you know as well as I do it's private. I wish you luck," he said, then held out his hand to shake.

As I took hold of his hand, I felt a piece of paper. We shook, and I shoved the paper into my pocket just as the elevator door opened. Aaron walked me into the property room. Diane's hit and run file, such as it was, rested on the counter. It would not be unusual to have a box or boxes of items, clothing, tools, and a ton of things. Diane's hit-and-run file was actually a manila envelope with a file inside the envelope.

Aaron headed back up to his office, and I settled into a cubicle. I pulled the piece of paper from my pocket. It looked like it had been torn from an adding machine, a little more than two inches wide and maybe an inch and a half long. A phone number and a street address were written on it, just below the name Humphrey. I shoved it back in my pocket and opened the manila envelope.

The file had a series of photos, not only the ones I'd seen up in homicide a few days ago but photos of Diane's body. I had a lump in my throat remembering her from high school. Obviously, I'd never seen her naked, and the black and white images were anything but sexy. As a matter of fact, I found them heartbreaking. There was a plastic evidence bag with cloth squares from Diane's clothing with barely pinhead bits of paint. Based on the notation on the paint chip evidence bag, they had never been examined to determine the manufacturer of the vehicle, let alone the particular model. I took out my cell phone, photographed the evidence bag, and then photographed three of the battered body photos.

I returned everything to the manila envelope and returned the envelope to the property counter. I signed out, and the sergeant behind the counter phoned Aaron.

"You all set?" Aaron asked ten minutes later as he stepped into the property room.

"Yeah, thanks, Aaron."

"You learn anything?"

"Yeah, I've got a long way to go to link this to Grumley, and the photos were heartbreaking. I never saw her after she dumped me on our graduation night, and the photos, well, not fun, but they've given me the incentive to try to determine if Grumley was involved."

"If I can help, let me know."

"Thanks, Aaron. I appreciate it. And thanks for the info."

"I don't know what you're talking about," he said. We took the elevator up to the front lobby, and I headed out to my car.

Twenty-eight

Once back in my car, I pulled the slip of paper from my pocket and put the address into the GPS on my cell phone. The place was just a couple of miles away in a section of town known as Frogtown, just northwest of downtown. Back in the 1850s, the area was a large swamp, apparently with lots of frogs. Over the years, the swamp was filled in, homes were built, and the name remained.

The area has seen better days. Today, the majority of the homes are over a hundred years old and have been turned into multiple rental units. The population is somewhat transient, and the crime rate is high. From a distance, the address, 715 Charles Avenue, appeared to be a brick house, but as I got closer, it became obvious the siding was covered with asphalt shingles in a brick pattern. Based on the condition of the shingles, it seemed a fair guess that they'd been on the house for at least seventy years. The wood trim on the windows and doors was a faded, peeling red. A washed-out green velvet couch with stuffing hanging from the corners was on the front porch. Five black mailboxes hung just to the left of the front door.

Could this be where Don Humphrey lived?

I drove around the block and headed down the alley. Sure enough, there was a white Jeep Liberty parked in the dirt area behind the house. I couldn't remember Humphrey's exact license number, but the first three letters, MEW, were the same, and that was good enough for me. Quite a few windows in the house had air conditioners set in them.

Based on the house and the location, it seemed logical that things weren't going very well for Humphrey. Aaron's comment about him not being able to get licensed made sense. For the briefest of moments, I considered slitting all four tires on the Jeep, but the possibility of Humphrey automatically thinking it was me and him coming up with some kind of payback dismissed that idea. Instead, I drove back to the office.

Morton was awake and met me at the door. I left a *'Back in 15 Minutes'* note on Louie's computer and took Morton for a quick walk. We'd just gotten back to the office, and I'd poured myself a coffee when there was a knock on the door. It opened, and a muscular-looking guy stepped in.

"Hi, are you Dev Haskell?"

"Yes," I said, no doubt sounding overly cautious after last night's break-in. He was dressed in blue jeans and a strappy gray t-shirt. He had very large biceps and forearms and a muscular chest. A six-pack stomach was apparent beneath the t-shirt.

"Kevin White sent me. Told me you had a break-in." I immediately relaxed as he turned around and looked at the damaged doorframe.

"Yeah, you can see the boot print on the door. The guy kicked it in sometime in the middle of the night. The pieces of the frame are leaning over there against the wall. I was going to nail them back in place, but Kevin seemed adamant. Maybe he's seen some of my attempts at carpentry."

He smiled at my last comment and said, "Yeah, if you put that back up there, all it's going to do is make it easier for the next guy. Instead of kicking, they'll just have to shoulder it open. I got some items out in the truck that will do a much better job. If it's okay, I'll bring them up and get started."

"Yeah, that's just fine. I really appreciate it. Can I help you carry them up?"

"No offense, but things will actually go faster if I do it. Any problem with setting up some sawhorses outside your door?"

"No, that should be okay. I'll just run over to the hairdressers and let them know you're going to be working out there for a while."

"Okay, I'll start hauling things up. Oh, I'm sorry, my name is Brian.

"Nice to meet you, Brian, and thanks for coming on such short notice."

"Kevin wanted it done today. Apparently, he owes you."

"No, he's just a good guy," I said.

Brian headed down the stairs, and I hurried over to the hairdressers. As I stepped inside, Marie, the owner, peeked around the corner. "Oh, hi, Dev. Thinking about touching up your highlights today, or do you want a pedicure? We've got a special on toenail designs. I'll give you an extra ten percent off, just because."

"Yeah, thanks, Marie, but I'm okay. Hey, a guy is going to be fixing our doorframe, and he'll be working just outside of our office. A couple of sawhorses, there'll be some hammering going on for a bit. Is that okay?"

"A working man out there in front of your office. We may just have to—" She suddenly stopped and stared past me. I turned as Brian climbed to the top of the stairs carrying two metal sawhorses and a large red metal toolbox.

"Is that your man?"

"Yeah, that's Brian. Is that going to be okay?"

"You can tell that hunk to take as long as he wants. If he needs anything at all, he can just come and talk to me," she said and raised an eyebrow.

"Yeah, okay, ahh, thanks, Marie."

"Oh, believe me, he's welcome in here any time."

Brian must have made at least five trips up and down the stairs. He was inside measuring the frame and the door and then outside running some high-pitched tool, then back inside measuring another section of the doorframe. Eventually, he stepped back inside the office with an electric drill in his hand and proceeded to remove the door. When he carried it out, I suddenly had a view of the hairdressers.

Marie and two of her employees were in the lobby. Two women with plastic capes were seated in chairs. All of them were watching Brian as he worked. Marie saw me staring at them and gave a fake little clapping of her hands. She said something I couldn't hear, and they all laughed.

Fifteen minutes later, Brian had removed the door-frame and was in the process of replacing it with half-inch steel panels. He screwed them in place and pro-ceeded to reattach the door. Once the door was reat-tached, he installed a new lock system. All in all, it took the better part of two hours which sounds like a long time, but I knew it would have probably taken me a week, and in the end, I would have done it wrong.

"You want to come out here and try this, Dev. It's a lot more secure, but I want to be sure it works for you before I take off."

I stepped out of the office. Brian handed me a key and closed the door. "Go ahead, give it a try."

"What happens if it won't open?"

"No big deal. I'll just take a saw and cut the door in half. But first, let's see if it works before I have to do that."

"Okay. Say, thanks for entertaining the ladies," I said and indicated Marie and the gang still staring out the window.

He turned around and waved at them. "You kidding? They were great. Brought me over a couple of Cokes. One of them gave me a back rub for a few minutes. They've ordered pizzas. I want to haul this stuff back to the truck before the pizzas come."

"They ordered pizza?"

"Oh, yeah. They were clapping when I was moving the steel frame pieces and blowing me kisses. It was really fun."

"Does that happen often?"

"To tell you the truth, it never has, but free Cokes and pizza, not to mention all the laughs. It was great. So go ahead and try the door, so I can get this stuff out of here."

I placed the key in the lock and turned it. The door opened perfectly.

"Here's what I did for you." He went on to explain the changes he made while placing his tools back in the toolbox. He stacked one of the sawhorses on top of the other and finished up his explanation by telling me, "The next time someone tries to break in, they'll actually have to break the door down."

"This is great, Brian. I can't thank you enough. What do I owe you?"

He shook his head. "Kevin would fire my ass if I took any money from you. I don't know what you did for him, but he thinks you're pretty damn special."

"You sure? I could—"

"No way, man."

"At least let me help you carry this stuff out to your truck."

"Yeah, okay. Maybe just grab the toolbox. I'll take the sawhorses and come back for those steel scraps."

"Yeah, okay."

Brian picked up the metal sawhorses and hurried down the stairs. I lifted his toolbox and groaned. The thing must have weighed a couple hundred pounds. I slowly climbed down the stairs, one step at a time.

Once I made it to the ground floor, I set the toolbox down. Brian walked back into the building and said, "Gee, thanks, Dev. Here, I got it." He picked up the toolbox with one muscular arm and hurried outside just as the pizza delivery guy walked in and headed up the stairs with three pizza boxes.

I climbed back up the stairs. Brian came back in and took the stairs two at a time. "Oh, Dev, before I forget, here's the second set of keys for that lock. Just in case you lose a set, you'll still have these."

"Thanks, Brian. Actually, a guy shares the office with me so I'll give them to him. Don't let me keep you. I'm sure the ladies would love to feed you pizza."

He held out his hand and said, "It was very nice to meet you. Any problems with the door, you call Kevin, and he'll send me out right away."

I attempted to squeeze his hand. It was as hard as a brick. "I'm sure we won't have any problems. Great to meet you, Brian, and thank you for the wonderful work. Now, go on over and enjoy."

He grinned and hurried over to the hairdressers.

I tried the second set of keys in the lock. They worked perfectly. I closed the door behind me and noticed there was a switch on the back of the lock that allowed the door to remain unlocked. I clicked the switch and tried the door handle to make sure it worked.

"Dev, oh, Dev," Marie called from her open door. "Come on over. There's plenty of pizza and," she lowered her voice, "we want to thank you for having Brian work on your door. An absolutely marvelous afternoon. Come on."

I joined them for twenty minutes. It was obvious I was pretty much a third wheel. Brian was the focus of everyone's attention, and rightfully so. I eventually made my way back to the office. I brought a slice of pizza for Morton, which he devoured in three quick gulps. I placed a call to Kevin White but ended up leaving a message. "Hi Kevin, I can't thank you enough for sending Brian over to repair and update our door security. So very kind of you, and he is such a wonderful guy. Please let me know what I owe you for the new doorframe and lock. You shouldn't have to give away Brian's craftsmanship. He's in the process of finishing up. Thank you and all the best."

Twenty-nine

Louie never did make it back to the office. Morton and I headed home and sat in front of the TV until close to 11:00 before we headed up to bed. We were back in the office before 8:00 the following morning. Since we had the new steel doorframe and the lock had been changed, Louie wouldn't be able to get in, so I wanted to be there to let him in.

The boot print was still on the door, but when we stepped inside, everything was just as I'd left it. I put the coffee on, rinsed out both our mugs, and started an internet search on fired police officer Don Humphrey.

Maybe not surprisingly, there wasn't much to find. Which suggested that whatever the reason for Humphrey being fired, it probably wasn't some big news event, and the department had probably made it worth his while to leave quietly. That said, based on the rental unit he was living in, life did not appear to be going very well.

I attempted to locate some version of a private investigation firm using a variety of names: Humphrey Investigations, Humphrey Detective Agency, Humphrey Investigating, Humphrey Patrol, and on and on. Nothing came up, so either he wasn't using his name in the business title, or he made the whole thing up and somehow got Grumley to pay him.

Louie pulled in front of my car a little after 9:00. He was wearing a dark blue suit and a tie. He looked decent, at least for Louie, as he crossed the street and made his way up the stairs. He opened the office door, gave the door knob a funny look, and went to his desk. I got up, filled his mug with coffee, and set it on the picnic table.

Once he caught his breath and had some coffee, he said, "What's with the door?"

"Same door, brand new steel doorframe for a lot better security. I placed a new set of keys for you next to your computer."

Louie turned in his chair and picked up the two keys. "So the old set doesn't work anymore?"

"That's right. Get rid of it."

He did just that, tossing the old keys into his wastebasket. "It looks like the same door."

"Yeah, it is," I said and gave him a quick update on the steel doorframe, Brian, Marie and company ordering in pizza, and getting to know Brian better.

"You find anything out on whoever broke in here?"

"I'm pretty sure I know who did it. I'm guessing he's working for Arthur Grumley, and in short order, he'll find himself as lost as I was."

I kept thinking about Grumley's Mustang. As far as knowing much about cars, I could fill most gas tanks and check the tire pressure. Beyond that, I quickly found myself in someone's garage. I couldn't change the oil, and as far as working on an engine, I was absolutely worthless.

Grumley still had the car he was driving when Diane was killed. What were the odds? My phone rang. "Hi, Sandie, how are things with you?"

"More importantly, Dev. How are things with you? Last time you were over, I was all set for a wild, crazy night, and your mind had you off somewhere in la-la land."

"Yeah, I know. I'm sorry. I was in the middle of working a case, and all sorts of things were popping up in my thick skull. Can I beg forgiveness?"

"I don't know about begging, but you could earn it. You want to come over for dinner tonight?"

I was tempted to joke and ask what she was serving, but I knew that would be playing with fire. Instead, I said, "I'd love to. What can I bring?"

"Not a thing. I've got everything set up, including dessert. Tell you what, if you want to bring a bottle of wine, that would be fine. We'll be eating roast beef, baked potatoes, and roasted red peppers. I'm baking a pan of brownies for dessert."

"Sounds delicious. What time would you like me?"

"Oh, any time after 6:00 works for me."

"I'll grab some wine and arrive promptly at 6:00."

"Good. Oh, and rest up," she said, suggesting things were heading back toward normal.

I phoned Billy Flores and Luscious Dixon and checked in with them. Everything was going well. When Luscious wasn't eating, he was out checking the parking lot and the front of the building. Thus far, there hadn't been any trouble. I called Eleanor Monroe, the woman who had witnessed Diane Donnelly being hit by the car. I ended up leaving her a message. "Hi, Eleanor. This is Dev Haskell. Say, I resigned from the case involving the hit and run you witnessed back in 2006. Another individual has taken it over. I didn't give him any information, but someone broke into my office the other night and stole my file. If you're contacted regarding the hit and run, please call me before agreeing to see anyone. Sorry for the headache. All the best, Dev."

Louie headed over to The Spot at the end of the day, and I begged off and took Morton for a walk. On the way home, I stopped at the gas station and filled my car. The gas cost about the same as a case of wine.

While I was at the station, I walked back to where two guys were working on cars. They'd done everything from replacing a headlight to doing engine repair for me in the past. I talked to Sam and told him I was thinking of buying a 2005 Mustang, and was there a way I could check and see if panels had been repaired or replaced?

"You're thinking of buying a vintage Mustang? Do you have a place to store it?"

"I could probably move most of the stuff from the half of my garage I can't park in, and I could pull it in there."

"You sure you want to do this, Dev? I mean, most of the people I know who have vintage cars, well, they're car guys. You know? They can fix engines and stuff. No offense, but I don't think you can do anything like that, can you?"

"No, I can't, but I was thinking, if I needed anything, I could just call. More guaranteed employment for you."

"Yeah, okay, I'm all for that. So, one of the best ways to check to see if panels have been replaced without having to take things apart or crawl around underneath is to check the paint thickness."

"Paint thickness? How in the hell do I—"

"Not to worry. Just go online and check out a digital paint thickness meter. You're just looking, right? And you're not planning on doing anything like actually painting the vehicle, are you?"

"Can I use a brush?" He gave me a look. "Relax, Sam, I'm just joking."

He seemed to think for a moment. "Now, where was I? Oh, yeah, go online and check out a digital paint thickness meter. Get one for twenty-five, maybe thirty bucks. The things are battery-operated, it fits in your pocket, and you just hold it against the car, push a button, and it gives you the paint thickness. Depending on the make, a normal thickness might be something like two hundred microns. Measure a couple of areas on the car and come up with an average. If the car is, say, two hundred, and you measure an area that suddenly comes up maybe five hundred or seven hundred and fifty, that's been re-painted. The other thing you can look for is an orange peel effect to the finish. That's usually not factory work. Of course, paint on areas of trim, a color imbalance, all can point to the same thing."

"Okay, Sam, thanks. Much appreciated. I'll go online tonight."

"Glad to help, Dev. Good luck, and I look forward to working on your car."

Thirty

I pulled into Yarmo Liquor and picked up two bottles of Pinot Noir. The reason I went to Yarmo was because I wanted to see if the violin player was in the parking lot, and he was. I leaned on the trunk of my car and listened for four or five minutes, then clapped when he finished. I walked over and gave him all my cash, two dollars. His black eye was gone.

"Really enjoy your music. You have any more problems with those two guys?"

He shook his head and said, "No, not see them again."

"Good, I hope it stays that way."

"My brother is here, too," he said and glanced over at the guy sitting on the hood of a car. A black baseball bat was lying next to him. I gave him a wave, and he nodded.

"I hope it works for you. Hey, tell me your name. I'm Dev Haskell, by the way."

"Dev?"

"Yeah, that's short for Devlin. What's your name?"

"My friends call me Mateo. It is my name."

"Nice to meet you, Mateo. Thanks again for playing. You're very good."

"And you are very nice, gracias," he said as we shook hands.

I waved again at his brother on the hood of his car and climbed into my car. I drove out of the parking lot and headed up Davern Hill. I pulled in front of Sandie's house at exactly 6:00. I quickly checked for any stray vehicles. There were none, and I headed up the sidewalk.

She must have seen me pulling up because she opened the door before I could ring the doorbell. "Well, Mr. Right On Time. Come on in." Tonight she was wearing skintight cut-off jeans and a light blue halter top. I got a quick kiss and handed her the bag with the bottles of wine. "Come on back to the kitchen," she said and led the way.

Her halter top was backless, which suggested a very enjoyable evening.

"Now, I've got a chilled white wine ready to go, or if you want, we can open one of those reds. Whatever you feel like."

"Let's do the chilled white, and we can have the reds with dinner, or you can hang onto them for some other time."

"Well, here, if you'll bring these hors d'oeuvres out to the patio, I'll get the wine out of the fridge."

I grabbed the hors d'oeuvre platter and held the door open for her as she carried the ice bucket out to the patio. It was a clear evening. The sun was still up and warm, but the patio was beneath a giant oak tree that shaded half of the yard. She set the ice bucket on the table, and I set the hors d'oeuvre platter next to it.

"You mind doing the honors?" she asked and handed me a corkscrew.

I opened the wine bottle and filled the glasses. The wine looked bubbly. We clinked glasses and took a sip. It was light, sparkly, and perfect for tonight.

"So? You've been busy?"

"Well, yes and no." I went on to tell her about the Grumley deal, my quitting, and the burglary. Told her about Kevin White sending Brian over to do yeoman's work on the door. I didn't mention Diane Donnelly.

"Oh, boy. Well, let's see, I went and looked for shoes but didn't buy any. Oh, and I was grocery shopping yesterday. That's about the extent of all my excitement."

"Sounds okay to me. I'd love to get back to whatever normal is."

"You said this guy that came to your office broke into it that night?"

"Well, that's what I think, and based on the file that was stolen, it almost has to be him. Apparently, he was on the police force at one time, but they let him go. I'm not sure why, and I didn't find anything online mentioning it, so it was probably a mutual hush-hush deal between the police and him. I'm guessing he got paid some amount just to go away quietly."

She shook her head. "You deal with some crazy people, Dev."

"Yeah, well, it's the business, I'm afraid. What's new with you? Do you still have that lake place?"

"Yes and no. It's owned by my ex's siblings. Part of the divorce agreement was I get to use it for a certain number of weeks, just like everyone else. They schedule it out on New Year's Eve, although I just email my dates, so I don't have to see them personally. I know everyone, by and large, is trying to be nice, well, with one exception. But, to be honest, it's not relaxing for me up there any more. I'm just uncomfortable. Gary passed away four years ago, and each year, I've cut my time in half, and I haven't missed it. I'm in Florida and out to California and Arizona in the winter. Maybe a weekend up at the lake would be nice, but I can live without it. This year when it comes time to schedule, I'm just going to say thanks but no thanks."

"Will they be okay with that?"

"Oh, are you kidding? They'll love it. Four more weeks, they can be up there, and they won't have to deal with an interloper like me. Besides, the one sister is the textbook unhappy person, and she's always got a complaint. She doesn't like the way I folded the sheets. She doesn't like the wine I left. There's a mouse in the cabin, so it must be my fault. She's worn me out, and I actually feel a little guilty."

"It all adds up. I'm lucky I don't have any of that. I always thought—Oh shit," I said and pulled out my phone. Luscious Dixon. "I'm sorry, Sandie, I need to take this call."

"Not a problem. I should go in and check on the roast. Take your time," she said and patted me on the shoulder as she headed into the house.

"Yeah, Luscious. What's up?"

"Just giving you an update, Dev. Two of those pieces of shit were out front for a couple of minutes. Billy recognized 'em as being here before. I went out and nicely asked them to leave."

I could only imagine what his version of nice was like. "Did they leave?"

"They looked like they were going to try to give me a hard time. I convinced them otherwise."

"You okay?"

"Oh yeah, not a problem. As a matter of fact, Billy was all happy. He was patting me on the back. He even had one of the girls bring me out another dessert. I'm very happy. I just wanted to let you know what happened, and I'll be keeping an eye out."

"These two guys, was one of them in a leather vest, and the other one was wearing a gray hoodie with the sleeves cut off?"

"Oh, you met 'em before."

"Yeah, I had a run-in with them a week or so ago. Idiots. They hassled a kid playing his violin to get donations. I may have overreacted."

Luscious laughed at that comment. "That would be easy to do. Anyway, they decided the better decision would be to leave. Told me they'd be back with a friend, and I'd better watch out."

Damn it. "You want me down there?"

"I don't think that's necessary. Those two ain't no problem, and some other dude, nah, I just wanted to keep you up to date."

"Okay, any problem, you call me before you deal with them. I'm literally just a few minutes away, and I can be there right away."

"I appreciate that, Dev, but don't you worry none. Everything is cool."

"Thanks, Luscious, appreciate the call. Oh, and good work."

I disconnected and filled up Sandie's wine glass. I barely topped mine up just in case Luscious had to call back.

Sandie stepped out of the kitchen a moment later. "Everything okay?"

"Yeah, just the normal nonsense. I've got a good guy on it, and he was just giving me an update. How'd the roast look?"

"Wonderful. I took it out of the oven and covered it with foil. We can let it sit like that for ten or fifteen minutes," she said and took another sip of wine. We chatted about people we both knew, giving one another updates, a divorce, a baby, two new jobs, a couple moving out of state, and then we headed in to dinner.

Thirty-one

We chatted over dinner. I was still holding back on the wine. We'd finished a little after 8:00. Sandie moved us into the living room, and we were seated on the couch facing one another. I kept thinking the next three hours would be the prime time for these idiots to try something at Ranchero Flores, and I didn't want Lucious to get hurt.

"Well, there is something I wanted to ask you about, Dev."

"Oh, what's that? Do you need help with your taxes, or do you want to know who to vote for in the fall?"

"Very funny. No, I've got something coming up, and If it's okay with you, I'd like your help. No pressure. If you don't want to do it, I completely understand, and I'll find someone else to help me, I think."

"Don't tell me you want to get pregnant."

"What? Are you crazy?" she laughed and slapped me on the knee.

"I don't know. Why don't you just tell me what it is you want instead of laying groundwork that sounds like you're thinking of jumping out of a plane without a parachute."

She rolled her eyes. "Oh, if only. Okay, so here's the deal. I have a cousin getting married at the end of the week. All my siblings and all my cousins are going to be there. The wedding is up in Hibbing. It's a go-to-the-church wedding, spend the night in a hotel and have breakfast with a hundred other nosey extended family members the following morning. Everyone will be pointing and whispering at us. I've already booked a hotel room, and I may have told my family that I was bringing a date, sort of. But I never said your name."

I started to laugh.

"It's not funny," she giggled and slapped my knee again. She set her wine glass on the coffee table and refilled it, then raised the bottle toward me.

"No thanks, I'm okay. So, you're going to this wedding. A big extended family wedding."

"Yes, and my dopey sisters and my cousins have put all sorts of pressure on me, and well, I maybe embellished things a little bit."

"Embellished? Did you tell them you were seeing someone? Did you suggest you were in a relationship? Do they think you might be the next wedding?"

"I didn't use the word relationship."

"So you need some really smart, debonair, good-looking guy to escort you to this family affair?"

"Yeah, that's right, but since I couldn't find anyone like that, I decided to ask you."

Even I laughed at that. "Yeah, I'd be happy to go with you, Sandie. Call me tomorrow with the date you want to leave. I'll put it on my calendar. I'm presuming this isn't a t-shirt and blue jeans affair."

"No, it's a nice coat and slacks affair. I don't know about a tie."

"How about I bring a tie just in case. I'm presuming your folks will be there."

"Yes, they will. My dad really liked you, and my mom will just be glad I'm not sharing the room with another woman."

"What?"

"Just mother-daughter battles that I don't need to go into at the moment. Oh, thanks, I really appreciate this, Dev, and I'm sorry to dump this on you. It's a big affair. They've got some special band booked for the reception. It'll be fun, and you'll take a lot of pressure off of me. Well, and then you'll get the third degree from my sisters."

"Relax, I'll just tell them I'm on a weekend release from the St. Cloud prison." She stared wide-eyed for a moment. "Just kidding, Sandie, relax. I'll be on my best behavior. If I can remember how."

"Oh, stop. I've had enough wine and thank you. Really, I mean it. You've just eliminated a lot of pressure for me." With that, she set her wine glass on the table, took me by the hand, and led me into the bedroom.

The room was dark, and I was aware of Sandie slipping out of bed and going into the bathroom. I glanced at the digital clock on the dresser. It was 3:30. The next time I looked at the clock, it was 6:00. "Here you go," Sandie said and handed me a coffee. She was wearing a blue terrycloth bathrobe. "I'll have breakfast ready in just a bit. Grab a shower, and I'll call you."

She made blueberry pancakes for breakfast. I wolfed them down, had a second coffee, thanked her for a lovely night, and hurried home. Morton met me at the front door. He didn't wait for his head scratch but quickly trotted to the backdoor. I unlocked the door and let him into the backyard. I did a quick perusal of the house and amazingly didn't find a mess anywhere. I filled his food and water dishes and worked on my laptop until he'd finished breakfast.

We were the first ones in the office. There was no sign of a break-in. Amazing, two days in a row, and no one broke into the place. I made a fresh pot of coffee, chatted with Louie for a few minutes once he arrived, and then put Morton in the car. We drove over to Charles Avenue and Don Humphrey's address. I drove down the alley. His white Jeep Liberty was in the dirt parking area behind the house. He was parked between a faded blue Ford Focus and a Hyundai with a smashed left rear panel. I pulled to the end of the alley and parked on the street. I leaned against the hood of my car and glanced down the alley. I could just see a sliver of Humphrey's Jeep Liberty. If and when he left, whichever direction he was going, I'd be able to follow him.

I waited a good hour and got a half-dozen strange looks from people walking or driving past. Humphrey's Jeep finally backed out of the parking area forty-five minutes later and headed in my direction. I hurried back in my car and lowered myself below the dashboard as he drove past. When he was a block away, I glanced up, started the car, and followed him. He drove over to Dale Street and pulled onto I94. I was two cars behind him, which was perfect. The white Jeep Liberty was almost impossible to miss. From I94, he merged onto 35E and eventually turned onto Highway 36. I was pretty sure where he was going, and sure enough, he took the Stillwater exit, drove through town, and eventually turned onto Quinlan Ave North. Arthur Grumley's house was just down the road. I pulled over rather than follow.

Thirty minutes later, Humphrey passed me where I was parked on the shoulder of the road. I followed him back into town on the same route he'd taken earlier. He took the Dale Street exit and then pulled onto University Ave. I thought he would be heading home, but he passed the logical street to turn and drove four more blocks before turning into the parking lot for Dozey's bar.

It was a dive place with not the best reputation. I went around the block and pulled next to the parking lot. Humphrey's Jeep was there, along with four other cars. I waited for twenty minutes, decided he was probably going to be here for a while, and headed back to the office.

Louie was out of the office. I phoned Luscious and ended up leaving a message, which made sense because he taught his weightlifting class in the morning. "Hi Luscious, it's Dev. Just checking in since I didn't hear from you again last night. Hope everything went okay. Give me a call when it's convenient."

I called Billy Flores next. He answered right away. "Hi Dev, how are things?"

"Not a problem, but more importantly, Billy, how are things on your end?"

"You heard from Luscious last night?"

"Yeah, but that was early on. Told me he suggested those two idiots find somewhere else to hassle folks. Did they ever come back?"

"No, I think they were just acting tough or trying to. Obviously, it didn't work."

"So they didn't come back, and everything was okay this morning when you came in? No spray paint or broken windows?"

"No, everything was just fine. I gotta tell you, Dev, I really like the guy. Thinking maybe I might try to find a way to bring him in full time."

"That's great news, Billy. Keep me posted on what you do. He's a piece of work."

"Yeah, well, he's done a great job here. All the customers like him. A couple of regulars we worry about once in a while seem to have gotten the message. It's all going well."

"That's great. I placed a call to him this morning and left a message. I think he's teaching his weightlifting class right now. I won't mention your full-time idea to him if he calls me back."

"Yeah, thanks. I'm still trying to figure out a couple of things. Hey, I gotta run. A delivery just arrived," Billy said and disconnected.

No sooner had I gotten off the phone with Billy than I had another call. Monica's name was on the screen. "Hi, Monica. How are things?"

"Just fine, Dev. More importantly, how are you? I've been out of town at a conference and just listened to your message. Someone broke into your office?"

"Yeah, a couple of nights ago. The reason I called is they stole my file with the birth record, and my notes were in the file. Your name and phone number were in my notes."

"What does that mean?"

"Probably nothing. I'm pretty sure the break-in was committed by a guy named Don Humphrey. He says he's a private investigator, but he's not licensed, and he was fired from the police department. He apparently took over when I quit. I don't know how much he knows. I've been in touch with everyone else in my investigation, and no one was aware of him, and no one is interested in dealing with him. I just thought I should make you aware of the situation."

"Well, thank you. I appreciate the information. Fortunately, I haven't heard anything from this person. You said his name was Humphrey?"

"Yeah, Don Humphrey."

"I'll let you know if he calls. Everything else is good?"

"Very good, you stay safe," I said, and she disconnected.

Thirty-two

After I took Morton for a walk, I grabbed a BBQ sandwich for lunch and got a shoulder bone for him. I finished the sandwich in about five minutes. Morton was involved in a serious exploration of the bone. I debated driving back past Dozey's to see if Humphrey was still there, but then what? With the price of gas now up to almost five bucks a gallon, I decided to make a phone call instead. I had a burner in the bottom drawer of my desk, took it out, and dialed the number.

"Yeah, Dozey's," was how some guy answered the phone after a half-dozen rings.

"Is that piece of shit Don Humphrey in there?"

There was a brief pause. "He might be. Who the hell are you?"

"You tell him I got his number, and if he ever comes near my wife again, I'm going to deal with him up close and personal. Real personal," I said and hung up. It felt good to make the call. With any luck, I gave Humphrey something to worry about for the rest of the afternoon.

Hopefully, he'd have to cancel whatever his plans for the night had been and find a new bar.

"You're looking like the cat that swallowed the canary," Louie said when he stepped into the office a couple of minutes later.

I told him about my phone call.

"He's working for that jackass that was in here a few days ago? That Gummy guy?"

"Grumley, Arthur Grumley. Yeah, hopefully, my phone call will have him staying close to home and looking over his shoulder. All going well on your end?"

Louie nodded and said, "Fine if you don't go into any detail."

"I'm going to run a quick errand. You plan on being here?"

"Don't worry about it. My next appointment is over at The Spot at the end of the day."

"An appointment? Are you meeting someone?"

"Yeah, Mike, the bartender."

"Oh yeah. Of course. I should be back in an hour or so."

"Take your time, Dev."

Morton was too involved with his shoulder bone to bother to look up as I left. I drove over to O'Reilly Auto Parts and was directed to aisle 4, where there were three different digital paint thickness meters for sale. Two were priced at over sixty bucks, and the one priced at under thirty came with directions. It wasn't a tough choice. I bought a four-pack of AA batteries and headed back to the office.

I installed a battery in the meter and tested it on my car. No two panels on the car tested the same. One was at 230, another at 225, and then a bunch of areas in the 500-600 range. In other words, my car apparently had a lot of work done on it prior to me buying it at the police auction. I put the meter in the glove compartment and went up to the office.

At least Morton gave me a half-second glance when I walked in. Not that he got up or anything. I think he was just making sure I wasn't someone who was going to try to take his bone. Louie appeared to be in the middle of a nap, so I quietly closed the door, settled in at my desk, and turned on my computer.

I brought Arthur Grumley's mansion up on my computer and then studied the area around the house. The four-stall garage was attached to the house. I couldn't recall seeing anything that suggested an alarm system in the house, but I had to believe there was one. There was a window on the side of the garage and a short two-foot-high hedge running along the side of the garage. No image of the back of the garage was available.

I didn't know how long I'd been on my computer when Louie suddenly said, "I don't know about you, but I've had enough for one day. You thinking about making an appearance at The Spot?"

"I've got to take care of something tonight. Once I've dealt with that I'll try to make it over if it's not too late."

"Enjoy," Louie said and headed out the door. I locked up, took Morton for a walk, and headed home. I made a grilled cheese sandwich, then went upstairs and changed into a pair of black jeans and a black shirt. Grabbing a container of face paint from the basement, along with a can of insect repellent and a flashlight I returned to my car.

The sun was just beginning to set as I drove through the town of Stillwater. Parking on Quinlan Avenue about a half-mile away from Grumley's house, I walked into the woods and made my way to the paved trail that led to the mansion. I quickly made my way along the trail until I could see the open area fifty yards ahead, along with a corner of Grumley's house. I stepped into the woods and continued toward the house at a much slower pace.

The place looked the same, although at this hour there weren't any cars parked in front. I sprayed the insect repellant on me and then applied the hunter's black face paint to my face and hands. For a moment, I felt as if I was back in the army.

I sat and watched the house for the better part of an hour. A couple of rooms on the first floor had lights on, and one room up on the second floor was illuminated. I was wondering how long it would be before Grumley went to bed when suddenly the corner door on the attached garage rose, and a black car backed out. It looked like a Jeep, and I recognized it as the G-Class Mercedes that had driven Grumley to my office the other day. Grumley was behind the wheel. He pressed the button to lower the garage door and drove off down the trail, disappearing from sight.

After waiting a few minutes, I hurried across the open area. Fortunately, no motion detector lights flashed on. I stopped against the wall of the garage with the hedge and walked toward the window. Given the age of the place, I was hoping it was a double-hung window. Unfortunately, it wasn't, and it was securely fastened to the frame. I walked around to the back of the garage.

A well-kept lawn gently sloped down to a limestone wall. There was a large patio with a glass-topped table. Eight chairs were positioned around the table. What looked like a fire pit was surrounded by cushioned couches and chairs. An outdoor bar with four stools was behind one of the couches.

There were four windows in the back of the garage. None of them were double-hung, and I debated for a half-second about breaking one to get inside. I quickly decided that would be one of the dumber things I could do. I tried the garage doors, all four of them. They didn't budge. I went back to the windows and pushed the frames every which way. Nothing happened. Once again, I considered just breaking one of the garage windows and came up with the same response, dumb, dumb, really dumb. I walked back into the birch forest, sat down, and tried to find a solution. How in the hell was I going to get into Grumley's garage?"

Thirty-three

I'd been sitting in the dark with my back against a birch tree, racking my tiny brain for over an hour, and coming up empty-handed. Suddenly, a pair of headlights filtered through the trees. I remained very still and watched as Grumley's Mercedes wound its way along the paved trail and into the open area heading for the garage.

He didn't appear to be in any hurry. A thought immediately popped into my head, and I acted on it. I dashed out of the birch forest and was off to the left and maybe fifteen feet behind the Mercedes. The car slowed as it entered the garage. I crossed my fingers, picked up speed, and prayed to God that Grumley was focused on the wall of the garage as he pulled in and not glancing in his rearview mirror.

I had crouched down and was close enough to touch his rear bumper and the brake lights as he pulled into the garage and slowed. As soon as there was room, I hopped over to the rear of his Cadillac Escalade parked three feet away and slid underneath the car as the garage door closed. As I slid, I felt something squish beneath me.

I held my breath as I heard the driver's door on the Mercedes open and then another door. Both doors closed at about the same time. The horn suddenly honked, signaling Grumley had pushed the button to lock the car doors.

"Oh, wow, man. You got a really cool gig here, baby. This is going to be fun. Let's party, honey. I want to play," a woman said.

"That's what I'm counting on. What'd you say your name was?"

"Trixie, sweetheart, but you can call me anything you want. Donny told me anything with you is free tonight. So, you gonna mix me something to drink before we get started?"

"What are you in the mood for?"

"A lot more than drinking," she said and laughed just as I heard a door open, and they apparently entered the house. I heard the door close, and a second later, a lock clicked into place. I remained beneath the Escalade for another five minutes hoping they weren't still in the garage. I don't think I took a breath the entire time.

I slowly crawled out from beneath the Escalade and attempted to adjust my eyes. There was a foul smell, and I clicked on my flashlight and looked beneath the Escalade. There it was, dog shit, no doubt that dachshund of Grumley's. Apparently, I'd smeared it across the floor as I slid beneath the Escalade. Now it was all over the back of my jeans.

With the four windows on the back wall, I could make out the shapes of the cars. The Mustang was parked at the opposite side of the garage, closest to the wall of the house. I shined my flashlight on the garage floor and hurried over to the Mustang. I pulled the digital paint meter out of my pocket, placed it against the right-back panel of the Mustang, and pressed the button. 217 microns. I measured the other side and got the same thing. I cautiously squeezed around a recycle bin and stepped to the front of the vehicle. I pressed the button and got 220 microns. I stepped around to the front panel on the passenger side and measured. The thickness came up as 718 microns. I measured in four other places on the panel, 705, 721, 711, and, finally, 730 around the head-light. I wrote the numbers down on an envelope I pulled from the recycle bin.

Based on the little knowledge I had, that suggested the panel had been repaired or replaced and painted in a different method than the rest of the car. I took my car keys out and scratched the panel a number of times, col-lecting tiny 'chips' on my fingertip and then rubbing them off my finger and into a small Ziplock bag.

I walked back to the distant garage door. The one Grumley had raised to pull in. There were two illumi-nated buttons. The green button was labeled 'open,' and the red button was labeled 'close.' I took a deep breath and pushed the green button. The interior light in the gar-age immediately flashed on, illuminating the entire room. As the door began to rise, I bent down and stepped out. As soon as it had risen high enough for me to push the red 'close' button, I reached in and did that. The door stopped for a half-second and then closed. I stepped around to the side of the garage and stood alongside the window. The garage light went off a half-minute later, and I waited to see if it came back on, signaling Grumley had heard the garage door opening and was investigating. Luckily, it never came back on.

After five minutes, I peeked around the corner of the garage. There didn't seem to be any activity out front, and I hurried across the open lawn and back into the birch forest. I stopped five feet into the forest and looked at the mansion. The lights on the first floor were all off. The second-floor room was still illuminated, but the light was substantially dimmer.

"Enjoy your evening," I muttered and headed back to my car. Once I got to the car, I emptied my pockets and pulled off my belt. I waited for a car to pass, stepped out of my jeans, left them on the side of the road, and drove home in my underwear.

I was up early the next morning and drove to the gas station. I walked into one of the bays. Sam had his back to me and seemed to be searching for something in his toolbox. An SUV with a good deal of rust was raised up on the car lift. "Good morning, Sam," I said as I stepped into the bay.

He half jumped, turned, and looked at me. "Dev? What's wrong?"

"What?"

"What's the problem? The sun is barely up, and you're standing here. You just on the way home from last night?"

"No, no, nothing like that. I measured the paint thickness on that Mustang I told you about, and I wanted to get your opinion." I handed him the envelope where I'd written the numbers down on the back.

He looked at the envelope, then gave me a sort of funny look and shook his head. "So these numbers in the two hundreds are on different areas of the body?"

"Yeah, both rear panels and then the front panel on the driver's side. The numbers in the seven hundreds are on the front passenger side."

"You see any orange peel effect on that front passenger side?"

"No, I looked for it, but I didn't see any."

"Probably an expensive repair job, but whoever did it, did it right. Someone either hit something, maybe someone, or they were hit. My money's on them hitting something."

"If they hit something, is there any kind of timeframe where that's not much of a factor?"

He shook his head and said, "I'm not following."

"If this paint job was done, say, twenty years ago, would the reading be off for some reason? Maybe because it's old paint?"

"No, nothing like that. This front panel area with the high numbers was definitely repaired and repainted. That doesn't mean it wasn't done well. You may not even be able to tell except for these readings, but it was definitely worked on. I would guess the higher number, this 730, was probably around the headlight."

"Yeah, as a matter of fact, it was."

"Well, there you go. If you're serious about this vehicle, ask the seller if it was ever in an accident. If he says no, or he tells you that he doesn't know, you could mention this, and he might feel the need to reduce the price a bit."

"Thanks, Sam. I'll keep that in mind."

"Good luck. I hope it works out for you," he said and went back to searching through his toolbox.

I had the coffee going by the time Louie made it into the office. His mug was waiting for him on his picnic table. He sat and stared at me for a long moment as he sipped his coffee. Finally, he said, "Were you involved in playing some weird zombie sexual role thing last night?"

"What?"

"Your face, it's got these weird shadow-like things on it. I don't know. Were you maybe pretending to be a vampire or something?"

"No. You know, a woman gave me some different kind of skin cream, and I thought I'd washed all of it off, but I guess not," I said.

"Yeah, okay, skin cream, sure."

Thirty-four

Not much happened for the rest of the day until just a little after 3:00, when I got a call from Diane Donnelly's father. "Dev Haskell?"

"Yes, Mr. Donnelly. Is everything going okay?"

"I'm not sure. This person you mentioned, Humphrey. This Don Humphrey, the detective, he called this morning."

"What did he want? Oh, and he's not a detective, sir. Actually, he was fired from the police force a few years ago. He's no longer with the police, and he is not now, nor has he ever been, a detective or licensed private investigator."

There was a pause. "I was afraid of something like that. He phoned this morning around 11:00. I was out on the golf course, and Marilyn took the call. He's coming over at 5:00 this evening. He didn't leave a phone number, so we don't have any way to contact him and tell him not to come."

"Okay, did he tell her he was a detective?"

"I believe so, but I can't be absolutely sure. He told her he had some questions regarding the hit and run and wanted to talk with us."

"Did he mention the adoption?"

"Yes, he did and said he wanted to talk to that family as well."

"Did your wife give him any contact information for the Whites?"

"No, she didn't have it available at the time, but Marilyn told him she would be able to find that information by this evening."

"Okay, I'll be over in the next ninety minutes. Don't worry. Everything is going to be just fine. I appreciate the call."

"Sorry to interrupt your day. Is there anything I should do in the meantime?" Donnelly asked.

"Yeah, tell your wife not to worry. Everything is going to be fine. I'll see you shortly," I said and disconnected.

I phoned Aaron LaZelle and crossed my fingers. Amazingly he answered on the second ring. "Yeah, Dev."

"Hi Aaron, I need your help. I just got a call from Diane Donnelly's father. Apparently, Humphrey phoned them this morning while Mr. Donnelly was out on the golf course. His wife took the call, and Humphrey is going over to their house at 5:00 tonight."

"So call him and tell him not to come."

"I was hoping for a little more than that. Here's the deal. If he called, he got their name and number from the file that was stolen from my office. That's the only way he'd be able to contact them. When he talked to the wife, he referred to himself as a detective."

"A detective? He's not on the force anymore, and he never was a detective."

"Yeah, I know that. So here's a guy using stolen information and impersonating a police officer. Is there someone you can send over to their house before the 5:00 meeting and arrest this piece of shit?"

"I can do better than that. I'll be there myself. I kinda remember the house from high school, but give me their address just in case."

I gave him the Donnelly's address on Pinehurst Avenue.

"What time did you say he's supposed to be there?"

"5:00, Aaron, that's a little more than ninety minutes from now."

"Maybe head over there now, just in case Humphrey decides to make an early appearance. Park down the block. I'll be there as soon as possible, and Dev, thanks for the call. We always want to nip this sort of thing in the bud. See you shortly."

I phoned Donnelly back and told him I was coming over now. He sounded relieved. Hopefully, there wouldn't be any trouble, but just to be on the safe side, I took Morton home and let him out in the backyard with a water dish and a biscuit. I placed my Glock in the sticky holster, pulled my shirt out, shoved the holster into the waist of my jeans, and headed over to the Donnelly's.

I parked across the street and down three doors. I glanced up and down the street, checking for a white Jeep Liberty. Thank God I didn't see one. Donnelly opened the front door when I was halfway up the side-walk.

"Can't tell you how glad I am to see you, Dev. Come on in. Marilyn is in the kitchen." He lowered his voice. "She's pretty upset she took the phone call and talked to this guy."

"It's not her fault. I'm sure he gave her a good story. He did the same thing to me the first time I met him. He came across as this really nice guy who just wanted to help, and then that night, he kicked the door in at my office. He stole the file with all my information on the birth and the baby."

"Well, come on into the kitchen. She wants to tell you how sorry she is."

"That's not necessary. Like I said, I'm just glad you called." I followed him into the kitchen.

"Marilyn, Dev is here," he said as we stepped into the kitchen.

Mrs. Donnelly was sitting at the kitchen counter. An untouched cup of coffee was in front of her. Her eyes were red and puffy from crying.

I took one look at her and wrapped my arms around her. "Oh, Mrs. Donnelly, don't you worry. Everything is going to be fine."

"Oh, I'm just so, so, sorry. I don't know what I was thinking. Why didn't I just hang up the phone? I can't believe I was that stupid. Now I've caused all sorts of problems. I feel awful, just awful. What are you going to do?"

I pulled back a little just in time to see another tear run down her cheek.

"Actually, you may have helped us, all of us."

"Helped? Oh please, even I know that's not possible."

"Did he tell you he was a detective?"

"Yes, that's why I agreed to meet with him at 5:00."

"So what that proves is he is impersonating a police officer. He's not a detective. He's not on the police force, and he's not a licensed private investigator. I know a police officer who will be joining us, and he'll deal with this."

"Will I have to meet with this person?"

"Neither you nor your husband are going to meet with him."

"Are you going to arrest him?" Mr. Donnelly asked.

"That's going to be up to the police, but I would think they won't be too happy with this guy pretending to be a police officer. As a matter of fact, I would not be surprised if—" The doorbell suddenly rang.

Mr. and Mrs. Donnelly both got a worried look on their faces.

"Stay here. I'll deal with this," I said and stepped into the dining room. I closed the kitchen door behind me and headed for the front door just as the doorbell rang a second time.

I looked through the peephole in the front door. Aaron LaZelle and a woman I recognized but couldn't remember her name. She was dressed in jeans and a faded black t-shirt from a Rolling Stones concert. The t-shirt had the open mouth with the red lips and the tongue sticking out. US CONCERT TOUR 2005 was in faded white letters across the bottom.

"Oh, am I ever glad to see you two," I said as I opened the door.

Hi, Dev, I think you've met Janet Lincoln before," Aaron said as I stepped back so they could come inside.

"Yeah, been a while, Janet. Nice to see you again and thank you both for coming on such short notice."

"An ex-cop, fired no less, and impersonating a police officer. I'm looking forward to dealing with this," Lincoln said.

Aaron smiled and raised his eyebrows as he stood behind her. "Where are the Donnelly's?"

"They're both out in the kitchen. Mrs. Donnelly is kicking herself for even answering the phone, let alone agreeing to meet with Humphrey."

"With any luck, he'll say something stupid, and it will just make our job that much easier," Aaron said.

"You didn't drive in a squad car, did you?"

"Oh, please," Janet said.

"Let's meet the Donnelly's," Aaron said, and we walked back to the kitchen.

Thirty-five

As we stepped into the kitchen, I said, "Mr. and Mrs. Donnelly, I'd like you to meet Lieutenant Aaron LaZelle and Detective Janet Lincoln."

"Bill Donnelly," Donnelly said and extended his hand to Aaron and then Janet. "This is my wife, Marilyn. Thank you for coming."

"Yes, and I'm the fool who caused this problem," Mrs. Donnelly said.

"You did no such thing and thank you for having Dev get in touch with us. Before we get started, I have to tell you we met once before," Aaron said.

Both Donnelly's got a questioning look on their face.

"I was in your daughter's high school class along with Dev. It was back in 2003, the night of our high school homecoming. Six girls were here getting ready, and the boys arrived. We ate all the delicious frosted cookies you had on a platter, and then we headed off to the homecoming dance."

"Did we take your picture?"

"All the girls' parents were here, and there were a lot of cameras flashing," Aaron said. "I never had the chance to thank you for the start of a memorable evening, so thank you both very much. Better late than never."

That seemed to relieve some stress. "I'll have to go through the photo album and see if I recognize you," Mrs. Donnelly said.

Aaron smiled and nodded. "What we would like to do is have you and your husband in the back room. Dev, I'd like you to be with the Donnelly's. Janet will answer the door, ask Mr. Humphrey a couple of questions, and then, depending on his answers, we will either arrest him or send him on his way. Whichever happens, you will not have to deal with him."

"You can arrest him for making his phone call?" Mrs. Donnelly asked.

"No, but we can arrest him for impersonating a police officer. It's normally a misdemeanor offense, but with Mr. Humphrey's history, we should be able to raise the stakes without too much problem. Did he happen to mention what he wanted to discuss?"

"Only that he wanted to talk to me, well, or to us, regarding the adoption of Diane's baby, and he wanted the name of the adoptive family. God in heaven, why didn't I just hang up on the man?"

"Maybe God had a bigger plan, and he wanted us to be involved tonight," Janet said. That seemed to calm Mrs. Donnelly.

At 4:30, we moved into the back room and closed the drapes. Aaron and Janet Lincoln stepped out to the front room a few minutes later. From where they sat, they could view the street and would be able to see Humphrey's white Jeep Liberty coming either up or down the street. I'd given Humphrey's license plate number to Aaron, and he'd sent a text to someone, which made me think there were probably other officers in the neighborhood.

At 5:03, I got two beeps on my cell phone from Aaron, signaling that Humphrey had just pulled up in front.

"He's here," I said to the Donnelly's, seated on the couch across from me. Mr. Donnelly placed his arm around his wife's shoulder. A moment later, the doorbell rang. We heard the front door open and the voices of a woman and a man, but they were too distant to make out what was being said.

Approximately five minutes later, Aaron stepped into the room and said, "Okay. All finished. Nothing to worry about."

"Did he leave?" Mrs. Donnelly sounded anxious.

"We'd like to talk with him a little further, so he's on his way down to the police station. He did tell us he wanted to leave this for you," Aaron said and handed Mrs. Donnelly a box of chocolate-covered caramels from Regina's Candies, a local candy store.

"Oh, well, I'm not sure—"

Mr. Donnelly reached across his wife and took the box of candy. "Tell him thanks."

"If it's all right with you, I'll be on my way. Dev, we might need you for some follow-up information," Aaron said.

"Great to see you both," I said to the Donnelly's as I rose from the chair. "Thank you for the call, and Aaron, thanks for your quick response. I'll follow you out."

Mr. Donnelly led us to the front door. We shook hands. He thanked us two more times and closed the door behind us.

There was a black and white squad car out on the street. "How many people did you have here?"

"Enough to do the job. Janet was wired and posed as their daughter. She asked if he was with the police, and he said yes, and that he was a detective investigating the hit and run of her sister. Then he handed her this," Aaron said and handed me a card with Humphrey's picture. The thing looked like a five-minute effort to make a fake ID. The card listed Humphrey as 'Chief of Detectives.'

"He thought this would work?" I grinned and handed the ID back to Aaron. "He said he was investigating Diane's hit and run? You think he was serious?"

Aaron shook his head. "No, he was just bullshitting his way in. The funny thing is, as I was placing the cuffs on him, he said that he had information Grumley had given him, and he'd be willing to share it if we let him go."

"So that's why he's on his way to the station?"

Aaron nodded. "Don't know how credible it is, but you've alluded to Grumley and the hit and run. If we could close a cold case, it would be worth it. We'll find out if there's anything worthwhile. I figured you might want to take a front-row seat in the viewing room."

"You bet I would. Who's going to be talking to him?"

"Janet and I will. You interested?"

"Absolutely. I'll see you down there."

Thirty-six

On my way down to the police station, I stopped at home and let Morton inside the house. I had no idea how long the interview with Humphrey would go, so I made myself a quick sandwich and drove down to the station. No need to rush.

When I arrived, I waited for twenty minutes before being escorted to the viewing room attached to Interview Room 3. The viewing room was arranged like a small movie theatre with three rows of six chairs. Each row was raised slightly higher than the row in front of it. The room was dark, and Interview Room 3 was lit up and occupied by Don Humphrey. He was not wearing handcuffs, and he wasn't shackled to a chair or the table. As a matter of fact, he was eating a sandwich and potato chips and sipping from a can of Coke.

I was the only one in the viewing room for close to a half-hour. Eventually, another guy stepped into the room. I recognized him as the detective that had been working at a desk when I read the report on Diane Donnelly's hit and run. He had told me to take a seat at the desk next to him. "Owen's desk," was what he had said. He never did tell me his name.

When he stepped in, he gave me a nod, walked to the opposite end of the front row, and sat down in the last chair.

"Hey, my name is Dev Haskell. We met before. I was reviewing a cold case file from 2006, and you told me to sit at Owen's desk. I'm sorry, I forgot your name," I said, even though he'd never told me his name.

"Charlie Thomas. Nice to see you again."

"Good to see you, Charlie. Any idea when things are going to get going here?"

"They're finishing up the preview, so not too long," he said.

Two other guys stepped into the room. They both looked familiar, but once again, I couldn't recall their names. A few minutes after they entered, the door opened, and Roger O'Leary, the retired detective I'd met for coffee in Afton, entered. If Roger was here, that suggested something regarding Diane Donnelly's hit and run was hopefully going to be discussed.

"Hi Roger," I said and gave him a little wave as he scanned the room.

He smiled, nodded at someone else, and then settled in next to me. "How's it going, Dev?"

"You know the gig, Roger. Never enough time in any given day. Great to see you here. Are they expecting something on the Donnelly hit and run?"

"I hope so. I was just talking with LaZelle and the woman. I've already forgotten her name."

"Janet Lincoln. I was with her and LaZelle this afternoon. I resigned from the case I was working, and a couple I had interviewed were contacted by Humphrey. He said he wanted information on a family. He told them he was a detective. Anyway, they brought him down here. Do you know, did they actually arrest him?"

"I believe they've had a discussion with Humphrey regarding something mutually beneficial," O'Leary said just as the door to the interview room opened. Janet Lincoln and Aaron LaZelle stepped into the room.

"Before we get started, do you need anything, Don? Another soda or a coffee?" Aaron asked.

"I'm good. Let's get this started, so I can get out of here."

"We feel the same way, Don, believe me," Aaron said as they sat down.

"We want to thank you for agreeing to come down this evening," Lincoln said.

"Not like you gave me much choice. By the way, I checked, and telling someone I'm a cop is nothing more than a misdemeanor. It wouldn't be worth your time to fill out the paperwork."

"That's true in most cases, Don, but as we mentioned, your case is a little different. First of all, you left the department under the auspices of a written agreement that states, among other things, you would not attempt to join another force nor present yourself as an officer. You seem to be in violation which could lead to the removal of any and all benefits. Basically leaving you without a source of income.”

“You kidding? I can barely make it on the so-called benefit I’m getting now.”

“All the more reason to help us out, Don,” Aaron said. “You told us you had information you were willing to share. We’d like to hear what that information is.”

“I’m going to need some promises first. I want to be able to get a PI license. I want my record to be expunged. I want my retirement benefits reinstated.”

Aaron shook his head and said, “I’m sorry, Don, but that’s not going to happen. You’re lucky you didn’t receive a five-year sentence for your offenses. You were running a brothel, Don. The women were peddling themselves along with drugs, and you protected them. It was in the interest of the department that we quietly sent you on your way, which we did, and you were thankful for it at the time.”

“You were never able to prove anything, and you know it,” Humphrey said.

“Maybe we should take a little closer look. You sure you want to start an investigation like that?” Aaron replied.

A name clicked in my mind. I leaned over and said, “Hey Roger, you got a pen on you?” He nodded and pulled a pen from the inside of his coat.

“Thanks,” I said. I pulled out a business card and wrote on the back of the card. *Woman with Grumley the other night, Trixie. Donny lined it up. Everything was free.'* "Back in just a minute," I said and hurried out of the room. A uniformed officer was standing in front of the door to the interview room. He watched as I approached.

"Hi, I'm in the viewing room. Can you get this to Aaron LaZelle? Humphrey just made a statement, and I think this might help the interview," I said and handed him the note on the back of my card.

He seemed to think about that for a moment and then nodded.

"Thanks." I turned and hurried back to the viewing room.

"Everything okay?" Roger asked as I settled back into my chair.

"I hope so," I said and handed his pen back. A moment later, there was a soft knock on the door. Lincoln glanced at Aaron. He nodded, pushed his chair back, and hurried to the door. There was a short, two-sentence conversation I couldn't make out, and Aaron came back to the table. I thought he might be suppressing a smile but couldn't be sure.

"So, Don, you told us you had something you would be willing to offer."

"I just got done telling both of you what I want in return. Starting with my record being expunged and getting my retirement benefits reinstated."

"And I just got done telling you it's not going to happen. Here's the deal, Don, and this is why you need to cooperate. We're painfully aware that you're continuing in the direction that led to your dismissal. That wasn't part of the deal. You've violated the promise you made to us that—"

"I don't know where you're getting your information, LaZelle, but you got nothing on me. You think I'm going to fall for your bullshit, the two of you. I've been around the block a few times."

"Yes, I guess you have, Don. Let me ask you a little question. What'd you have to pay your girl Trixie to take care of Arthur Grumley the other night?"

"I…umm…I don't know what you're talking about. Besides, she was with me the entire night. And she's an adult, at least that's what she told me."

"Oh, boy, Donny. I fear you're going to be facing a lot more serious charges than a petty little misdemeanor. Maybe we'll just let you think about this overnight while we line up our case. Let me call the guards, and they'll escort you back to your cell."

Humphrey seemed to think for a brief moment, but once Aaron stepped from his chair, he said, "Okay, okay, hang on there. I may have made a little mistake, but it was only the one time and—"

"Not good enough, Donny. We need something and quick, or you're going to end up with two to four years to think about it."

"Oh, shit. Just sit down, damn it. Come on, sit down, LaZelle. If I tell you, I want the charges from today dropped. That's it."

"I'll see what we can do. But you're going to have
to tell us what you know first."

Thirty-seven

Humphrey seemed to think for a long moment. LaZelle and Lincoln just sat politely and waited. It suddenly seemed as if they held all the cards.

O'Leary leaned toward me and said, "Does this have anything to do with you running out of here a minute ago?"

I shrugged and said, "I just made a little suggestion. LaZelle is the one who made him jump."

Humphrey shook his head and said, "Okay, okay. Christ almighty, so here's the deal. I signed on to do an investigation for this Arthur Grumley guy. He lives out Stillwater way. Does some kind of online stuff. I'm not sure what, but apparently, he makes some pretty good dough. He fathered a child back in 2003. He was just a high school kid at the time. Some girl from school he didn't even know very well. Anyway, he knocks her up. They make a deal that she won't list him as the father, and that's what happens. He's not listed anywhere. She never tells anyone it was him. The adoption is lined up before the kid is even born. My guy Grumley never ever sees the baby, and he doesn't want to. Two or three years later, he stumbles on some computer idea, not Facebook, but something like that, and he starts making money, lots of money."

"Is he in a relationship with the woman?"

"That's the strange part. As far as I know, he hadn't seen her in years, not since she found out she was pregnant. But all of a sudden, out of nowhere, he gets all worried about her wanting a chunk of his profits. Worried about having to pay child support and all that shit."

"But she gave the baby up for adoption, didn't she?"

"Oh, yeah, and it's not like she called him looking for money or anything, but you gotta understand this guy. He has a way of looking at things, and there's no alternative. It's all about him. His way or the highway. With this woman he knocked up on a one-night-stand, his thought was she was eventually going to come after him looking for money, and maybe a hell of a lot of money because he stumbled onto this internet thing and was making a lot of dough, big time."

"So, how do you know all this if you've only been working for him for a week?"

"Well, he was one of my better customers. He liked the ladies, and he liked the treats."

"You mean the drugs?"

"Yeah, you might say he's addicted but not to drugs. He loves to party with one or two women, and when he does that, and he's been drinking, and then they get him to snort something, well, he just starts telling all sorts of stories, bragging, you know. Now, I don't know how true the stories are. I just know when he tells them, they sound like the real deal."

"So you've never actually heard him."

"Oh, but I have. You see, the girls record him on their cellphones. He doesn't know that, but they do."

"Do you have these recordings?"

"I might know where some flash drives are that you could listen to."

"That would probably go a long way in getting you off the hook."

"Just so you understand. I want to go on the record that these are recordings of an inebriated individual who has been snorting cocaine, and I'm of the opinion the tales may not, in fact, be true. Okay? That's why I never provided them to you as evidence. I don't want to be linked to hiding evidence on a murder."

"Of course, Don. That only makes sense. We won't charge you with withholding evidence. I mean, who doesn't shoot the shit after a couple of beers?" Aaron said.

"We're talking way more than a couple of beers, Aaron."

"Yeah, I get that. We're also going to need the names of the women involved. We don't intend to prosecute them, but we're going to want them to testify, should we need them," Lincoln said.

"I can give you names, but I can't guarantee they'll agree to that."

"You let us worry about that," Lincoln said. "You have access to these recordings?"

"I believe the flash drives are in a safe place."

"So take us back to this woman who had the baby. Has she tried to get in touch with Grumley?"

"Were you listening to me? She can't get in touch with him. She's dead. He killed her. Ran her over with his car, years ago."

"And he never got caught?"

"Apparently not. He's still out there, bragging about it. Uses it as a warning to my girls, just in case they're thinking of trying to blackmail him. He tells them he still has the car. By the way, none of them like him, but he pays so well they put up with him for a couple of hours. Once he passes out, they call me, and I go pick them up."

And there it was, just like that. Grumley intentionally killed Diane. I didn't really hear anything else until Lincoln said, "This concludes our interview, at 21:25 hours." Two officers walked into the interview room and led Humphrey away. Lincoln gathered up their files and headed out of the room. Aaron clicked off the recorders, stepped out of the room, and a moment later came into the viewing room.

"You two okay?" he asked O'Leary and me.

"Oh, my God, Aaron, well done. Just like that, and you've got a name and presumably a recording of the guy admitting to it," O'Leary said.

"Yeah, we've got someone on the way to Humphrey's place now. The flash drives are supposed to be taped to the back of the refrigerator. We'll see. Dev? Hey Dev, you okay?"

"What?"

"I said, are you okay? You look a little out of it, man."

"Oh, sorry. I guess I'm just a little in shock. All these years, and suddenly, you may have a recording of Grumley telling someone that he killed Diane. And for what? Because he thought she might want his money even though she hadn't contacted him in three years and was just trying to get on with her life?"

"Yeah. Hell of a price to pay for a one-night-stand as a kid."

"You know, all the stuff you read about some of these high-tech characters, or hear on the news, in a sad way, it's not surprising," O'Leary observed.

"I think I'm just going to head home, Aaron. Keep me posted."

"You okay, Dev?"

"What? Oh, yeah, not to worry. It's just been a long day," I said and headed out of the viewing room. "Dev, hey Dev," Aaron called as I was halfway down the hall.

I turned and watched as he approached. "You sure you're okay?"

"Yeah, don't worry. I'm fine. Just a hell of a thing to hear, and like I said, it's been a long day."

"We're going to get Grumley. With any luck, they'll get hold of the flash drives, and we could have him behind bars as soon as tomorrow."

"That would be good. Once again, too bad we don't have the death penalty in the state."

"A person like Grumley, we lock him up for fifteen or twenty years, and he's gonna wish we did have the death penalty. Did you ever find out if he has any family?"

I shook my head. "I was only out at his house once, but I didn't see any hint of a family. If Humphrey's story is correct and he was a regular hiring working girls, that would suggest there isn't a wife in the house. The one time I was out there, I didn't see anything like a swing set or a basketball hoop that suggested kids. That said, I was only there once for maybe thirty minutes."

"You're going home?"

"Yeah, that interview took the wind out of my sails."

"Maybe hit the sack and try to get a good night's sleep. Hopefully, I'll be calling you with some good news tomorrow."

"Yeah, thanks, Aaron." I headed out of the building and climbed into my car. It took all the mental strength I had not to drive out to Stillwater and Grumley's place. But then what? Would I shoot him? Maybe chase him around that open space in my car? No, a quiet, early-to-bed night with Morton sounded like a much wiser idea. I pulled my car into the driveway and went in the back door. Morton stepped out of the den to check on me. He must have been taking a nap on the couch before it was time to go up to bed. I put a frozen pizza in the oven and grabbed a beer from the fridge.

We settled in front of the TV, and I ate a couple slices of pizza and was just drifting off to sleep when my phone rang. Luscious Dixon.

"They're back, Dev. Three of them."

"You're down at Ranchero Flores?"

"Yeah, Billy spotted them in the parking lot. I'm going to go out and—"

"Can you wait till I get there? I'm heading to my car now. I'll be there in ten minutes. Two are better than one," I said.

"Yeah, but hurry up, man. They start doing something to customers' cars, I'm going to have to deal with it."

Thirty-eight

I made it down to Ranchero Flores in a little over six minutes. I also ran two red lights, but thankfully, no cops saw me. I parked at the curb two doors down from Ranchero Flores and hurried in the front door. Billy was pacing back and forth behind the cash register.

"Oh, wow, that was fast. Thanks for coming, Dev. Luscious is at the back door, watching them out in the parking lot. So far, they haven't done anything, but they got that big muscle-bound guy with them tonight, so I think they're looking for trouble."

"Did you call the police?"

"Yeah, but no sign of them yet."

"Okay, you stay here and calm down. I'm going to check with Luscious."

I walked past the half-filled bar area and through the almost empty restaurant. Luscious was standing at the backdoor, looking out the window.

"Anything happening?" I said.

He turned, smiled, and said, "Oh, man, am I ever glad to see you, Dev. Nothing yet, but it's probably just a matter of time. I think I should go out there and try to talk them down."

"Yeah, probably right. Be better if the two of us go. Let me go first," I said, and before Luscious could respond, I pushed the door open and stepped into the parking lot. The two idiots in the leather vest and the sleeveless hoodie were in the middle of the parking lot with their backs to me. They appeared to be talking to the big muscular guy. The last time I saw him, the cops had suggested he leave, which he did, but not before telling me, "I'll see you around."

"Hi fellas, can I help you?"

Leather vest turned around and grinned. He was carrying what looked like a tire iron at least eighteen inches long. Perfect for changing a tire, smashing a car window, a headlight, or cracking my thick skull.

"Oh, perfect. Can this get any better, Goro?" he said, slapping the end of the tire iron against his left hand and taking a step toward me.

The big guy grinned as he focused in on me and said, "I knew I'd see you around, sooner or later. I'm gonna take you and—Luscious? What the hell are you doing here?"

"Goro? I was gonna ask you the same thing. I work here, dude. Security. What are you doing out here? You should be home resting. You got a lifting competition in two days."

"Yeah, I know. I had to come out and see about working a little something we got going."

"Sounds to me like it ain't going too good. You working with these two? You know the two of 'em beat up a violin player last week? A violin player, and it took the two of 'em," Luscious said.

"You going to let him talk 'bout us like that?" Leather Vest said.

"Shut your mouth, fool. The man's my weight trainer. Show some damn respect."

"The dude's name is Luscious, and you want me to—Ouch, ow, ow, you're hurting me, Goro. I can't, ow, ow." Goro's massive paw was squeezing the back of Leather Vest's neck. When he half-threw him onto the ground, the tire iron bounced across the pavement. He turned to look at the guy in the hoodie.

"I'm cool, Goro. I'm cool. Leaving right now," Hoodie said and headed out of the parking lot.

Leather Vest was back on his feet. He reached for the tire iron, but Goro stepped on it and growled, "Leave it." Leather Vest nodded and hurried out of the parking lot.

"Hope I didn't mess things up for you, Goro. But they hired me to keep them two away. They been causing problems and threatening little old ladies and stuff."

Goro shook his head and said, "Sorry, Luscious. I didn't know you were working here. I'll keep 'em away."

"This here's a pal of mine, Dev Haskell. He helps me out a lot."

"Nice to meet you, Mr. Dev," Goro acted as if we'd never seen each other before.

"Nice to meet you, Goro. You lift with Luscious?"

He nodded, and Luscious said, "He's in the Midwest weightlifting competition in two days. You best be home resting up. You coming in to lift tomorrow morning, Goro?"

"Yeah, I'll be there."

"Good, be happy to see you. It keeps the rest of the folks energized and focused."

Goro nodded and said, "I should probably head home. There won't be no trouble here. I'll make sure."

"Thanks," Luscious said.

"Nice to meet you," I called as he walked out of the parking lot and up the street. Luscious picked up the tire iron and said, "He's a good guy. Just loses his way every once in a while."

"You think he'll keep them away?"

"Oh, yeah. If they know him at all, they'll know they best not cross him."

"Well done, man. Everything nice and perfect, and you didn't even break a sweat."

We headed back inside. Luscious stepped into the kitchen with the tire iron. I went up to the front of the restaurant. Billy wasn't pacing anymore, but he still looked worried.

"Well?" he said.

"Relax, Luscious handled it perfectly. Suggested they find something better to do, and they left."

"No problems? Anyone hurt?"

"No one hurt. Luscious told them he was working here, and apparently, that was enough to send them on their way. Probably a wise move on their part."

Billy served us dessert in the back booth. If he thanked Luscious once, he thanked him a half-dozen times. I headed home once my plate was clean. Morton was already asleep up in the bedroom. I climbed into bed and slept soundly until my alarm woke me.

Thirty-nine

We were in the office well before Louie. I had the coffee going and was on my third cup by the time Louie pulled in behind my car. I filled his mug and set it on the picnic table. After catching his breath for five minutes and sipping some coffee, he said, "So, you do anything last night?"

I told him about Luscious and Goro at Ranchero Flores and about Humphrey's arrest and the flash drives he said he had.

"Is he going to turn the flash drives over to the police?" Louie asked.

"I think he already has. Aaron said something about them being taped to the back of Humphrey's refrigerator. He made it sound like they were going to get them last night. With any luck, they're listening to them as we speak."

"That would be great," Louie said.

I phoned Monica and left a message. "Hi, Monica. This is Dev. Just calling with an update. Apparently, the police are close to arresting Arthur Grumley, the guy attempting to find the child who was adopted. Hope to have more information later today. I'll give you a call once I know more."

I debated calling the Donnelly's and decided it would be better to see them in person. I took Morton for a quick walk, and then we drove over to the Donnelly house. Mr. Donnelly answered the door.

"Everything all right?" was how he greeted me. Clearly, he was still stressed out about the Humphrey situation.

"Yes, in fact, I can give you an update. Things seem to have improved with the arrest of Don Humphrey here yesterday. He had some information that was pertinent to Diane's death."

He looked at me for a long moment, but I wasn't sure he was seeing me. He seemed lost in deep thought. "Diane's death? I'm not following."

"Could I talk to both of you?"

"What? Oh yeah, yes, I'm sorry. Come in, come in. Marilyn was just going through some photos. In fact, we found two of that officer yesterday, the LaZelle boy."

"Oh yeah, Aaron LaZelle. Probably from homecoming when all the girls were getting ready here."

"Marilyn," he called as I stepped into the house.

"I'm in the living room," she said.

We walked into the living room. Mrs. Donnelly was seated on the couch. Two photo albums were on the coffee table, and a stack of loose photos was next to the albums. A half-dozen photos were lined up on the couch next to her.

"Marilyn, Dev says he has some information."

"Hi, Mrs. Donnelly, looks like you've been busy."

"Oh, I think I found the homecoming pictures with the LaZelle boy. But you don't seem to be in any of them."

"That's because Diane and I weren't dating until the following January."

"Oh, so you didn't take Diane to homecoming?"

"That's right."

She shook her head. "Oh, who can keep track? Well, it's nice to see you again. Sit down, please."

"Thank you," I said and settled into a wingback chair across from her. Mr. Donnelly moved the photos off the couch and sat down next to her.

"I wanted to stop by because some things have happened as a result of that arrest yesterday."

"Oh, thank you again for getting the police involved. I'm not sure what we would have done if we'd had to deal with that person. I simply don't know what I was thinking when I agreed to meet with him."

"Well, it seems to have worked out for the best. The police interviewed him last night, and he said he had recordings of Arthur Grumley that should be helpful in an ongoing investigation. Hopefully, the police have the recordings and are listening to them as we speak. I hope to hear from them later today. With any luck, it will result in the arrest of Arthur Grumley."

"I hope they lock him up and throw away the key," Mr. Donnelly said.

"And this is the person who got Diane pregnant?"

"Yes, ma'am."

She seemed to think about that for a long moment. "Yes, locking him up would be a good start."

"I'll let you know as soon as I hear something. Hopefully, it will be later today."

She nodded and reached for the handful of photos her husband had moved to the coffee table. "Take a look at these. I think the LaZelle boy is in there."

I looked at the photos. Two of them were definitely Aaron. He looked like he was about ten years old, with a babyface and longer hair. "Yeah, these two are Aaron LaZelle."

"I knew it," she said and began gathering up the loose pictures and returning them to a Ziplock plastic bag. I took that as an indication that it was okay for me to leave.

"Well, it was good to see you. I'll let you know when I get an update from the police."

"Now here, you take these and give them to the LaZelle boy," Mrs. Donnelly said and handed me the two pictures.

"Thank you. I'll make sure he gets them," I said.

Mr. Donnelly walked me to the door. "Thanks for stopping by, Dev. This whole thing has brought her back to another time. Well, actually, it's done that to both of us," he said and shook his head.

"If I hear anything from the police, I'll give you a call. No point in upsetting her."

He nodded and said, "Yeah, thanks. I'd appreciate that."

I tossed the two photos on the passenger seat, took a biscuit from the glove compartment, gave it to Morton, and we drove back to the office. Louie was gone. The coffee pot was almost empty and still on. I turned it off and dumped the remnants down the sink. Aaron called me just after 2:00.

"What's the word?" was how I answered.

"Well, the flash drives definitely have more than one recording of Grumley saying he intentionally hit Diane Donnelly with his car. On one of them, he said that he had waited for her to appear on three separate evenings. Just his description of the hit and run makes it pretty clear he isn't making it up."

"Did you arrest him? He lives in a big Stillwater mansion. Did they talk to the guy that answers the door? His name is Tony."

"Yeah, I think that's one of the persons they talked to. The Stillwater detectives were there last night and didn't get an answer when they knocked on the door. They went there twice last night, and they were waiting in front of the place this morning when the staff began to arrive. They searched the house, but there was no sign of Grumley anywhere."

"Did they look in the garage?"

"The garage? Dev, they looked everywhere, including the garage. He wasn't there."

"Yeah, I get that. I was wondering what car he took."

"Yet another crazy twist. Apparently, he's driving around in a 2005 red Mustang. They've put out an APB on the car."

"Good. Did you send anyone out to Stillwater?"

"No, we let them handle it. As soon as they arrest him, he'll be transferred to us."

"Okay, thanks for the call. If and when he shows up, keep me posted. You still have Humphrey?"

"Yes, we do. He's attempting to be helpful, but for the moment, Grumley seems to be missing in action."

"Damn it. Okay, thanks for the call. Hopefully, he'll turn up," I said and disconnected.

Forty

I decided it might be wise to alert Kevin White just to cover all the bases. I placed a call and left a message. "Hi Kevin, Dev Haskell. When you have a moment, give me a call. Some things have changed on this end, all good, by the way. I'll bring you up to date. Thanks."

Forty minutes later, I called him again. "Hi Kevin, Dev Haskell calling. If you would give me a call, please. The police have arrested a man pretending to be a Private Investigator. He had tapes of his client apparently admitting to killing Patrick's biological mother back in 2006. Please give me a call when you get this. Thanks."

I waited for another two hours. This didn't seem like Kevin White, at least the little I knew of him. I figured there was no point in leaving a third message. I sat and thought for a long minute and then decided the hell with it. I left Louie a note, climbed in my car, and headed out to White Acres, Kevin White's place in Prior Lake. As I drove, I grew more concerned with every passing mile. I made the half-hour drive in twenty-two minutes. I turned onto Murphy Boulevard, and a couple of minutes later, I turned into White Acres.

The last time I was here, there were two pickup trucks parked in front of the red barn that had been converted to an office structure. Today, the pickups were gone, but a red, make that crimson red, 2005 Mustang with a spoiler on the back was parked in front of the barn. I opened the glove compartment and took out my pistol. I backed up and parked by the house, then got out of the car and quietly closed the door.

I walked along the barn and peeked around the corner toward the patio that was just outside of Kevin's office. Kevin and his wife, Colleen, were seated on the couch. They did not look happy. Facing them, and with his back to me, was Arthur Grumley.

Despite the fact that Grumley had apparently somehow dodged the police, he seemed to be calm. I couldn't see a gun anywhere. In fact, Grumley was actually laughing, although the Whites looked pretty serious. There was a noise off to the left. I looked over to see a tractor just turning into a field, pulling a small tank. The tractor began to head toward the building behind the barn. Patrick White was driving the tractor. He was wearing a face mask, but there was no mistaking his red hair.

The Whites and Grumley watched the tractor approach. Grumley said something, and Kevin White shook his head. Kevin and Colleen didn't look comfortable. As the tractor drew closer, Grumley suddenly stood, and that's when I saw his pistol. I saw it for just a second, but it was all I needed.

Grumley took a couple of steps toward the tractor and then waved his arm at Patrick, signaling him to join them. The Whites remained seated. As the tractor approached, I stepped out from behind the barn and started to hurry toward them, hoping the noise from the tractor would cover my approach. Patrick had to see me coming, but if he did, he didn't acknowledge me. He smiled and gave a wave to Grumley. Grumley signaled again with his arm, encouraging Patrick to join them.

Patrick drove up alongside the patio and stopped the tractor. The engine was still running, and I was at least fifty feet away.

I could clearly see Grumley's pistol. He was holding it in his right hand behind his back. From the front, it would have appeared as a casual stance. Patrick gave a friendly wave to Grumley. He raised his index finger, signaling something like one second or one minute.

Just as Grumley began to point the pistol, Kevin was on his feet and shouted something. I couldn't shoot because Patrick was in the line of fire. If I missed Grumley, there was a good chance I might hit Patrick.

Grumley suddenly turned and spotted me running toward him. He raised his pistol and fired a shot just as Patrick grabbed the hose connected to the tank behind the tractor and began to squirt Grumley.

Whatever he was spraying caused Grumley to drop his pistol and stagger a few feet. His arms were flailing left and right, up and down, and he was screaming. Patrick aimed the hose at Grumley's face and continued to spray him.

Kevin shouted something. Patrick stopped spraying and turned off the tractor.

Grumley sank to his knees, vomited, cried, and vomited again.

"You guys okay?" I asked just as Colleen kicked Grumley's pistol across the patio.

"Yeah, we're okay. You all right, honey?" Kevin asked Colleen.

"Yes, thanks to Patrick. Come here and give me a hug, you wonderful boy."

"I can't, Mom, I'm covered with insecticide."

"Thank God you were here, Haskell. This lunatic was going to shoot all of us. Said he just wanted to talk, and then he pulled that gun."

"You didn't get my messages?"

"He made me leave my phone in the office."

I took my phone out, dialed 911, and handed it to Kevin. "Get the police here. They can deal with him. He's going to be locked up for a long time."

Grumley remained on his hands and knees, coughing and crying.

I shook hands with Patrick and said, "Nice to finally meet you. Sorry it's under this circumstance."

"Mom and Dad told me about you. This was kind of cool. I've always wondered what would happen if you squirted someone with that stuff."

Grumley groaned and coughed some more.

The Prior Lake Police arrived in just a few minutes. They ended up having Grumley strip down, and then they hosed him off. They wrapped him in a calf blanket, handcuffed him, and hauled him off to jail. He was still coughing and crying when they led him away. Two detectives interviewed us and took our statements. A tow truck eventually arrived and hauled the Mustang away.

Once Patrick had a shower and changed, I chatted with him and his parents for the better part of an hour. I thanked him at least a half-dozen times, and we all agreed that we would get together with Mr. and Mrs. Donnelly once things settled down.

On my way home, I placed my phone on speaker and gave Aaron LaZelle an update on the afternoon's activities. They were in the process of having Grumley transferred to the St. Paul jail and expected him to be in their custody by the end of the day.

When I finally made it back to the office, Louie and Morton were already over at The Spot. I checked my messages online and then walked over and joined them.

"The usual?" Mike asked as I stepped in the door. "Yeah, and whatever Louie is having." I walked to the end of the bar. Louie was on his stool, and Morton was curled up at his feet. Two pork rind bags, already empty, rested on the bar next to Louie.

"Busy afternoon?" Louie said and then leaned forward, twitching his nose. "What the hell is that smell?"

"Insecticide," I said and went on to tell him about my afternoon.

"What in God's name was this guy thinking? Apparently, all the money in the world, and he tracks down the biological son he has no relationship with? Is he nuts?"

"Yeah, I'd say so. Based on the attempted murder charges he'll be facing after this afternoon and the hit and run murder of Diane Donnelly, he'll have plenty of time to consider how wise a decision those two incidents were."

"You just can't make it up." Louie shook his head.

We only stayed for one beer and then headed home. I undressed next to the washing machine, tossed my clothes in, then headed for the shower.

We were in front of the TV, watching a movie of no social value, when the phone rang. Sandie calling.

"Hi, Sandie, what's up?"

"Just calling to remind you, Dev. We're going to the wedding this weekend up in Hibbing. Clean clothes, no jeans."

"I haven't forgotten. I'm really looking forward to it," I lied.

"You are? Oh, that's great. We're going to have a really fun time. I just know it."

"What time do you want me to pick you up?"

"Actually, please don't take this the wrong way. But I want to take my car. No offense, but as long as we're going to be playing the part of the cool, romantic couple, it would be nice to have a decent car. Don't you think?"

"Whatever you want, Sandie."

"Oh, thank you. I'll pick you up around 1:00 Friday afternoon. I'm getting my hair done that morning."

"I'll be waiting for you."

"See you then, and thanks for doing this, Dev. I really mean it."

God, the wedding was already becoming a pain, and it was still a couple of days away. We headed up to bed once the movie was over.

Forty-one

Louie beat us into the office the following morning. He'd even made a fresh pot of coffee. We had been chatting about everything and nothing when I asked, "Hey, Louie, you got anything going on this weekend?"

"No, I'll be at the Spot Friday night. I plan on sleeping in Saturday and heading back to The Spot Saturday evening. Same thing on Sunday. Why do you ask?"

"I forgot I've got to go to some family wedding with Sandie and play the part of a nice guy."

"You think you can do that?"

"I'm not sure, but I'm going to try. Anyway, the wedding is about five hours north, and I need to find a place for Morton."

"Oh, not a problem. I'll take him. No big deal."

"You sure? I can board him if you think—"

"Dev, I just told you it wasn't a problem. Relax."

"I'll bring him down Friday morning and then take off around noon if that's okay."

"Yeah, sure, whatever works."

"I'm supposed to dress up for this thing, no jeans. She was adamant about that."

"So, what are you going to do?"

"I'm going to have to buy an outfit, slacks and a sport coat."

"You might want to think about a shirt, too. Doesn't sound like a t-shirt is going to work, and maybe a tie while you're at it."

"God, I'm kicking myself for even agreeing to do this."

"Oh, I don't know. There just might be some benefits for you along the way."

"Promise?"

"That's your department, Dev."

I went clothes shopping after lunch. I can't understand how people like to shop for clothes. I just want to get them and get out. I drove over to the Milbern clothing store. They specialize in suits. To say I was out of the demographic was an understatement, but I had a nice sales guy who helped me out. I ended up taking the boring route. I got a navy-blue sport coat, gray slacks, and a blue and white striped shirt. The slacks had to be tailored, but they would be ready in the morning, and I would be all set a full day before the wedding.

Louie was just getting ready to leave for The Spot by the time I got back to the office. I took Morton for a nice long walk, and we headed over to join him. Just before we went inside, my phone rang, Aaron LaZelle.

"Hi Aaron, what's up?"

"We've had your friend, Arthur Grumley, since yesterday evening. He's aware of the charges he's facing out in Prior Lake, and we've made him aware of the charges he is going to face on the hit and run. We will be interviewing or, rather, interrogating him in an hour. We have the recordings of him bragging about the incident, statements from the women he was bragging to, and he has indicated that he will admit guilt in turn for a reduced sentence."

"Reduced by how much?"

"Normal time for a hit and run death is fifteen years and a ten grand fine. Here's the deal. This wasn't normal. This was an intentional murder, so he's looking at potentially forty years. Then once this trial is finished, he's back in Scott County for his Prior Lake trial."

"Have you spoken to the Donnelly's?"

"I have, but only in regards to Grumley's arrest for the hit and run. I didn't tell them about the upcoming interrogation, the women's statements, or the recordings."

"Thanks, I'm not sure they could listen to him. They've had to deal with the loss of a daughter for the past sixteen years. They don't need to hear this jackass spout off."

"You interested in attending? I called Roger O'Leary, and he'll be here."

"Yeah, I'll definitely be down there. Is it going to be you and Detective Lincoln?"

"Yes, she's going over the recordings again as we speak. Grumley is lawyered up, but the recordings of him are so devastating, not to mention the Prior Lake incident waiting in the wings. Hopefully, they'll cross their fingers, and Grumley will cut a deal."

"What kind of deal? He murdered Diane."

"Yeah, but we'd be willing to agree on twenty years if he pleads guilty to the four counts of attempted murder out in Prior Lake. The two sentences served consecutively will put him away for at least forty years."

"Okay, I get that. Can I suggest one more thing?"

"I'm listening."

"The guy has one hell of an estate. As far as I know, he has no children other than Patrick White, the son he wanted no part of. Is there something that could be arranged for Patrick, maybe college tuition or a yearly stipend from Grumley's finances?"

"I don't know, but it's certainly worth a try. In fact, we may be able to add that to our list of demands regarding the fifteen-year plea on the hit and run."

"I'll see you in an hour," I said, and Aaron disconnected.

Rather than go into The Spot, I took Morton home and then proceeded down to the police station. This time, Roger O'Leary was already in the viewing room. Once again, we would be watching the proceedings occur in Interview Room 3.

"Hi, Roger," I said as I stepped into the room.

"Good afternoon, Dev. I've been looking forward to this day for a very long time. Always nice to have a cold case cleared."

"Yeah, congratulations on that. Did you talk to Aaron this afternoon?"

O'Leary nodded and grinned. "Gave them a copy of my file and spoke with both him and Detective Lincoln for almost an hour this morning."

"Yeah, I had a call from Aaron just a little while ago."

"You were out in that mess in Prior Lake, weren't you?"

"I was. Thank God for the son Patrick dealing with Grumley, or you'd quite possibly be looking at three or four murders, including mine."

"How in God's name did Grumley think that would be a good introduction to his biological son? Nice try. I'm here to kill you and your parents. I'm thinking that action will serve very nicely when it's sentencing time," O'Leary said just as the door to Interview Room 3 opened and a handcuffed Arthur Grumley entered the room with his lawyer. Grumley was dressed in an orange jumpsuit, orange socks, and flip-flops.

The two guards attached Grumley's handcuffs to a chain bolted to the floor.

"Is that really necessary?" his attorney said.

"Policy, sir. Four counts of attempted murder. The murder of a woman sixteen years ago. To answer your question, yes, it is necessary. The officers should be here shortly. Is there anything you need?"

"I'd like a corned beef on rye," Grumley said and laughed.

His lawyer shook his head and said, "We're fine, don't need anything. Thank you."

Once they left, Grumley leaned forward and said, "Come on, relax, Charlie. I'm screwed, and I know it."

"Arthur, please. There are liable to be people in the viewing room. Remember our agreement. You are not to say a word. I will speak for you, please."

"I don't give a damn. To hell with anyone watching, and I can damn well speak for myself," Grumley said. He turned toward the viewing room and gave us the finger.

"Charming," O'Leary said to me.

A moment later, Janet Lincoln and Aaron LaZelle entered the room. They sat down and opened the files in front of them. Lincoln gave the date, time, and everyone's name and then asked each person present to state their name. I thought Grumley might try to make a joke or some stupid comment, but he didn't. His lawyer was named Charles Evans.

"Mr. Grumley, we're here today with regard to the death of Diane Donnelly, the victim of an intentional hit and run on May 26th in the year 2006. She was struck on Randolph Avenue in the city of St. Paul between 8:10 and 8:25 PM. Hit by a 2005 Ford Mustang. We have a number of recordings of you confessing to this incident if you would like us to play them."

Grumley's attorney raised his hand to stop Grumley from whatever he was about to say. "The individuals who have submitted these tapes seem to have no relationship whatsoever to Mr. Grumley, and their credibility is questionable at best. I would like to—"

"Charlie, you're just going to drag this out, and we're going to end up no further ahead. The gals in the interviews were all great in the sack. Why the hell do you think I told them what I'd done? They loved it. They knew I was someone they better not cross."

"Arthur, please. We've discussed this. I'll do the talking."

"Well, I don't like what the hell you're saying, and I'm paying the bill. You work for me, Charlie. Now, I think that—"

"I would like a word in private with my client, please."

Lincoln and LaZelle nodded, closed their files, and headed out of the room.

Once they were gone, Grumley's lawyer said, "Arthur, what in the hell do you think you're doing? You're not helping one damn bit."

"Charlie, shut the hell up. I just want to get this bullshit over with. Hey, whoever the hell is watching this," Grumley said and flashed his middle finger again toward the viewing room.

When Lincoln and LaZelle reentered, Grumley said, "For the record. I'm in charge. Diane Donnelly forced me to have sex with her so she would become pregnant. She never wanted to work, and she wanted me to have to pay her for the rest of her life. I decided I didn't want to do that."

Forty-two

Forty-five minutes later, Janet Lincoln, O'Leary, and I were all sitting in Aaron LaZelle's office. The blinds were pulled, and we were sipping whiskies from red plastic cups. "I still don't get why, after all these years, he admitted to intentionally running over the girl. Everyone says he's smart, but after running her over, he hung on to the car. It just doesn't make any sense," O'Leary said.

"I think a big part of the reason is he holds the opinion that he's better than everyone else. At the end of the day, it was just luck of the draw that he scored big in the internet world. But that convinced him that he really was better than everyone else. This interview was just the latest in a series of things he's probably done. He essentially fires his lawyer, and the next thing he says, he solved a potential problem. It was simple. 'I killed her.' Not that it makes a difference that she never attempted to contact him. By all indications, she wanted nothing to do with the man," O'Leary said.

I drained my cup.

"More, Dev?" Aaron asked, reaching for the bottle.

"No. Thanks, but I'd better not. Oh, say, Aaron, before I forget. Something from the Donnelly's for you."

Aaron got a strange look on his face as I pulled an envelope from my back pocket and handed it to him. He glanced at all three of us, then opened the envelope and grinned.

"Oh, God, will you look at this?" he said. He laughed, then handed the two homecoming pictures to Janet Lincoln.

She looked at the photos and smiled. "Oh, good Lord. How old were you, ten?"

"No, that was my senior year in high school. We were going to the homecoming dance, and all the girls met up at the Donnelly house. All their parents were there taking pictures. Girls, no doubt in the process of deciding older guys would probably be a lot more fun than us."

"Were you at this thing, Haskell?" O'Leary asked as Lincoln handed him the pictures.

I shook my head. "No, I started dating Diane the following January. She dumped me on our graduation night. I didn't know it at the time, but she was a couple of months pregnant and went to stay with her aunt until the baby was born." I shook my head. "You know, at that age, you think you have all the answers, and you don't know shit."

"Well, it's taken sixteen years, but justice is finally going to be served," O'Leary said.

"Yeah, better late than never. Aaron, are you going to call the Donnelly's?" I said.

"I will, but I think I will give them the official announcement tomorrow morning. Were you planning to stop by their place tonight?"

I glanced at the watch on O'Leary's wrist. It was 6:50. I could be at the Donnelly's in fifteen minutes. "Yeah, in fact, I should maybe head over there now. Hopefully, this will bring some closure for them. I'll tell them you'll be calling in the morning. Any idea when the sentencing will be?"

Aaron shook his head. "Depends on how he pleads to the four attempted murder charges. We'll be asking for twenty years, five more than the state standards on an accidental hit and run, and we're requesting consecutive sentencing on the charges."

"Thanks for doing that. I'll call you tomorrow. Janet, Roger, thank you for bringing this to a close and getting Diane Donnelly some justice, finally."

Lincoln nodded.

"Thank you, Dev. It took a while, but you got him," Aaron said.

I pulled in front of the Donnelly house. I rang the doorbell twice but never got an answer. I could hear voices coming from the back. I walked around the side of the house and opened the gate on the white picket fence.

As I stepped into the backyard, I saw the Donnelly's seated in lawn chairs with another couple. I turned to head back out of the yard when Mr. Donnelly called, "Well, speak of the devil. John, this is the man I was telling you about. Join us, Dev. This is my brother, John, and his wife, Madeline. We were just telling them about you."

"Nice to meet you," I said as Donnelly's brother stood, and we shook hands.

"Can I get you a glass of wine, Dev, or maybe a Coke?"

"No, no, thanks. I, umm, I'm sorry to interrupt. I didn't realize you had guests. I'll stop over tomorrow, and we—"

"If you've got information, Dev, we need to hear it. After waiting all these years, the sooner, the better. John and Maddie are aware of the situation," Mrs. Donnelly said.

"Go ahead, Dev," Mr. Donnelly said and stepped over to his wife.

"Okay, Arthur Grumley has been arrested. He had his lawyer present in the interview with Lieutenant LaZelle and Detective Lincoln. Not even halfway through, Grumley fired his attorney right there and took over. The first thing he did was admit to the hit and run."

Mrs. Donnelly's hands flew up to her face, and she was suddenly crying. Her husband wrapped his arms around her. Donnelly's brother made the sign of the cross, and a tear ran down his wife's face.

It took a minute, but Mrs. Donnelly regained control and said, "Oh, thank God. I was so worried he'd be let off. Oh, my prayers have been answered. What happens now?"

"Lieutenant LaZelle will call you tomorrow with the official word. They're going to ask for a twenty-year sentence that will be served consecutively with whatever his sentence will be on the attempted murder charges in Scott County."

"Dev was one of the people this guy was going to kill. It was in the paper. So, he's going to go to jail?" Mr. Donnelly said.

"Oh, yeah. Could well be forty or fifty years, total, if he lives that long. A charge of four attempted murders won't be taken lightly, especially since he agreed to plead guilty to Diane's death."

"Oh, thank God, and thank you, Dev," Mrs. Donnelly said. She rose from her chair, wiped the tears from her face, and gave me a long hug.

"Diane is looking down and smiling at you," Mr. Donnelly said.

All four Donnelly's were hugging one another as I left. I grabbed Morton from home, and we headed down to The Spot. Morton got his pork rinds. I had a beer and chatted with Louie.

We headed home and had just settled in front of the TV when my phone rang. Monica calling. My first thought was God works in mysterious ways, and maybe it was a last-minute invitation to spend the night.

"Hey, good looking, what's up?"

"Oh, hi, Dev. Hope I'm not interrupting anything."

"No, not at all. In fact, I was just talking to Morton."

"Morton, your dog?"

"I was kidding, Monica."

"Oh, yeah," she said, not really sounding like she meant it. "Hey, the reason I'm calling is, I was hoping we might get together this weekend, and I completely forgot I'm meeting up with my siblings. I'll probably need a wild and crazy night when I get back. You up for getting together next Monday evening? I'll make dinner, and you can make me exhausted. How does that sound?"

"It sounds like a great plan. I've got a crazy weekend, too. How 'bout I call you on Monday?"

"That will be perfect. Enjoy your weekend."

"You, too. Talk with you on Monday."

Forty-three

The next morning, Morton and I made it down to the office at 9:00. Even showing up late, we still beat Louie by a half-hour. Just before lunch, I drove over to the Milbern clothing store. I tried on my new slacks and jacket. They looked great. I took them home and hung them in the closet rather than leave them in the car where they'd either get stolen or Morton would stretch out on them. I had one beer with Louie at the end of the day, and we headed home.

We had a quiet evening watching a movie and went to bed after the news. The following morning, I loaded the car with Morton's food and water dishes, his rawhide bone, and the forty-eight-pound sack of dog food.

Louie wandered into the office around 9:30. I filled his mug with coffee and had a fresh blueberry muffin from the bakery waiting on his picnic table for him. We chatted for the better part of an hour, then I said goodbye to Louie and Morton and headed home.

I called Sandie and told her I was ready whenever she wanted to pick me up. She pulled into the driveway, took one look at me in my camouflaged shorts and t-shirt, and made me change. Fifteen minutes later, we were heading north toward Hibbing. I was wearing clean jeans and a sports shirt.

"Okay, so we're going to meet my extended family. My brother's name is Tommy. My sisters are Debbie, Mary Alice, Teresa, and Laura. Now, my cousins, there's a bunch of them. The one getting married is Jo Ann. Her sisters are—"

"Sandie, how about I just remember Jo Ann's name and your brother Timmy's name?"

"It's Tommy, Dev."

"Oh, okay, could have sworn you said Timmy. Anyway, I'm going to forget all the names, so I'll just introduce myself, tell them I've heard nice things about them, and pretend to be a wonderful guy."

She nodded and said, "That's probably a better idea."

"Anyone I should watch out for?"

"Just be on your best behavior. They'll be watching you, and after a glass or two of wine, they'll start asking you how long we've been dating and do you have any plans, meaning marriage. Oh, and just for the record. I don't want to marry you, Dev. No offense, but I'm sure you don't want to marry me either. Have you ever had people or friends direct you, and if you'd just follow their direction, they absolutely know you'd be happier? Then you look at them, and even though they're your friend, you don't want to be like them."

"Yeah, there's quite a few people out there who wonder when I'm going to grow up."

"What do you tell them?"

"I tell them the truth. I don't want to grow up."

She laughed at that. It was a four-and-a-half-hour drive and that included stopping for gas. I paid seventy bucks to fill the tank. It was just after five when we pulled into the Hampton Inn in Hibbing. Sandie had a reservation, but we used my credit card. We had just entered our room on the third floor when her cellphone rang.

"Hi, Carol, are you here? Oh, you did? Yes, my boyfriend. Yeah, we can do that. Okay, see you in a bit," she said and disconnected. "Well, that didn't take long. They're all downstairs in the bar. Someone saw us check-in."

"Okay, you want to go downstairs and meet them?" I hung up the three clothes bags and placed Sandie's suitcase on the chest of drawers. I wheeled my suitcase over to the far side of the bed and left it on the floor. I handed her the black leather case that was labeled Saint Laurent Paris.

"Oh, thanks, my makeup. Let me just put this in the bathroom," she said. She stepped into the bathroom, closed the door, and came out twenty minutes later.

"Everything okay?"

"Just freshening my makeup. You ready?"

"Let's go," I said, and we headed downstairs. Just before we stepped into the bar, Sandie took hold of my hand, and we entered. There was a table with two guys and a table with a couple. And then in the back there were four tables pushed together with a crowd of at least two dozen people. The women were all seated around the tables drinking wine or mixed drinks. Their spouses made up the outside ring and were mostly drinking bottles of beer.

"Sandie! Oh, Sandie, you finally made it," someone called, and we headed in that direction. The noise level of conversation seemed to go up a notch.

"Oh, hi. Great to see everyone. This is my, umm, friend I told you about, Dev Haskell. I'm not going to introduce you all because he'll just forget your names. Please be on your best behavior. He's very nice," Sandie said.

The group said a collective, "Hi, Dev."

"What can I get you from the bar?" I asked.

"I think just a white wine. I'd better pace myself."

I headed over to the bar and ordered the wine and a beer. Sandie had settled herself into a chair at the table. I handed her the wine and then dragged a chair over from an empty table and set it between two guys.

They immediately introduced themselves, and their names went in one ear and out the other. Over the course of the next two hours, Sandie had five glasses of wine. The conversation noise level went up another notch or two. I was still on my second beer.

"Hey, we're going to grab something to eat. You want to join us?" one of the guys half-whispered to me.

"Yeah, let me get another wine for Sandie. You going to the restaurant here?"

"Yeah, we'll save you a seat," he said, and we went in opposite directions.

I brought the wine back to Sandie and told her I was going to get something to eat. She nodded, said, "Thanks, Baby," and blew me a kiss.

There were six of us seated at a round table in the restaurant. It was a lot quieter. One of the older guys pulled his hearing aids out.

"They get burned out with all that noise in the bar, Billy?"

"No, I just have to turn them on. Had them off going in there. Can't stand all the shrieking and talking."

"Yeah, and no one listening to anyone else," another guy said.

"Will they get something to eat?" I asked.

They all shook their heads. "Catching up on gossip. Right now, Sandie will be getting the third degree," one of them said, and they all laughed.

We stayed in the restaurant for ninety minutes. That's a long time to eat a cheeseburger. It was a good thing none of the women were driving when we returned. No one was feeling any pain. By 11:00, a few couples started to leave. We were back in the room forty-five minutes later. Sandie was in the bathroom for twenty minutes removing makeup and applying creams. I was in there for five minutes, and when I came out, I was greeted by deep snoring. I climbed into bed, pulled the pillow over my head, and was asleep in sixty seconds.

I was up just before 7:00. I shaved, showered, dressed, and left Sandie a note that I was down at breakfast. I joined four other guys at a table, forgot their names immediately, and ate breakfast. I did learn that the previous night's get-together with the guys in the background and the women catching up on what everyone was doing was pretty standard for the once or twice a year meet-ups. I thought it was actually a pretty nice thing. A number of the couples, in fact, most, had kids in junior high or high school. There were three kids in college, and one had just gone into the service. They seemed to be solid, good, interesting families just trying to make it through life.

I took a plate of blueberry pancakes and sausage up to Sandie. It helped. She was in recovery mode after last night's wine, but she would be fine by the time the wedding rolled around at 3:00.

Forty-four

It took me about fifteen minutes to dress for the wedding. Sandie started getting ready just after the noon hour. She liked my outfit and, fortunately, decided that I didn't need a tie. I put the tie in my coat pocket just in case. I drove to the wedding while she put the final touches on her makeup.

We were nodded at and got a couple of hugs from family as we entered the church. Sandie pulled a sales tag off my coat sleeve that I had missed. We chatted with her folks. Her mother's hair was even more orange than I remembered. I shook hands with her father and got a hug from her mother, who whispered, 'Oh, thank God," in my ear.

It happened during the eulogy, with the minister going on about this grand occasion and how wonderful the couple was. We were seated about halfway back in the church. The place was full, and I was looking around the congregation, trying to see if I recognized anyone.

The bad news is, I did. There she was, Monica, on the groom's side of the aisle. Apparently, this wedding was her 'meet up with her siblings.' I stared for a long moment, hoping I would see something that would make my initial recognition wrong, and it wasn't her. That didn't happen. Instead, it was almost as if she could feel my stare. She moved her shoulders as if trying to get comfortable and then glanced over her shoulder in my direction. Her eyes widened, and her mouth half-opened. The couple behind her picked up on it and looked over at me.

"Let us pray," the minister said, and everyone stood. So did Monica, and then she glanced over at me two more times.

The bride and groom kissed and marched down the aisle all smiles, followed by the bridesmaids and groomsmen. The church began to empty one pew at a time. Since Monica was across the aisle and two pews ahead, she stepped into the aisle before I did. Based on the way people were lined up, I thought she was alone, but a guy suddenly took her hand. She made a point of looking in the opposite direction as she walked past.

We remained on opposite ends of the room at the reception. Thank God it was close to two hundred people. Seating was assigned, and we were at different tables. I felt as if a pair of eyes were burning into my back.

The tables were cleared and moved from the dance floor. The band began to set up, eight musicians and a singer. They played two or three numbers and then did a solo for the bride and groom and then the parents of the wedding couple. I stayed back in a corner, constantly looking in case Monica approached armed with a steak knife.

The band played another number, where almost everyone danced, and then someone had the microphone and said, "Mr. Dev Haskell. Dev Haskell, please come to the dance floor."

I thought for sure it would be both Monica and Sandie, each with a steak knife.

I set my beer bottle on the table, took a deep breath, and made my way through the crowd.

"Dev, what did you do?" Sandie said and quickly left the table with her sisters, who were no doubt giving her the third degree. She caught up to me, and we stepped out onto the dance floor together.

"Here he is, ladies and gentlemen, my hero. Dev Haskell. He saved my life just two weeks ago. Please give a round of applause for my hero," Mateo said.

He was holding his violin, and as people applauded, his brother with slicked-back hair stepped to the microphone and said, "It's true, two men were threatening Mateo, and Mr. Dev stepped in and beat them both. They never laid a hand on him. Only because of him, we are here today. Dev, here is a special song for you now. To all you beautiful women, you must dance with our hero. It will bring you good luck."

With that, Mateo started playing his violin, the entire band began to play, and Sandie and I started to dance as Mateo's brother sang in Spanish. After maybe twenty seconds, Jo Ann, the bride, tapped Sandie on the shoulder and stepped in. I danced with the bride's mother, the groom's mother, a number of women, and then Monica.

After a couple of steps, she smiled and said, "So, which one of us feels like the bigger asshole?"

"Oh, I'm sure I do."

"Just for the record. That's an on-again, off-again friend of mine. My sisters and my mother are always trying to set me up, so he's pretending to be my guy. Just so you know."

I started laughing.

"What's so funny? You don't know how tough a family can be on a girl."

"Actually, I do. That's exactly what I'm doing here. The woman I'm with needed someone to play the same part."

An older woman tapped Monica on the shoulder. She gave me a peck on the cheek and said, "Don't forget to call on Monday," and stepped away.

I introduced Sandie and two of her sisters to Mateo and his brother during one of the band breaks. We stayed and danced until the end, then had a couple of glasses of wine at the bride's parents' home. We made it back to the hotel around 2:00 AM.

"Oh, what a night, Dev. What a night. How much did you pay those two?"

"What?"

"The singer and the violin guy. How much did you pay them to say that about you?"

"Nothing, Sandie. I didn't even know they were going to be here. That really happened. He was getting pushed around by these two thugs at Sibley Plaza. They wanted him to pay them protection money. Then they were hassling a pal who owns a restaurant, and I was with a guy who ran them off."

"You really did that, beat them up?"

"Yeah. I like his music, and they were going to hurt him."

She stepped closer and said, "You are just full of surprises," as she began to unbutton my shirt.

Epilogue

We made it home in one piece. Sandie dropped me off at my house and drove away before I'd unlocked the front door. I tossed my shirt in the laundry basket and pulled on a faded t-shirt I got at a Fleetwood Mac concert back in 2018. I headed down to The Spot. Louie and Morton were there, along with six or seven other people. Morton casually looked up at me and then jumped to his feet. I gave him a big, long scratch behind the ears. I bought Louie a drink, stayed for one beer, and then headed home.

I called Monica on Monday, not sure what reaction I might get. She sounded just fine and came over for dinner. Steaks on the grill and Monica overnight.

The following week, Arthur Grumley, Arty-Farty, was sentenced to twenty years in Stillwater Prison, and his trial date for the attempted murder charges in Scott County was set for November. The day after his sentencing, I met with Diane's parents out in Resurrection Cemetery. I was at the black granite family gravestone with the name Donnelly in gold letters and Diane's parents' names. Diane's gray granite gravestone with the image of a dove in flight had dried grass clippings on it, and I brushed those off before her folks showed up, then laid a dozen white roses on the stone.

They arrived and parked just opposite the family plot and behind my car. There was a long moment of sadness, and then they both took a deep breath and smiled.

"Oh, Dev, did you bring those roses?" Mrs. Donnelly asked.

"I did. I don't know if you remember, but the corsage Diane wore to our senior prom was white roses."

"Oh, my, actually no, I don't remember. Oh, that's so kind of you. I know she would just love that. She loved roses, and she—Well, now who is this?" she asked as a shiny white pickup pulled in behind their car.

"A very special surprise," I said.

The doors on the pickup opened, and Kevin and Colleen White stepped out. The rear door on the driver's side opened, and Patrick 'Rusty' White walked around the front of the pickup carrying yellow roses.

One look at the red hair, and Mrs. Donnelly said, "Oh, Bill, is it…"

"Hello, Donnellys, it's been far too long," Colleen said. "Patrick, say hello to your grandparents, Mr. and Mrs. Donnelly."

"Bill," Mrs. Donnelly said as she grabbed her husband with both hands, and tears rolled down her cheeks.

"I think we should meet him, Marilyn," he said and led her forward.

"Oh I've always wanted to meet you. Your daughter is my biological mom. My name is Patrick, but everyone calls me Rusty because of my hair. I guess it's like my mom's."

Mrs. Donnelly ran a hand over his hair and said, "Oh, Diane. Diane."

"I grew these roses for her," Rusty said. He handed the bouquet to Mr. Donnelly, hugged Mrs. Donnelly, and didn't let go.

Now a tear ran down my face.

The End

Thanks for taking the time to read <u>Hit & Run</u>. If you enjoyed the read please consider leaving a review, it really helps.

Just click on the link below.

Don't miss the sample of the next book in the Dev Haskell series, Suspect Santa, on the following pages.

Sneak Peek

Suspect Santa

Second Edition

MIKE FARICY

Prologue

After filling her wine glass, I held it out to Layla. It was our fifth date, not counting the night we'd met at a mutual friend's birthday party. Tonight was the first night in her bedroom. She had a two-bedroom condo in the Blair House Condominiums, a five-story Victorian brick building built back in 1887. Layla's unit was all the way up on the fifth floor. The ten-foot ceilings had elegant plaster crown molding. The woodwork throughout the place was oak with beautiful oak floors, all original to the building. Gorgeous stained glass panels were across the tops of double-hung windows. Her living room and the master bedroom both had fireplaces with glazed antique tiles.

She leaned over, kissed me on the cheek, and took the glass. "Thanks, baby. You are so nice. I'm really surprised."

"Surprised? Are you kidding? I'm one of the nicest guys in town. Why are you surprised?"

"Oh, you know, just what I've heard," she said and extended the glass toward me. I clicked it with my beer can. We were leaning on the pillows piled up against the carved headboard of her four-poster Victorian bed. The walnut dresser, with the carved leaf drawers and antique mirror, seemed to fit the room perfectly. Antique wooden chairs were on either side of the dresser.

"Is that some fancy formal jacket hanging on the back of the chair?" I asked and raised my beer can in the direction of the red velvet jacket with the white fur trim and brass buttons.

"Don't be silly. That's my elf coat."

"Your elf coat? Are you into something? Are you married? I thought—"

"No, Dev. I'm not married. Are you?"

"No, of course not. Who'd have me?"

"Yeah, good point. No, that's my Santa's elf coat. This will be my third year playing an elf in Santa's Workshop. I just love doing it. I take time from work, and we have hundreds of children. They're just darling. All on their best behavior, they tell Santa what they want for Christmas, and he says he'll try, but he can't make promises. You know, I really enjoy doing it, and it's an opportunity to give back something to the community."

"Sounds nice."

"You should think about doing it sometime, Dev. The kids are so wonderful. They really believe in Santa, and the older ones, even if they don't really believe, they're still hedging their bets, just in case. I think you'd be good at it. The guy we had the last two years was such a crab. His name is Arthur, and I was sure he was drinking on the job, but we could never prove it. Unfortunately, I think he's going to be back again this year. God, he's had an entire year to get even crabbier, if that's possible," she said and took a large sip of wine.

"Yeah, I would probably like to do that. I wish I wasn't so busy," I lied and gave a quick glance to see if she had picked up on it.

"I'll put your name on the alternative list. You never know. Maybe Arthur will break a leg or fall down the stairs. Or maybe someone's dad will just hit him for being such a jerk. One can only hope."

"He's that bad?"

"Surprisingly, yeah, he is. He's certainly not fun like you. It would be nice if you were there. Besides, I've never made love to Santa before. At least that I can remember." She set her glass on the bedside table and snuggled up to me.

I'd showered, shaved, and had been home for an hour before Morton wandered into the kitchen. I gave him the proverbial head scratch and let him out into the backyard. It was cold, and there was about six inches of fresh snow on the ground. Morton stood on the back porch, looked over his shoulder at me, and gave me a look as if to say, *Really? I'm supposed to go out there with the snow up to my knees and do my duty? You gotta be kidding.*

He was back inside three minutes later. As soon as I closed the door behind him, he shook the snow off and onto the floor, the walls, and the back door, then headed over to his food dish. I attacked the melting snow with a handful of paper towels.

We were down at the office before Louie Laufen, my office mate, arrived. I got the coffee going and was halfway through my first mug when Louie pulled up in his faded Ford Fiesta. He parked behind my car and gingerly crossed the street, trying to avoid the patches of ice. A moment later, I heard the stairs creaking and groaning as Louie made his way up to the office.

He opened the door and stood there red-faced and gasping for breath. He gave me a slight wave that signaled *Don't say anything* as he entered. I filled his mug with coffee, set it in front of him on the picnic table he used as a desk, and went back to looking out the window. The blinds were drawn on the apartment building across the street, so there was no point in taking my binoculars out of the desk drawer.

After a few minutes and a half-dozen slurps of coffee, Louie said, "So, did Layla spend the night at your place again?"

"No, as a matter of fact, I graced her condo with my presence. She made a wonderful dinner, lasagna, garlic bread, and apple pie for dessert. We had wine, chatted, and I was home around 6:00 this morning."

"Was that your first time there?"

"I'd been there before, but it was my first time spending the night. She has a really nice place. Up-to-date kitchen, and it's on the top floor, so you really don't pick up any street noise. How was your night?"

Louie shrugged and said, "Just the usual. Over at The Spot until about 9:00 then home. Watched, I forget what, on TV and went to bed after the news. I'm in court this morning at 11:00. With any luck, I'll be back in the office before 2:00. I—"

My phone ringing cut Louie off. Well, the ringing and me looking at the caller ID, shaking my head, and saying, "Damn it, Tubby Gustafson. This can't be good."

One

Louie looked over after the fourth ring and asked, "You going to answer that?""Yeah, I know. I know." I picked up the receiver and said," Good morning, Haskell Investigations."

"Save it for someone who cares, Haskell. I've got a car waiting out front for you. You've got two minutes to get down there."

"Actually, Mr. Gustafson, sir. I'm…umm…I'm still at my house. I've got a doctor's appointment, and I—"

"Don't fool with me, Haskell. I know you're at that dump you refer to as your office. Now, you can either get in the car waiting for you or drive yourself to the emergency room, where they'll place a cast on both your broken legs. Your choice."

"I'm heading out to the car now, sir," I said as I turned off my computer.

"Wise choice, Haskell," Tubby said and hung up.

I grabbed my jacket, gave Louie a wave, and headed for the door. Morton watched me but didn't move from his pillow.

I stepped out of the building, nodded at the thug seated behind the wheel of Tubby's black Cadillac Escalade, and waited for a bus to pass.

"Thanks for joining us, Haskell," a thug I knew as 'Lollipop' greeted me. He was seated in the passenger seat and wasn't smiling. "I was thinkin' we were going to get to go up to your office and remind you how Tubby don't like to be kept waiting."

"Just finishing up a report and wanted to check it for typos."

"What's them?" the driver asked.

"Yeah, sure you were," Lollipop said. "Don't kid a kidder. You were probably scanning that apartment building with your binoculars, hoping to catch some unsuspecting woman who doesn't know she's got a pervert living right across the street."

The thug behind the wheel chuckled, stepped on the gas, and took off down the street before I'd even closed the car door. It slammed shut as he accelerated.

"Better buckle up. We wouldn't want to lose you along the way."

I did just that, clicking the seat belt and then adjusting it from whatever fat guy had been seated here before me. I laughed to myself, thinking it had probably been Tubby Gustafson.

At no surprise, we ran two yellow lights and a red one and made it to Tubby's mansion on the River Boulevard in record time. But then, that was always the case when traveling in Tubby's car. It used to surprise me that his car was never pulled over for speeding, at least as far as I knew. Now, I'm not the least bit surprised. It's the way things work. People with money get whatever they want, and a blind eye is always turned toward them. Guys like me, the working stiffs, or maybe *sometimes* working class, we have to follow the rules or else. We pay the taxes, pay full price, pay, pay, pay. Folks like Tubby Gustafson, wealthy, privileged, and boss of the world, well, at least his world, get to do whatever they want. The rules folks like me have to deal with don't apply to the likes of Tubby Gustafson.

The Escalade pulled into the circular drive and stopped opposite the front door to Tubby's mansion. A couple of armed guys were on either side of the front door, leaning against the wall. They watched as I climbed out of the car.

"Good luck, Haskell," Lollipop said, sounding like he meant anything but as the car pulled away and headed back out of the massive front yard.

"Assume the position," a guy said and rose out of the lawn chair parked in front of a space heater. He smelled like cigar smoke as he patted me down, then finally said, "He's good. Let him in."

One of the guys leaning against the wall reached over and opened the door.

"Thanks," I said and stepped into the foyer.

A muscular guy was seated just inside. He looked up from the comic book he was reading, carefully set it on the oak bench, and stood. He patted me down again, and just as he finished, Fat Freddy Zimmerman, Tubby's second in command, appeared.

"It's about time, Haskell. Follow me."

I followed him past the staircase with the gilt-framed painting of Tubby holding what looked like important documents. An unsuccessful attempt to make Tubby appear honest and upstanding. We walked down the hallway to Tubby's office door. Fat Freddy knocked on the door as he opened it. I followed him into Tubby's office.

A massage table was positioned in front of the fireplace with the landscape painting above it. Naked Tubby was stretched out on the table. Fortunately, a white terry cloth towel covered most of his large rear. The fat from his massive figure hung over the sides of the massage table. Two attractive women, dressed in black thongs and smiling, were currently massaging Tubby's hairy, dimpled shoulders. Unfortunately for the two of them, they weren't wearing latex gloves. They ignored Fat Freddy and me and continued kneading Tubby's fat figure with their bare hands.

I was thinking Tubby might be asleep. His eyes remained closed, but he suddenly said, "Thank you for interrupting your otherwise busy day, Haskell. I want you to check someone out for me. Frederick, if you would present the file, please."

Fat Freddy seemed to come to attention and said, "Happy to do so, sir." He stepped over to Tubby's enormous antique desk. At the moment, the desk was devoid of everything but a phone, a crystal pen holder, and a thin manila file folder. Fat Freddy picked up the file, took two steps, and handed it to me.

Still keeping his eyes closed, Tubby said, "I'll expect you to provide me with a full report on this individual no later than one week from today."

"Anything you can tell me in advance, sir?" I said and opened the file. There were two pieces of paper. One was a copy of a photograph of a man, I guessed maybe mid-forties. The second page had what appeared to be a very short bio on the guy. His name was Alex Chillcot and, apparently, he lived on the East Coast, Newark, New Jersey, to be exact.

"Everything you need will be in that file."

"Is this Chillcot guy in town? Would you happen to have an address, a phone number, an email, or maybe a place of employment?"

Tubby gave a sigh. "Once again, Haskell, you never fail to disappoint. That is for you to determine. No questions? Good. Send him on his way, Frederick."

"But sir, how am I supposed to—"

"Come on, Haskell, let's go," Fat Freddy urged me toward the door.

"I'm just trying to figure out what you need here, sir."

Another sigh from Tubby. He raised his head so that his triple chin oozed into one, opened his eyes, and shook his head. He stared at my faded Bob Seger t-shirt.

"Haskell, just get me anything and everything you can on this character. Is that too hard to understand?"

"No, sir. It's just that I—"

"Stop. It's just that you never, ever get the damn message, Haskell. Seek and ye shall find. Do I make myself clear?"

"Yes, sir, perfectly," I said and followed Fat Freddy out of the office. Once back in the hallway, I said, "Freddy, what does he want to know about this Chillcot guy?"

"Were you listening to what he just said? Anything and everything, Haskell. Is that so hard to understand? Address, phone numbers. Where he's working. Does he have a wife? A woman? Is he in a relationship? Why the hell is this so difficult for you to figure out? Just do what you're supposed to do. Find out everything you can on this guy."

Two

I asked Louie, "So you've never heard of this Chill-cot person? You're not aware of a pending case where he might be a witness or a defendant?"

Louie shook his head. He finished chewing the meatball in his mouth and took another bite of his sandwich. "Mmm-mmm, it's not ringing a bell with me. Haven't seen anything in the paper or on the news. Did you Google him?"

"Yeah, I did, but there are a couple dozen guys out there with the same name. No image of what they look like. They're scattered all over the country, so it really wasn't much help."

Louie swallowed and took another bite. "Mmm, I would think, since Tubby wants this information, that might mean the guy is living or maybe moving into this area. Could he be a potential competitor? Maybe he's someone who worked for or with Tubby, and he's disappeared."

"I checked online, and there's no report of a death or accidental injury by anyone with that name."

"What about this?" Louie said and then licked meatball sauce from his fingers. "What if he was some sort of business associate of Tubby's, and he's suddenly turned to witness protection? Maybe that's why Tubby wants to find him."

"I didn't think of that, but it certainly could be the case. The only thing is, if someone did something like that, it would be a name I think I would recognize. This guy's name doesn't ring a bell at all."

"All I can say is good luck," Louie said. He picked up the Styrofoam tray and began to lick off the tomato sauce. Suddenly, a big glob dropped out of the tray and onto his shirt and tie.

"You might want to deal with that sauce on your shirt, Louie."

"What? Oh, for the love of—" He attempted to remove the sauce using his finger, which only served to smear a larger stain on his shirt.

I watched him make a mess of the process for another minute, then picked up the phone and called Aaron LaZelle, my pal in homicide. I was ready to leave a message when he picked up.

"Yeah, Dev, how can I be of assistance? Oh, and by the way, if you've been arrested again, you're on your own."

"Not even funny, Aaron. Thanks for answering. Just wondered if the name Alex Chillcot rings a bell with you?"

"How are you involved with him?"

"Actually, I'm not. I got strong-armed into checking the guy out for Tubby Gustafson. He gave me a file with the guy's picture and a very brief description. Lives in Newark, New Jersey, age forty-six. Nothing mentioned about employment or family. As far as I know, the guy could be a schoolteacher or a minister."

"I think you can assume if Gustafson is interested, the guy isn't involved in either one of those occupations. The name rings a bell. I believe he's involved in gambling, obviously not the legal form. You should talk to Tommy Bishop. You know him?"

"That name sounds familiar, but I can't picture him."

"He's a detective in Special Investigations. Give him a call. In fact, let me send your call to the main desk, and they'll transfer you. Oh, and by the way, it's your turn to buy lunch."

"Thanks, Aaron. I—" but he'd already forwarded my call to the main desk.

"St. Paul Police Department," a male voice said a moment later.

"Hi, I just got transferred to this number. I'm trying to reach Detective Tom Bishop in Special Investigations."

"One moment, please, and I'll connect you."

A few seconds later, the phone was ringing. After a half-dozen rings, I listened to the message, "This is Detective Tom Bishop. I'm unavailable to take your call at the moment. If you would please leave a message, I'll get back to you just as soon as possible. Thank you."

A moment later, I heard the beep. "Hi, Detective Bishop. My name is Dev Haskell. I got your name from a long-time friend, Lieutenant Aaron LaZelle, in homicide. If you would give me a call back, I'd appreciate it." I left my number.

"LaZelle didn't know anything?" Louie called. At the moment, he was standing next to the sink. He had the left side of his shirt untucked and was scrubbing the sauce stain with the rag in the sink. The rag hadn't been washed for a month, maybe two. His effort just seemed to make the stain that much worse.

"He gave me the name of a guy who might know something. I'll see if he calls back." I went on the computer and started going through the list of guys named Alex Chillcot. There were a number of individuals in the UK, a handful scattered around the US, none of whom even remotely resembled the image in the file Tubby had prepared. It was getting close to 4:00, and I was thinking of taking Morton for a walk when my phone rang.

"Haskell Investigations."

"I'm calling for Dev Haskell."

"Speaking."

"Hi, Dev. My name is Tom Bishop in Special Investigations. I'm returning your call."

"Oh, yeah, I got your name from—"

"Aaron LaZelle, yeah, I know, you mentioned it, and actually, I just got off the line with him. He said you were okay."

"He probably said that because it's my turn to buy lunch, and he didn't want to screw that up."

Bishop chuckled at that. "You're the P.I. that works for Gustafson, aren't you?"

"Yes and no. I've done some things for him in the past, never been paid, by the way, but on occasion, he throws me a bone. He asked me, actually, asked is his term. My version of things is he told me to find out everything I could on a guy named Alex Chillcot. If I didn't do that, I'd have plenty of time recovering in the hospital to consider my mistake. He told me Chillcot was from out on the East Coast, Newark, New Jersey, actually. He gave me a file with a picture of the guy and three sentences describing him. Nothing earthshaking and absolutely nothing that would help in any investigation. I've been searching online and came across a bunch of guys over in the UK, a couple of obituaries, and nothing on anyone from Newark, New Jersey."

"Yeah, Chillcot keeps a pretty low profile. I'd be interested in seeing the file Gustafson gave you. Would you be willing to let me go through it?"

"Not a problem. Any information you could pass on to me would be a big help. I literally have found nothing. I should warn you. I was serious when I said all I have is a picture of the guy, actually a copy of the picture, and just that he lived in Newark."

"You have time to meet in about an hour?"

"Today? Yeah, sure, Tom. You name the place."

"There's a bar not far from the station called Alary's on East Seventh."

"Yeah, I know the place. I'll see you there in an hour."

"Okay, thanks,"

"Oh, I'm wearing a Bob Seger t-shirt if that helps."

"I already checked out the department's Dev Haskell file. I saw a couple of pictures of you." Bishop laughed at that. "As a matter of fact, Aaron mentioned you and Detective Manning used to be at each other."

"You name the crime committed, and Manning had me first on his list," I acknowledged.

"I'll see you in an hour, Haskell, and don't forget the file," Bishop said and hung up.

I closed things down, clipped the leash on Morton, and locked the door as we headed out. We walked for three blocks and then climbed into the car and went home. I let Morton into the backyard and debated changing my Bob Seger t-shirt, then remembered I told Bishop that's what I was wearing. I coaxed Morton back in the house with a biscuit and headed out the door.

Three

I was able to grab a parking place just around the corner from Alary's Bar. There's a patio in back, but since it was winter, that wasn't going to work. I walked into the place and was in the process of unzipping my jacket when a voice called from across the bar, "Haskell, over here."

A guy smiled and waved me over. It was close to 5:00, and you'd think the place would be filling up with folks stopping in after work for a drink, but Bishop was one of only two guys seated on that side of the square bar. The last time I had been in the place, all the bartenders had been scantily clad, attractive young women. Today there was only one bartender. He was an older guy with a beer belly and crew cut. Thankfully, he was wearing jeans and a St. Paul Saints sweatshirt instead of being scantily clad.

I headed over to Bishop. As I came around the corner, I extended my hand. "Tom Bishop?" I said.

"Nice to meet you, Dev. Please, call me Tommy."

"Okay, hey, thanks for making the time to meet me."

"Yeah, I have to warn you. I can't stay for long. We've got a foster child for a couple of days, and the wife is going to need a hand in about thirty minutes."

"What'll it be?" the bartender asked.

"I'll have a Summit IPA. You want another?" I asked Bishop.

He shook his head. "Thanks, but it's strong coffee, and one is my limit at this time of day. I'm on the short leash tonight. You said you had a file from Gustafson?" he said, looking at my empty hands.

I reached inside my jacket and pulled out the two pages of the so-called file from Tubby Gustafson. "Here's what I got from him. An image of Chillcot and three sentences on the guy."

He unfolded the two pages, smiled when he saw the copy of the photo, and shook his head as he read the three sentences. "Man, no wonder they want you to investigate. First of all, this photo is out of date by probably ten years. The description they gave you is obviously worthless. Any idea why Gustafson is interested in him?"

"I have no idea. If I had to guess, I'd think maybe he was involved with some mob out east, turned state's evidence, and is hiding somewhere in a witness protection program."

Bishop nodded and said, "Maybe half-right. Basically, what happened is he ripped off someone or some mob family back in New Jersey. He is, or rather was, connected. So instead of getting his brains blown out, he was able to return the funds. He paid a fee and got the boot out of town. Not sure of the exact numbers, but we're talking a seven-figure payment."

"So a million bucks?"

"At least, but his choice was pay or be killed, so he paid and headed west. That was back in late July or early August. At the time, the word was he was headed to Kansas City. Not exactly clear on what changed that, but the bottom line is he's coming here. That suggests Gustafson either owed someone a favor or he's doing a favor for someone back east and will be compensated."

"Is there a file on Chillcot? I mean, has he done time? I couldn't find anything on the guy," I said just as the bartender set a beer mug in front of me. I tossed a ten-dollar bill on the bar and nodded at the bartender. He tapped the ten on the bar and left.

"Not surprising you didn't find anything. Chillcot was, or maybe still is, connected. It's the main reason he was allowed to leave, as opposed to taking a bullet between the eyes. He has always been a behind the scenes operator. He's got dirt on just about everyone, and the rumor is, should anything happen to him, that information will automatically be sent to the powers that be."

"Meaning the DEA?"

"Yeah, among others," Bishop said.

"What sort of information?"

"Everything from tax evasion to details on a number of illegal operations and even affairs with women. Some of the wives of the higher-ups could make life very difficult. From what I've heard, it's not just the info, but in the case of the sexual dalliances, there are actual pictures."

"So all that information serves as the guy's safety net?"

"Exactly. It's actually pretty clever. I don't know this, but I'm guessing the information is stored up in the cloud somewhere. Something happens to Chillcot, and that info floods out. You can just imagine. On the one hand, the information on you gets out, and you're screwed, charged, and arrested. On the other hand, maybe you're not charged, but the information is out there, and there will be people so pissed off that the safest place for you may be behind bars. It's really pretty ingenious."

"So, Tubby Gustafson is concerned because Chillcot is coming here. Does that mean that Chillcot has something on Tubby?"

"It could be, but my sense is he doesn't have anything on Gustafson for two reasons. First, Gustafson is out here in Minnesota. Secondly, Gustafson is a big player here in town. But he's never made a move or even expressed an interest in doing something that would put him on center stage. He's clearly content in the business as it is, right here in the world's biggest small town, St. Paul."

"I can't argue with your theory, but then why does Tubby want the information on Chillcot? It sounds like he's not going to have any trash on Tubby."

"Because the problem with Chillcot is that Gustafson is suddenly going to have a competitor on the scene. A competitor who is backed up by some very strong individuals. A competitor who knows the business, whatever the business is, gambling, women, drugs, you name it. And, over time, Tubby Gustafson will either be pushed to the side, if he's lucky, or simply eliminated."

"Why wouldn't Tubby just take him out?"

Bishop shook his head. "That would be the logical reaction, except if he takes Chillcot out, suddenly all the bad information, the double-crosses, the stealing, the dalliances see the light of day, not to mention all the prosecutable information. No, if Gustafson took him out, he'd be dead within twenty-four hours, and he knows it."

"You're making this Chillcot character sound untouchable."

"Exactly."

"Do you know when and where Chillcot is going to land?"

Bishop smiled. "I have some ideas, but with all due respect, I'm not at liberty to pass them on. I can tell you this. Word is he's purchased some Victorian mansion down on Summit Ave. Somewhere in the four hundred block."

"I'm just a few blocks from there. I'm not aware of any place with a for sale sign on it."

"Could be it will be more of a private transaction if that translates. I've got a place in mind, a corner lot, double lot, as a matter of fact."

"The homes are so big they're all double lots along there. A corner lot? That wouldn't happen to belong to a state senator? Delvin Durkin, a member of our illustrious state legislature?"

"Former member of the legislature. If you'll recall, Durkin didn't file for another term. I've never heard this, so it's just a guess on my part, but like all the connected people out east, your man Chillcot found out something and made Senator Durkin an offer he couldn't refuse. Namely, sell Chillcot the house or else."

"Oh, man, no wonder Tubby wants any and all information on this guy. Does he have a family?"

"He has a former wife. They divorced almost thirty years ago. She has custody of their two children, or I should say, had custody. A boy and girl. I believe the son is thirty-four or five. He's a practicing dentist down in Orlando, Florida. The thirty-two-year-old daughter lives out in Denver. Last I heard, she was an RN in a neonatal facility. Both children took their mother's surname when they turned twenty-one."

"What's the mother's name?"

"Diane Olsen. That surname ends with the letters 'en.'"

"No ties to the old man's business?"

"To my knowledge, they haven't seen him since the divorce thirty years ago. The former wife filed a restraining order against him prior to their divorce, and as far as I know, he's respected it. Hey, nice meeting you, Dev, but I should probably take off. If I know what's good for me, I better get my butt home. My wife will be trying to make dinner, and I'm on kid duty."

"How many do you have?"

"Just one at the moment, a ten-year-old boy. We do foster care."

"You're lucky," I said.

"Don't we know it. If I can be of any help, feel free to give me a call, or you can send me a private message to this email address. Always interested in what you learn," he said and extended his hand with a business card.

"Thanks, much appreciated, Tommy. Anything I can help you with, just let me know. Well, except for babysitting. I would probably be a bad influence on kids."

He laughed at that and headed out the door.

I finished my beer and headed home. I drove through downtown, up Ramsey Hill, and past State Senator Durkin's house on Summit Avenue. Sure enough, there was a moving van parked in front, actually a large semi-truck. At the moment, two guys were carrying a brown leather couch out the front door and down the half-dozen granite steps to the semitrailer. Not a fun job in the best of weather, let alone a Minnesota winter evening.

I pulled into my garage and entered the house through the back door. Morton trotted down the hallway and into the kitchen. I gave him a head scratch and said, "Outside, Morton. Outside?" as I opened the back door.

He looked at me like I was nuts.

"Outside?" I repeated.

He actually took two steps backward.

"Okay, I get it," I said and reached into the cookie jar where I kept his biscuits and tossed one to him. He caught it in midair and hurried out of the kitchen so he wouldn't have to share it with me.

Four

The following morning Morton and I were in the office well before Louie. I had the coffee on and was in the process of emailing Bishop at his private site, telling him about the moving van last night at Senator Durkin's house. I heard a grinding noise out on the street and turned to look out the window just in time to see Louie pull his faded Ford Fiesta in behind my car. When he turned his car off, a large cloud of black exhaust exploded out the back and then just sort of hung in the air for a long moment. Louie made his way through the slush on the street and into the building. The formerly white snow on the boulevard next to his car was now covered with black debris.

The staircase leading up to the second floor began to creak and groan, and a moment later, red-faced Louie entered the office. He gave me his usual wave, set his briefcase on his picnic table, and draped his black wool coat over the back of his office chair. I stepped out from my desk, grabbed Louie's coffee mug, filled it, and set it in front of him. He replied with a polite nod.

I went back to my desk and began typing notes from my conversation with Tommy Bishop the night before. At least I had the beginnings of information on Alex Chillcot for Tubby Gustafson.

"I thought you were going to come over to The Spot last night," Louie said a few minutes later. "Were you working or playing?"

"I met up with a cop. Turns out he had some information on Alex Chillcot. Nothing specific, just general stuff, a lot of hearsay, but it was more than I got from Tubby."

"Anything interesting?"

"Yeah," I said and began to fill Louie in on what Bishop had told me.

When I'd finished, Louie thought for a long moment and then said, "My sense is that, far from wanting to help someone out, Tubby Gustafson is probably worried about this Chillcot character coming to town and cutting into his business. You said he wants any and all information. Sounds like he's already in the planning stages."

"Yeah, okay, but the way Bishop described it to me, this Chillcot is basically untouchable."

Louie shook his head. "Possibly, or does Tubby just have to come up with a plan that's untraceable? What if Chillcot's in a plane crash? A car accident with a teenage driver? Or what if he simply disappears without a trace? Is Tubby Gustafson supposed to protect this guy? Or is he just being a nice guy and going to welcome him to the city?"

"I get what you're saying. So Tubby is worried about the guy moving in on his business, and he wants as much information as possible on the guy so he can get rid of him and not face any problems."

"There's one more part to this, Dev."

"What's that?"

"You don't want to be fingered as the person who gave Tubby Gustafson the information on Alex Chillcot. In some people's minds, that could make you just as guilty as whoever pulls the trigger, plants the bomb, or does whatever it is that removes Chillcot from the picture. I'd say it seems a pretty safe guess they're going to eliminate this guy. It's just a matter of how. Be careful who you deal with. Be careful what and who you ask about this guy, Dev. Even talking to this Bishop, nice guy and all, but if something should happen and word got out you were checking on Chillcot, you could end up with an awfully big target on your back."

A little later, I took Morton for a walk up to Roosters BBQ and got two Memphis-style pulled pork sandwiches to go. I couldn't get Louie's comments regarding my research of Alex Chillcot off my mind. Thus far, I'd only spoken to two people, Aaron LaZelle, and Tommy Bishop. I felt safe on both counts, but Louie's thoughts served as a note to the wise, or in this case, me.

I was back in the office with the sandwiches fifteen minutes later. Neither Louie nor I said much during lunch, but that wasn't unusual. Amazingly, Louie only had one small drop of BBQ sauce on his white shirt, and that was on the left sleeve. When he finished, he pulled on his suit coat, which covered the stain, not that he even noticed. He placed two files in his briefcase, wrapped a scarf around his neck, pulled on his black wool overcoat, and headed over to the courthouse for his 2:00 appearance.

As soon as his car started and he drove away, I called Sarah Debbens, a real estate agent I dated briefly last year. She answered on the second ring.

"Hi, this is Sarah."

"Hey, Sarah, a voice from the past. This is Dev Haskell."

I could almost hear the air being drawn out of the room. After a long pause, she said, "Hello, Dev. If you're looking to have me represent you in the sale of your home, I'm afraid at the moment, and for the foreseeable future, I'm simply too busy to take on another client."

"That's great news, Sarah. I'm glad the business is working well for you. Listen, I don't want to take up too much of your time. I just wondered if you know who had purchased the home at four-forty-one Summit Avenue? I drove past last night, and there was a large moving van out front. I just live a couple of blocks from there, and I wondered—"

"If you'll recall, I'm perfectly aware of where you live."

"Oh, yeah, I didn't mean to suggest anything. I just wondered if you—"

"Is that all you want? Or is this some lamebrain attempt at apologizing for the damage you did driving my car through the garage door?"

"Actually, I was driving because you had been over-served, and I was just trying to help. The last thing you needed was to be arrested for driving while intoxicated and—"

"And you took advantage of me in my car and turned out to be just as over-served."

"Well, yeah, that part was unfortunate, but I—"

"I'm checking the records now. If I give you the information, will you promise to get off the line and never, ever call me again?"

"Yeah, sure. If that's what you want."

"That's exactly what I want," she said. I could hear her fingers on the keyboard. "Okay, here we are, four-forty-one Summit, the home went for, wait a minute, this can't be right. It says that home went for six-hundred-and-fifty thousand. That house, in that location, should go for at least three times that."

"Does it list the name of the buyer?"

"It should. Let me check. The buyer is, wait a minute. What? A company named Alpha Publishing? That doesn't make any sense. Something's not right here. Are you still doing that detective thingy?"

"Yeah, my company is called Dev Haskell Private Investigations."

"So, are you investigating this sale? Something definitely doesn't seem right here. This is way off."

"No, I'm not investigating that sale. I was just driving past, and there was a moving truck, actually a big semi-trailer out front. Two guys were carrying a couch out of the house and into the truck."

"Something's not right here. Well, unless maybe it's some sort of family deal, a property trade or something. I mean, this can't be the sale price. There has to be more involved here."

"And you said the company listed is Alpha Publishing?"

"Yeah, have you ever heard of them?"

"No, they're not ringing a bell with me."

"And you just drove past and wondered? You're not investigating?"

"No, honest, Sarah, I just wondered if it had sold."

"Strange, very strange. Well, listen, Haskell. I'd normally say it's been a pleasure to talk with you, but in your case, I think I'll just hang up." Click.

To be continued . . .

Thanks for checking out the sample of <u>Suspect Santa</u>. It's shaping up to be a rather complicated Christmas season and things have barely started. Better grab a copy and see what happens, Dev Haskell doing his best in the Holiday Spirit . . .

Books by Mike Faricy
Crime Fiction Firsts

A boxset of the first four books in four crime fiction series:

Russian Roulette; Dev Haskell series
Welcome; Jack Dillon Dublin Tales series
Corridor Man; Corridor Man series
Reduced Ransom! Hot Shot series

The following titles comprise the Dev Haskell series:

Russian Roulette: Case 1
Mr. Swirlee: Case 2
Bite Me: Case 3
Bombshell: Case 4
Tutti Frutti: Case 5
Last Shot: Case 6
Ting-A-Ling: Case 7
Crickett: Case 8
Bulldog: Case 9
Double Trouble: Case 10
Yellow Ribbon: Case 11
Dog Gone: Case 12
Scam Man: Case 13
Foiled: Case 14
What Happens in Vegas… Case 15
Art Hound: Case 16
The Office: Case 17

Star Struck: Case 18
International Incident: Case 19
Guest From Hell: Case 20
Art Attack: Case 21
Mystery Man: Case 22
Bow-Wow Rescue: Case 23
Cold Case: Case 24
Cash Up Front: Case 25
Dream House: Case 26
Alley Katz: Case 27
The Big Gamble: Case 28
Bad to the Bone: Case 29
Silencio!: Case 30
Surprise, Surprise: Case 31
Hit & Run: Case 32
Suspect Santa: Case 33
P.I. Apprentice: Case 34
Rebel Without a Clue: Case 35
Puppy Love: Case 36

The following titles are Dev Haskell novellas:
Dollhouse
The Dance
Pixie
Fore!
Twinkle Toes
(*a Dev Haskell short story*)

The following are Dev Haskell Boxsets:
Dev Haskell Boxset 1-3
Dev Haskell Boxset 4-6
Dev Haskell Boxset 7-9
Dev Haskell Boxset 10-12
Dev Haskell Boxset 13-15
Dev Haskell Boxset 16-18
Dev Haskell Boxset 19-21
Dev Haskell Boxset 22-24
Dev Haskell Boxset 25-27
Dev Haskell Boxset 28-30
Dev Haskell Boxset 1-7
Dev Haskell Boxset 8-14
Dev Haskell Boxset 15-19
Dev Haskell Boxset 20-24
Dev Haskell Boxset 25-29

The following titles comprise the Jack Dillon Dublin Tales series:
Welcome
Jack Dillon Dublin Tale 1
Sweet Dreams
Jack Dillon Dublin Tale 2
Mirror Mirror
Jack Dillon Dublin Tale 3
Silver Bullet
Jack Dillon Dublin Tale 4
Fair City Blues

Jack Dillon Dublin Tale 5
Spade Work
Jack Dillon Dublin Tale 6
Madeline Missing
Jack Dillon Dublin Tale 7
Mistaken Identity
Jack Dillon Dublin Tale 8
Picture Perfect
Jack Dillon Dublin Tale 9
Dublin Moon
Jack Dillon Dublin Tale 10
Mystery Woman
Jack Dillon Dublin Tale 11
Second Chance
Jack Dillon Dublin Tale 12
Payback Brother
Jack Dillon Dublin Tale 13
The Heist
Jack Dillon Dublin Tale 14
Jewels To Kill For
Jack Dillon Dublin Tale 15
Retirement Scheme
Jack Dillon Dublin Tale 16
The Collector
Jack Dillon Dublin Tale 17

Jack Dillon Dublin Tales Boxsets:
Jack Dillon Dublin Tales 1-3
Jack Dillon Dublin Tales 4-6

Jack Dillon Dublin Tales 1-5
Jack Dillon Dublin Tales 1-7
Jack Dillon Dublin Tales 6-10

The following titles comprise the Hotshot series;
Reduced Ransom! Second Edition
Finders Keepers! Second Edition
Bankers Hours Second Edition
Chow Down Second Edition
Moonlight Dance Academy Second Edition
Irish Dukes (Fight Card Series)
written under the pseudonym Jack Tunney

The following titles comprise the Corridor Man series:
Corridor Man
Corridor Man 2: Opportunity knocks
Corridor Man 3: The Dungeon
Corridor Man 4: Dead End
Corridor Man 5: Finger
Corridor Man 6: Exit Strategy
Corridor Man 7: Trunk Music
Corridor Man 8: Birthday Boy
Corridor Man 9: Boss Man
Corridor Man 10: Bye Bye Bobby

Corridor Man novellas:
Corridor Man: Valentine
Corridor Man: Auditor

Corridor Man: Howling
Corridor Man: Spa Day

The following are Corridor Man Boxsets:
Corridor Man Boxset 1-3
Corridor Man Boxset 1-5
Corridor Man Boxset 6-9

All books are available on Amazon.com
Thank you!

Contact the author:
- Email: mikefaricyauthor@gmail.com
- Twitter: @Mikefaricybooks
- Facebook: Mike Faricy Author
- Website: http://www.mikefaricybooks.com

Published by

MJF Publishing

www.ingramcontent.com/pod-product-compliance
Lightning Source LLC
Chambersburg PA
CBHW070510310726
48976CB00002BA/398